THE
CROSSROADS

ALSO BY ALEXANDRA DIAZ

The Only Road

THE
CROSSROADS

ALEXANDRA DIAZ

A Paula Wiseman Book

Simon & Schuster Books for Young Readers

NEW YORK   LONDON   TORONTO   SYDNEY   NEW DELHI

SIMON & SCHUSTER BOOKS FOR YOUNG READERS
An imprint of Simon & Schuster Children's Publishing Division
1230 Avenue of the Americas, New York, New York 10020
SIMON & SCHUSTER BOOKS FOR YOUNG READERS
is a trademark of Simon & Schuster, Inc.
For information about special discounts for bulk purchases, please contact Simon &
Schuster Special Sales at 1-866-506-1949 or business@simonandschuster.com.
The Simon & Schuster Speakers Bureau can bring authors to your live event. For
more information or to book an event, contact the Simon & Schuster Speakers Bureau
at 1-866-248-3049 or visit our website at www.simonspeakers.com.
Jacket design by Krista Vossen
Interior design by Hilary Zarycky
The text for this book was set in Bembo.
Manufactured in the United States of America
0818 FFG
First Edition
2 4 6 8 10 9 7 5 3 1
Library of Congress Cataloging-in-Publication Data
Names: Diaz, Alexandra, author.
Title: The crossroads / Alexandra Diaz.
Description: First edition. | New York : Simon & Schuster Books for Young Readers,
[2018] | "A Paula Wiseman Book." | Sequel to: The only road. | Summary: Jaime, twelve,
and Angela, fifteen, discover what it means to be living as undocumented immigrants in
the United States, while news from home gets increasingly worse.
Identifiers: LCCN 2017061228 | ISBN 9781534414556 (hardcover) | ISBN
9781534414570 (e-book)
Subjects: | CYAC: Illegal aliens—Fiction. | Immigrants—Fiction. | Homesickness—
Fiction. | Schools—Fiction. | Brothers—Fiction. | Cousins—Fiction. | Refugees—
Fiction. | Guatemalan Americans—Fiction.
Classification: LCC PZ7.D5432 Cr 2018 | DDC [Fic]—dc23 LC record available at
https://lccn.loc.gov/2017061228

To the refugees and immigrants who truly make this world great.

CHAPTER ONE

"Are you sure I have to go? There's only six weeks and three days left of school anyway." Jaime twisted the straps of his new backpack around his hand. "I can help you with your work, Tomás, I know I can."

The large brown building seemed to have been dropped from space into a field of cacti and scattered bushes that the locals called trees. The glass gleamed from the windows and the stucco and brick walls still had that new, un-broken-in, graffiti-free look that made the whole building less welcoming. New in every way. But to Jaime Rivera, who was used to chipped cinder blocks and slatted windows that opened and closed with a hand crank, this school building looked completely alien.

Tomás put an arm around Jaime's shoulders but kept

driving down the two-lane highway toward the solitary building in the middle of the desert. On his other side, his cousin Ángela shifted the new backpack on her lap to reach for Jaime's hand.

"I'm scared too," she said just loud enough for Jaime to hear.

They'd talked about it all week. Tomás and Ángela. Mamá and Papá back in Guatemala. Even Abuela had her one-minute say in it. Everyone agreed, "The children need their school," and "They should be grateful for this opportunity." It's not that Jaime didn't want to go to school. It's just that going in August would be better than going now, today, in the middle of April.

Today. Only a week after coming to live with his brother, Tomás. Only a week since he arrived in southern Nuevo México. A week since he and Ángela had crossed *la frontera* into los Estados Unidos.

Tomás parked the truck in a big parking lot near the glass front door. These people really liked their glass. "Alright. The sooner we do this, the sooner you'll see everything's going to be okay."

Jaime didn't believe him. He glanced at Ángela and then scooted out of the driver's side door Tomás held open for him. With a second slamming door, Ángela got out too. At fifteen, she was going to a different school, one ten minutes away and in the middle of town. They'd driven past it yesterday when they'd gone grocery shopping. That school at least had character, with its old paint and holes in the fence. Not like this prison with its fence of pointed iron rods to keep kids trapped, as if there were anywhere to go from here.

They walked together, Jaime clinging to Ángela's hand again and Tomás leading the way. Through the glass front doors they came to another set of glass doors, which were locked. You needed to be buzzed in or have a special pass to get through those doors. Definitely a prison.

All the paperwork had been filled out already, and there was nothing stopping the inevitable. Even the lady to escort him to his cell, a young woman with dyed maroon hair, was present.

She entered through the locked glass doors in ripped jeans and at least three shirts layered over each other in a punk-rocker sort of way. "Hi, I'm Ms. McAllister. Do you speak English?"

Jaime understood enough to shake his head no.

This "Meez Macálista" didn't miss a beat. She switched to decent Spanish even though she was a *gringa*. "Don't worry. The Spanish teacher is sick today but I can help you out. Say good-bye to your dad and—"

"*Hermano*," Tomás corrected, and then continued in English as he held out a hand. "I'm his brother, Tom."

At his side, Ángela gave Jaime a look out of the corner

of her eye. Tomás liked to show off that he spoke near-perfect English, but they were still not used to him being "Tom."

"*Mucho gusto.*" Meez Macálista shook his hand and continued in Spanish. "Let's get him to class. You can pick him up at three o'clock outside the glass doors. Sixth graders don't need to wait with a teacher."

Ángela wrapped her arms around Jaime as best she could with his bag protruding from his back. The bones of her back stuck out more than they should, more than they used to.

"You'll be okay," she whispered in his ear with a sniff that held back tears. "I wish you could be with us to drop me off at my school."

Jaime let his hands dig into her spine and wing bones. "I'll be there to pick you up."

Tomás hugged him too, and then he and Ángela left the office through the glass door.

Meez Macálista let him watch until the truck was completely gone before putting a hand on his shoulder. "Come. Mrs. Threadworth will be wondering where you are."

She used a plastic card around her neck to open the locked glass door and walked down the vast hallway.

"Unfortunately, our school district doesn't have much money," the teacher continued talking in Spanish. "It's probably too late in the year to get you a special class to help you learn English, but hopefully, it won't be too hard for you."

Nothing Jaime saw seemed to indicate they were a poor school district—they had plumbing and electricity after all. On the contrary, it was one of the most well-maintained buildings he'd ever been inside. It looked just as new as the outside, with shiny floors that would make you slip if you where only wearing socks, and walls without chips or dirt smudges. Next to each classroom was a large bulletin board with class projects on display—maps labeled with all the states of El Norte, essays in English written in the best handwriting possible, the kindergarteners showing off their capital and lowercase letters. When Meez Macálista stopped, they were in front of a door with pictures of science projects. Jaime gulped. He'd never been good at science.

Meez Macálista knocked on the door and then entered without waiting for permission.

Four rows of six desks were squeezed into the room, where all but one desk was filled. Twenty-three pairs of eyes stared at him like he was some kind of alien. He ran his hand through his new crew cut and felt the sharp spikes of too much hair gel.

"Come in." The teacher gestured with her hand as he entered. Her voice was deep, and with just those two words, Jaime knew this was not a teacher to upset.

"What's your name?" she asked.

A few of the twenty-three pairs of eyes blinked and continued to stare at him. Which was the way out? Two rights and a left and he'd be by the glass doors? He wasn't sure. Just as he wasn't sure whether the glass door was unlocked from the inside.

"He doesn't speak English," Meez Macálista volunteered, and then returned to Spanish. "Mrs. Threadworth asked what your name is."

Great. Now the owners of the forty-six eyes thought he was stupid as well as alien. "Jaime Rivera."

His teacher continued in English, "Where are you from?"

He shifted from one foot to the other. If he told the truth they might guess he didn't have any papers. But if he lied, he'd never be able to convince them he spoke good enough English to be from here. Back home, in his regular school, he'd learned some English but he wasn't like Tomás and Ángela. Languages didn't come easily to him.

He understood more than he could speak and knew what Meesus had asked, just as he had the first question. He forced his mouth to answer. Just to prove to them all he wasn't stupid. "Guatemala."

"And how old are you?"

The panic rose more than ever. He was pretty sure he understood the question, it was the answering he wasn't sure about.

"Telv."

As expected, all twenty-three mouths burst out laughing. Jaime could feel his face burning and wondered if he'd accidentally said a bad word.

The teacher said something that made them quiet down and then turned to Jaime, said something else, and pointed to the empty desk in the corner next to the window. He took the hint and squeezed his way to the desk. From the front of the room, Meez Macálista, his only Spanish ally, waved good-bye and left.

The teacher continued talking and writing things on the whiteboard. He didn't even know what subject she was talking about. The eyes no longer stared at him but the kids also didn't have books open that gave any indication of what was going on.

Jaime glanced from the clock (only 8:52) to the window. Right away he noticed it was just a pane of glass—there was no way to open it. Back home the school's slatted windows were always open during the day to let in light and a breeze. How he wished for a breeze.

Outside on the ledge sat an interesting bug. Dark, six legs, and antennae. If he dared, he would pull out his sketchbook and draw the insect. Instead, he traced the outline on the desk with his finger. No, not six legs. Only five. One of them must have broken off.

He was just adding pretend leaves to his drawing when

the teacher dropped a book on his desk that squashed the invisible bug.

The teacher must have said something along the lines of "read this" and then returned to the rest of the class. Jaime lifted the book but all he saw was an old metal desk. No bug drawing. And no more bug outside.

The book was one of those first word books for babies that had a picture of something and then the word underneath. Except reading in English wasn't exactly the same as reading in Spanish. At least he already knew that "orse" was really pronounced "horse" and "beerd" was really a "bird." Still, he kept at it through 9:14 and 9:39, until disaster hit. He had to go. Bad.

"Meesus?" he asked while raising his hand.

"Yes, Jaime?"

"I go bat-rume?"

She waved in the direction of the board and said something he didn't understand but sounded like "seen out," which didn't make any sense. Maybe it was her who hadn't understood.

9:51.

"Meesus? I go toh-ee-let?"

This time what she said sounded more like "sign out" but he still didn't know what that meant. He crossed his legs. 9:56. Time to be more blunt.

"Meesus! Pee-pee."

The twenty-three mouths laughed and then the twenty-three pairs of eyes turned to sneak glances at him before laughing again.

"Please sign out." And again she nodded toward the board.

10:02.

He squeezed his legs tighter. Okay, "please" he understood, no problem. And "out" meant outside. But it was that "sign" word he couldn't figure out, and the whole whiteboard pointing was a complete mystery. Maybe the outhouse was behind the whiteboard? But he remembered passing the bathrooms on the way to the classroom.

10:09. He couldn't hold it any longer.

"Meesus!" He ran for the door without waiting for her response. But his movement relaxed his muscles and before he made it to the door, he felt wet warmth trailing down his legs.

CHAPTER TWO

It was a while before Meez Macálista's voice echoed into the boys' bathroom. "Jaime? ¿*Estás aquí?*"

Jaime didn't answer. His pants were still wet and the laughter kept playing in his head.

She left without checking the stalls and Jaime made sure his door was locked.

Boys came and went every few minutes, sometimes talking with others, sometimes forgetting to flush or wash their hands. A few even spoke in Spanish. No one noticed Jaime locked in the corner stall.

One boy came in a few times, but only to eat chocolate. Even without seeing him, Jaime knew it was the same kid. The crackle of the wrappers and the smell of chocolate gave him away each time. Choco-chico, as Jaime began to call him, had just left for the third time when Jaime was about to escape. But a herd of children stomped by outside the bathroom in loud voices and he lost his nerve.

"Jaime?" Meez Macálista returned. Jaime ignored her. She called again, saying something in English before her shoes squeaked into the boys' room. He lifted his sneakers off the floor so she couldn't see him from under the gap. Her own shoes, hot pink with leopard spots, stopped in front of the stall. "Jaime, I know you're in there."

He kept silent and still. Any minute she would pick the latch or look under the door.

Except she didn't. Judging by her shoes, she leaned against the wall in front of the stalls and crossed her ankles instead. "Please come out. It's lunchtime. Aren't you hungry?"

Yes, he was hungry. Back in the classroom was his new backpack, which had his new Teenage Mutant Ninja Turtles lunch bag, which had a ham and avocado sandwich, a banana, a bag of salt and vinegar potato chips, and a carton of milk. They had gone to a huge store the day before that sold everything imaginable, and Tomás had let him and Ángela pick out all their favorite foods. His stomach rumbled just thinking about it. So much for being quiet. But that wasn't enough for him to come out. He knew what it was like to be hungry; he'd spent days in near starvation. Skipping one meal was nothing. It would take a lot more than a few funny noises from his stomach to change his mind.

Meez Macálista seemed to think the same thing and sighed. "I can't force you, but I've talked with your teacher. This school has a strict no-bullying policy so no one will say anything to you."

A snort came out of Jaime's throat before he could stop it. He knew kids, and knew they would say whatever they wanted. He just wouldn't be able to understand what they said.

Meez waited. Maybe she understood what his grunt meant because she sighed after a few minutes.

"I can't stay. It is—" she paused as if she were trying to remember the Spanish word for what she wanted to say, "—not allowed for me to be here in the boys' bathroom. If you want to hang out with me instead, my room is to the left outside the bathrooms, left down the next hall, and all the way to the end. You'll hear the music."

Music? Did this mean Meez Macálista taught music? Did kids play the *chinchines* made from the dried gourds he'd seen along the side of the ranch road? Or was it just singing? He was about to ask when Choco-chico entered (the wrappers in his pocket were extra loud this time) and Meez Macálista excused herself before she got into trouble.

Jaime waited for Choco-chico to leave before pulling out some toilet paper and seeing what kind of sculptures he could make out of the paper. Lots of things, apparently. By making small balls and snakes and licking his fingers to make the paper stick, he ended up with a zoo of animals parading on the floor by the time the toilet paper ran out and the final bell rang.

Now was the time. He grabbed his two favorite paper animals, a horse and a dragon, and left his sanctuary, camouflaged in the crowd of kids with no one noticing him. Everyone talked and speed walked toward the glass front doors which, thank goodness, weren't locked from the inside. And there, waiting among all the parents, was Tomás.

Jaime rushed to his big brother and almost knocked him over by jumping on him.

"Hey, good to see you too! Where's your backpack?"

Jaime looked down at his scuffed sneakers and shrugged. "I don't know."

It wasn't a total lie. He didn't remember where the classroom was.

"Did you lose it?"

Again Jaime shrugged.

Tomás sighed and pulled out his phone to check the time. "Let's go look for it before picking up Ángela. I can't afford to get you a new one."

Jaime took a step back. He looked down at the state of his pants. They were dark blue and from his angle he couldn't notice any stains. Tomás's hand stayed on his shoulder, pushing him forward. After all these years of working as a cowboy and herding cattle for a living, Tomás didn't seem about to let one twelve-year-old boy go astray.

The teacher was still in the classroom grading papers. Jaime's backpack lay slumped on his seat. Jaime dug in his heels, ready to bolt, but Tomás pushed him in.

"Hi, I'm Tom Rivera, Jaime's brother," Tomás told the teacher in English.

As they talked, both of them kept looking his way. He didn't need to understand the words to know they were talking about him. They ended their talk with a handshake, and Tomás motioned with his head for them to leave. Jaime didn't need to be told twice. With his backpack strapped on and the two toilet paper creatures still in his hand, he was out of the classroom before Tomás.

They were almost at the truck when Tomás spoke up.

"Next time you need the bathroom, just write your name on the right-hand corner of the board and you're excused."

Really? That simple? Then why hadn't she said so!? Why did she have to use fancy words like "sign out?" How hard was it to beckon him to the board, have him write his name, and then point to the door. He was smart. He would have gotten it. Instead, she had practically ignored him as she waved vaguely in the board's direction. Weren't teachers supposed to know how to explain things so kids would understand?

He ate his sandwich while they drove to get Ángela. The avocado had gone brown but it still tasted pretty good.

Maybe a squeeze of lemon would help next time he made the—

"Wait. What do you mean, 'next time?' I have to go back?" Jaime gasped.

"Tomorrow. Education is a good thing," Tomás said.

"You didn't finish school," Jaime pointed out.

"I did," Tomás reassured him. "Once I got here, I studied for my certificate."

"But back home, lots of kids my age don't go to school," Jaime reminded him. Home. What he wouldn't give to be back there where everything was familiar.

"That's because there's no free transportation to get them to school: uniforms, books, and supplies cost too much; and parents need their kids to start working instead. In this country, kids are required by law to go to school."

"Well, maybe I don't want to be in this country."

The truck bumped and banged as Tomás pulled over and slammed on the emergency break. The truck leaned dangerously toward the ditch on the right.

Tomás unclipped his seat belt to turn and glare at Jaime. Gravity and surprise pushed Jaime against the passenger door. He couldn't remember ever seeing his brother so angry. And scared. "Don't even joke about that."

"I—"

"Gangs killed Miguel, our own cousin, and then they wanted you to take his place, and Ángela to be their—"

Jaime did his best not to have to hear Tomás say the words. He knew what would have happened to him. As much as being a drug dealer turned his insides, it would have been a million times worse for Ángela.

"I don't want to join the Alphas." Jaime defended himself as Tomás continued talking about what their parents had gone through to get them here safely. "But I don't want to be here either."

"Well, maybe you'll get your wish. Do you know what's going on in the news? Every day it seems like there's a statement about immigrants and who should be allowed to stay in this country. There's talk of a massive wall and deporting all of us."

"But you have papers. A work visa," Jaime frowned. He and Ángela didn't.

"Do you think that's going to make a difference? Officials capture first and let lawyers answer later. *If* you can afford a lawyer, and we can't. So where does that leave us? Back in Guatemala, me unable to get a job that pays enough to survive, and you and Ángela facing what you ran away from. Making everything we've all been through for nothing. *Qué maravilla.*"

Jaime ran a hand through his hair he'd gelled perfectly that morning, not looking at his brother. Outside the window, the nothingness of the scarce vegetation seemed to mock him.

"I know it's rough to hear the truth, but you're here to stay. So you. School. Tomorrow." Tomás left no space for arguing as he popped the emergency brake and pulled the truck back on the road.

They drove up in front of Ángela's school and, like Jaime, she came running to them. But unlike Jaime, she not only had her backpack, she also had a huge smile on her face.

"Guess what!" Ángela jumped into the truck, squashing Jaime, who hadn't scooted over in time. "You know how I've always wanted to do more acting than the nativity play? Well, they're putting on this play called *The Sound of Music*, and my English is good enough that the drama teacher said I could be in it! I'll just be one of the ladies in the crowd, like a nun or partygoer, but I'll be in a lot of the scenes and there's a chance I might even be given some lines! Rehearsals are Mondays, Wednesdays, and Fridays, so I'm actually missing today."

"Your school is about an hour and a half there and back." Tomás shook his head no. "I can't take that much time off work to pick you up from rehearsals three times a week. I'm only doing it today since it's your first day. Starting tomorrow, you two have to ride the bus."

Jaime could feel the blood draining from his face at the mention of the bus. Great, more kids to make fun of him.

But Ángela either didn't know bus horror stories or had

selective hearing and ignored the bus slip. "I'm sure I can find someone to bring me back to the ranch after practice. One of the boys already said he could after Wednesday's rehearsal. I just need you to sign the permission form. It is okay, right?"

"Does it cost anything to be in the play?" Tomás asked.

"We're fund-raising to cover the costs."

"*Pues, sí.* If you can find rides and you want to." Tomás shrugged as if it weren't his decision to make. Tía, Ángela's *mamá*, would have asked a lot more questions and gone to the school to personally meet the drama teacher and the person driving her home, and then would have made Ángela promise that she still had to maintain good grades before letting her be a part of the play. Jaime's *mamá* would have done the same.

"I really, really do." She reached over Jaime to try and hug Tomás. Her arms just grazed his shoulders, squishing Jaime and his two paper critters in the process.

"Let us know when the shows are and we'll come," Tomás said while taking one hand off the steering wheel to reach over Jaime to pat her knee. "And if they're going to film it, be sure to put us down for a DVD to send to your parents."

Jaime was about to inform Tomás that Ángela's family sold the TV to help pay for their passage, but Ángela lunged once more to hug Tomás. As she returned to her side, her nose scrunched up. "Why does it smell like pee in here?"

From the main highway, they turned onto a dirt road, went through three cattle guards, and drove for about twenty minutes more. All the land around them belonged to Meester George, from the highway to the mountain in the distance that was once a volcano, and beyond. Jaime hadn't seen the entire property, but Tomás said it took a few hours by car to get from one end to the other.

All that land for a few thousand head of cattle, and a few humans. It was like living in a Western movie, and any minute Zorro or Pancho Villa would come riding through.

Coming down a small hill, a gust of desert wind blew a huge cloud of dust, temporarily blocking the big house from view. Jaime still hadn't even met this Meester George, who was away with his wife visiting their new grandchild. From what Tomás said, Meester George was a strict but fair man. He let Tomás drive his old truck and live rent-free in one of the trailers near the big house. And even then, he paid Tomás an honest wage. But in exchange, Meester George expected hard work and dedication.

They drove up to their trailer just as another cloud of dust rose from the west. Jaime squinted into the sun to watch the cattle coming closer. A lone cowboy rode his gray Appaloosa behind them and four dogs helped herd the cattle into the large corral. Well, three dogs herded the cattle, while the fourth created her own dust ball dashing to the truck.

"Vida!" Jaime greeted their one-eared brown and white mutt, who returned the salutation with kisses as if she hadn't known whether she would ever see them again. Jaime knew how she felt. After Ángela's boyfriend had found the dog half drowned and torn apart from a dog-fight ring in México, Ángela had literally stitched her back to life. Now Ángela's boyfriend was gone and Vida was all they had left of those friends they made along their journey. It had been hard to leave her behind that morning, but the cowboy, Don Vicente, promised he would take good care of her. And it looked like he had.

The ranch hand, Quinto, latched the corral shut once Don Vicente ensured the last cow was secure. The older man said a few words to the ranch hand before turning his Appaloosa on his hindquarters and trotting over to Jaime and his family in front of their trailer. According to Tomás, Don Vicente had worked here since before Jesús, and knew the ranch better than anyone. Don Vicente's wife, Doña Cici, had been Meester George's nanny when the owner was little, and now Meester George had grandkids of his own.

"Storm's coming," Don Vicente said in his way of barely moving his lips. He was a desert man from Chihuahua,

México, with a face so worn and darkened by the sun, Jaime wondered if it had stiffened like old leather and too many expressions could cause it to crack. If the old cowboy ever had the time to sit for a portrait (on his horse, of course), Jaime would love to sketch out his face in charcoals (not that he had charcoals, but still) and capture the depth on the page.

"Tonight?" Tomás looked at the blue sky. Not a cloud in sight.

Don Vicente shifted his worn straw cowboy hat and grunted his response.

Tomás looked back at the brown cows with white faces in the corral. Most were hanging around, waiting to see if they would get fed, while a few were checking out their three-sided shelter. "Is that all of them?"

"Last of the cows. Til the calves come."

Tomás swore and headed to the corral. Don Vicente watched him for a second but didn't urge his gelding to follow.

"Why's Tomás upset? Aren't calves a good thing?" Ángela asked.

Don Vicente took his time to turn back to them. "I bet we'll have at least four cows in labor tonight, right in the middle of the storm. They always pick the worst weather to calve. It's a survival thing. Fewer predators out when the weather's bad."

"Are you sure it'll be bad?" Jaime looked again at the sky. He still couldn't get over how blue it was out here. No pollution, no smoke. It was like someone spilled the blue paint bucket and forgot to mop it up.

"I'm guessing about a foot of snow."

"Snow? In April?" Both Jaime and Ángela squealed. "*¿De verdad?*"

"Yeah, weather here in Nuevo México always does what it wants," Don Vicente said with a groan. "Tomás and I will be up all night tending to the cows delivering in the freezing weather. Last year we lost three calves and one cow during a spring storm, and Mr. George will be upset if it happens again." This time Don Vicente did nudge his gelding toward the barn near the corral. From over his shoulder he called out. "That's a nice dog you got there. Quick to learn."

Jaime smiled as he scratched Vida's one ear and got a kiss back. Finally some good news for the day. Snow!

CHAPTER THREE

The intense glare of the sun reflecting off the white snow woke Jaime up. From the bed he shared with Tomás, he pressed his nose against the window, unable to believe it. He could see to the end of the earth, all white and magical against the intense blue sky.

Mist formed on the window from his breath, clouding his sight. What was he doing looking through the window when he could see it for real?

He slid on his shoes, no time for socks, and tiptoed to the other side of the trailer where Ángela slept, which during the day converted to a table and seating cushions. Vida jumped off Ángela's bed and greeted Jaime with a wag of her tail.

"What's going on?" Ángela asked half asleep.

"Snow. Or something like it."

Ángela turned toward her window and pushed aside the curtain. She jerked back from the glare, but with each blink her eyes widened for a second longer. An instant later, her shoes were on, she grabbed the blanket from her bed, and burst out of the trailer after Jaime.

The snow buried Vida completely and she had to jump from one place to the next. Their feet sank into the snow to almost knee height. With the sun causing every flake to glisten and shine, the view was even more mystical than it had been from the window.

"It's incredible, isn't it?" Ángela said as they stood there, mesmerized.

"Yeah."

"Miguel would have loved it."

They both looked up at the sky. Jaime would never forgive the Alphas for what they had done to Miguel. If it hadn't been for them, Jaime would still have his best friend. If it hadn't been for them, Jaime would still be with his family at home.

"I felt the same way when I first saw snow." Tomás came up behind them and put an arm around their shoulders. His cheeks were rough with stubble and his eyes were red from not having slept, but still he seemed relaxed and happy.

"Is it always this magical?" Jaime asked.

"Yes, until it melts and mixes with the dirt and muck, and then it's just a mess."

Jaime couldn't take his eyes off it, afraid he'd turn away and it would return to brown dust. "How long will it last?"

"A few days, maybe less."

"Can we play in it?"

"Knock yourself out. I'm going to bed."

"What about school?" Ángela asked. Jaime turned to glare at her. Why did she have to ruin a great day by mentioning the dreaded S word?

"Cancelled," Tomás yawned. "There aren't enough plows to clear the roads in time."

"*¡Así se hace!*" Jaime jumped in the air and cheered. Now there was no doubt. Snow was definitely the best thing ever.

Except that Tomás was staring at him as if he'd said a bad word.

"Are you two wearing your sneakers? And no coats? Are you crazy? Get inside before Abuela finds a way to teleport over here and scold me for letting you get sick."

Inside, Tomás threw them each a towel and made them strip from their soaked pajamas. Then he dug under his bed and came up with a couple of pairs of waterproof pants, a few hats and scarves that Jaime was sure Abuela had knitted before her arthritis got too bad, four individual mismatched gloves, and some thick sweaters. For shoes he told Jaime to wear the work boots he just took off and for Ángela he handed over his knee-high rubber mucking boots.

"With some thick socks they should be fine."

Jaime didn't know about Ángela, but by the time he was completely dressed, he felt like a giant, waddling coconut. Still, he couldn't keep from smiling as Tomás took photos of them in the snow with his phone to print and send home.

"Alright, you guys have fun and don't wake me up unless the world's on fire." Tomás waved from the trailer's door.

"Wait," Jaime said, looking over at the corral where the ground was already brown with mud and muck. "How are the cows?"

Tomás smiled as he rubbed his eyes. "We've got five new calves and the moms are all fine. We'll go see them when I wake up."

With their mismatched gloves, they scooped up the snow and tasted it. Jaime could only describe it like cold airy water, but still very satisfying. The snow didn't pack very well into balls but that didn't stop them from throwing it at each other and at Vida. The dog tried to catch the snow in her mouth and then seemed to be surprised that it disintegrated. Jaime got Ángela good in the back of her head in an explosion of snow that made her black hair look like she had a major case of dandruff. She got him back though with snow down his shirt. The cold stung his skin and made him squirm, but that didn't stop the fight.

From the big house, Doña Cici waved them over. One of the biggest houses Jaime had ever seen, it was made from thick logs, had three chimneys, and enough space to hold Jaime and Ángela's entire family in Guatemala, including all their distant cousins. Only Meester George and his wife lived in the main part, except when their children and grandchildren came to visit. Even with them away from the ranch, Doña Cici kept up with her job of cleaning the big house and cooking.

"I figured you might be hungry, and *sopapillas* are best eaten hot." She handed them poofed-up squares of bread dripping in honey butter.

"Do we have to go in to eat them?" Jaime asked, feeling his stomach pulling him in two. The *sopapillas* smelled heavenly and they hadn't eaten breakfast. But on the other hand, he knew the snow wouldn't last forever.

Doña Cici, small and squat with short dyed black hair and a wrinkled face, handed them each an extra one, and a crunchy dog biscuit for Vida. "The gloves can be washed. Come back for more if you'd like." She retreated into the elaborate kitchen, which, according to Tomás, really was large enough to cook for fifteen hungry ranch hands.

They had barely finished the *sopapillas* when Don

Vicente came out of the annex that had been added to the big house. It was where he and Doña Cici lived. He couldn't have slept for more than an hour after staying up all night with the cows, but he didn't seem the least bit tired. Meanwhile, Tomás's snores could almost be heard from the trailer a hundred meters away.

"I got an idea," the old rancher said.

They followed him to the barn, where he tacked up his gelding, Pimiento, and strapped a harness onto the horse. Then he attached an old leather hide to the harness so the horse could drag it along behind him in the snow. Excitement sizzled through his veins and Jaime hoped he wasn't wrong about what he thought would happen next.

Don Vicente gripped the saddle horn and swung a leg gracefully over his horse's back without using the stirrup. "Hop on the hide."

Jaime and Ángela piled on and grasped the edges as Don Vicente urged Pimiento to a walk.

"Faster!" Ángela called out.

"Hold on." Don Vicente nudged Pimiento into a trot. The hide slid over the snow, swinging from one side to the other with Vida following their trail. Don Vicente rode them along the dirt driveway, the only section of the ranch guaranteed to be clear of cacti and other obstacles, but not clear of bumps. A rut caught Jaime off guard and sent him rolling into the fresh snow.

"Wait for me!" He ran in the clunky boots to catch up and dove headfirst back on the moving sleigh.

"¡*Oye!*" Ángela squealed as Jaime's impact caused the hide to skid sideways and spray her in the face with snow.

"You two had enough?" Don Vicente called over his shoulder as Pimiento continued trotting in the snow.

"¡*No!*" they both shouted. Don Vicente grunted, or maybe that's how he laughed.

Back in the barn later, they helped Don Vicente remove the hide and harness from Pimiento. Don Vicente couldn't have been off the horse for more than a minute before he remounted and leaned over the gelding to brush the snow off the top of Jaime and Ángela's heads. "I better check on the newborns and then go out to the rest of the herd. When you get tired of the cold, Cici will make you some hot chocolate with *cajeta*. Almost worth getting chilled just to have some."

They watched Don Vicente weave through the deep snow as if he knew where the cacti stood hiding. Jaime waited until he was out of earshot before turning to his cousin. "What's *cajeta*?"

Ángela motioned her head to the big house where smoke rose from one of the chimneys. "Should we find out?"

"We have to make a snowman first," Jaime insisted. "It's like a snow requirement."

"But how do you make one?" Ángela asked.

Good point. He got on his hands and knees and pushed the snow into a pile. He pushed more and more until the mound was huge, but it wouldn't shape into anything that looked like anything. More like a blob. When he tried to put in two stones for eyes, they fell right through. Still, he managed to stick a twig in the side and place his hat on top of the pile.

"Look, it's me with a paintbrush!" He stood in his bulky clothes next to the snowblob so Ángela could notice the similarities.

"Wait, let me get Tomás's phone to take a picture."

"Don't wake him up."

Jaime found another twig and experimented holding it the way the snowblob held it, and then like a real paint-brush. Then he tried carving a face onto the snowblob with his twig, but that just caused its face to fall. Literally.

He used the twig instead to draw on the ground. Their feet had compressed the snow around the trailer so much that it was a perfect drawing board. He looked around for inspiration. The cows would be obvious except they were too far away to see the details. Besides, the last time he drew a cow, he'd fallen asleep on the train and his and Ángela's backpacks had been stolen. He focused instead on sketching the big house, the other trailers, the barn and corral, and of course the mountain volcano in the distance.

The bulky glove didn't allow for much precision so he pulled it off with his teeth and picked up the twig again. Much better. When he drew smoke from one of the chimneys in the big house, the grooves of the chimney he had already drawn collapsed, but he smoothed out the section with his gloved hand and re-etched it. There, perfect.

Except it wasn't perfect. His ears getting cold and one hand near numbness, he turned to the trailer wondering what was taking Ángela so long.

He stepped up the snow-covered metal steps, holding on to the railing so as not to slip. Still that didn't keep him from flying backward when the trailer door burst open. He landed on the snowblob, which wasn't as soft as it had looked.

"Papá just called," Ángela said, her tan face whiter than the snow. "The Alphas attacked Abuela."

CHAPTER FOUR

"Is she . . . ?" Jaime froze. *No, they couldn't. They wouldn't dare. Not Abuela.*

Ángela didn't meet Jaime's eyes. Instead she blinked rapidly, as if yesterday's desert dust had blown into hers. "She's alive. But barely."

Jaime let out the breath he was holding. *"¿Q-qué pasó?"*

"Come inside," Tomás called from behind Ángela.

Some automatic force moved his legs up the metal steps a second time while he imagined Abuela—gray hair pulled into a tight bun so no stray strand would land in the food. Her eyes narrowed as she scolded him and Miguel for sneaking bits of food from the pan when they thought she wasn't looking, but then her eyes would soften as she slipped them broken pieces of tortillas drizzled with honey, lime, and salt.

Inside the trailer a puddle of melted snow surrounded the door where Ángela had taken off her boots. Jaime stood in place, his thoughts still on his grandmother. Tomás's hair stood straight up and his eyes had that dazed look of someone who just woke up and was not ready to deal with the world. Ángela sat on the bed she hadn't converted back to the table, hugging her knees to her chest. "They've really hurt her."

Jaime snapped out of his stupor. "But why? Abuela is old and helpl—" but then he stopped. He didn't want to think of her like that. Like she'd become in the last few years with Abuelo gone and her arthritis taking over. Instead, he remembered her when he was five and some kids who became future Alphas were teasing him for coloring with pink (to be fair, he colored with all of the crayons, not wanting one color to get upset for not being used). Abuela had grabbed both boys by an ear, dragged them to the washbasin, and squirted blue dish soap into their mouths to clean out their dirty words. Then, under her glare, sputtering and spitting out suds, they both apologized. Word got around after that, that you didn't mess with Jaime and Ángela's *abuela*. The shattering of her power over bullies cut into his heart. How dare they.

"Why would the Alphas attack her?" Jaime asked.

"*Nosotros*," Ángela muttered.

"Us?" Jaime braced a hand against the aluminum door. The trailer had never felt so small, even though it was about the same size as his house back home. "But why? We're gone."

They'd left their family in Guatemala, almost died in México, and come to live here specifically to avoid the Alphas' attack. And for what, when they took it out on Abuela?

"I hope she told them where to shove it." Tomás swore and scooped three spoons of coffee powder into a mug of water before slamming it into the microwave. "In a Catholic, Abuela sort of way."

Ángela hugged her knees tighter. "Papá confirmed she said nothing about our whereabouts. You know she wouldn't."

No, she wouldn't. When Jaime had stopped Abuela from butchering one of their hens because she was "too pretty to die" (she had beautiful bluish-gray feathers that in the right light looked purple), Abuela had told the rest of the family she wasn't in the mood for chicken that night. When Rosita, Ángela and Miguel's older sister, got pregnant with Quico without being married, Abuela was the first one to know, and the one who helped Rosita tell the rest of the family.

Abuela would do anything for her family. And anything to defend them.

"Tell me everything Tío said." Jaime folded his arms across his chest, made difficult with Tomás's oversize winter coat still on.

Ángela focused her attention on Vida, who was lying on the bed belly-up showing the scar of the wound that had almost cost her her life. "Papá said Abuela was coming home after selling her tortillas at the market. They robbed her of the few coins she had earned. Then they started questioning her."

"About us," Jaime said with disgust. "They still want us." Through the window by Ángela's bed he could see the snow sparkling in the sunlight. As far as he was concerned, they couldn't be farther away from the Alphas who terrorized their jungle-bordered village. And yet they still weren't safe.

"More like pissed that we got away." Ángela buried her head in Vida's short brown and white coat while the dog abandoned the belly rub request to provide comfort kisses instead.

"It's not going to be hard to figure out you've come to me. It's no secret that I'm here." Tomás swigged his coffee, then spat it back into the mug as thick steam escaped from his mouth. "But I doubt they'd make the effort to travel all the way out here for you two. Not that they'd find the ranch anyway. You're safe."

"Safe here while Abuela is everything but safe." Jaime held his arms tighter across his chest. The whole thing made Jaime sick. "And then what? They beat her up when she didn't talk?"

Ángela shook her head but kept her teary eyes on Vida. "They pushed her down some steps."

This time Jaime swore along with Tomás. And Ángela wasn't even done sharing the news. "She broke her hip and was knocked unconscious. She'll probably never walk again."

"They're going to pay for this!" Jaime shouted. "They can't get away with abusing everyone."

Except they could. And they were.

"I'm going back." Jaime's voice changed from loud and angry to low and determined. "I don't care what happens to me. They have to learn their lesson."

"How do you plan to stop them?" Tomás asked.

"I don't know." Jaime took in the things around the trailer he had accumulated in just a week. He'd have to pack—food and a few clothes; his new sketchbook. Crossing back into México would be much easier than what he'd already been through. If he was lucky, immigration officers might give him a free ride all the way back to Guatemala for being somewhere he didn't belong. And once he was there, the Alphas would remember no one messed with his abuela.

How exactly he'd teach the Alphas a lesson he'd figure

out later. He picked up his new backpack from where he'd dumped it yesterday, but Tomás removed it from his hands.

"What do you plan to do? Kill them? Do you really want to be responsible for someone's death? You'd be no better than they are."

"I—" but Tomás was right. Jaime couldn't become like them. That's what happened to Anakin Skywalker in *Star Wars*—by trying to rid evil, he became evil. "I'm still going back."

"We can't," Ángela mumbled. "That's why they hurt her. To show us, and everyone else in the village, that no one can run away. They control everyone in the village. They told Abuela that if we ever showed our faces again, they'd kill us and the rest of the family. Except for baby Quico. They would keep him."

Jaime leaned against the door. The winter clothes he still had on almost suffocated him in the warm trailer. So it was true. He really wouldn't ever be able to see his family again. He didn't care if they killed him; he could live with that thought. His death would be worth it if only to be with his family again, to see Abuela and help her recover. But he couldn't be responsible for the murder of all of them as well. As it was, the guilt of Miguel's murder still hung over his head. If Jaime had walked from school with Miguel like normal, instead of staying home, maybe Miguel would still be alive.

And now Abuela. If she never walked again that would be his fault too. In trying to keep them safe, she had been hurt. No one could say it wasn't his fault.

"So we just stay here and do nothing?" Jaime demanded.

"For now," Tomás said.

Outside, their footsteps in the snow were starting to show patches of brown dirt. Jaime finally ripped off his winter clothes and threw them in a pile. Doing nothing. That was worse than everything else put together.

CHAPTER FIVE

No one answered Tío Daniel's phone the next morning when they called to check on Abuela.

"What does that mean?" Jaime asked as he put on a long-sleeve blue polo he could use as a uniform shirt.

"Probably that Tío Daniel ran out of phone credit." Tomás grabbed a coffee can from the small cabinet above the kitchen sink. Inside, Jaime could see a couple of dollar bills crumpled near the bottom and heard the rattle of coins sliding from one end to the other. From the looks and sound of it, there wasn't much money in there. Tomás's stressed expression as he shoved it back in the cupboard confirmed Jaime's suspicion. "In English they have a saying, 'No news is good news,' which means everything is okay until we hear otherwise. I'm sure we'll get an update once Tío can add credit."

"How long before that happens?" Jaime asked.

It was Ángela who answered. "Papá gets paid next week."

Next week might as well be next year. Too long to wait for an update. His parents had e-mail, but could only access it through the village computer where the proprietor charged by the minute and each page took forever to load. They might as well be on different planets for all the information Jaime could find out, except NASA had much better reception with Mars than Jaime had with his family in Guatemala.

"So more doing nothing," Jaime said.

Tomás glanced back at the cabinet that held the coffee can piggybank. "There's nothing we can do at the moment."

Ángela bowed her head and squeezed her eyes shut as if wishing very hard for something. Jaime did the same. *Dear God and Miguel, please protect our family and help Abuela feel better.* Jaime sighed. When he had prayed before, he felt Miguel's presence, but this time there was nothing. Like both God and Miguel didn't venture out here to the no-man's-land of cacti and cattle.

"Pray in the truck," Tomás said as he headed to the tiny trailer bathroom. "I'll take you to the bus stop today to make sure you don't miss it. But we have to leave in two minutes."

With Jaime's thoughts still on Abuela, they loaded into

the truck and drove along the dirt road to where Meester George's property ended and met the highway.

"Your bus number is thirty-six," Tomás reminded them as they waited in the warm truck. Yesterday's snow had melted except for a couple of spots underneath the bushes, but the morning air still held a chill colder than anything Jaime had experienced back home. Jaime turtled himself in the old hoodie Tomás gave him; they hadn't bought coats when they went shopping a few days ago. "After school, the bus will pick you up first, Jaime, then go to Ángela's school."

"I'm not taking the bus home today, remember? I have rehearsal," Ángela reminded them.

"You're sure you can get a ride home?" Tomás asked as he checked the time on his phone. A few minutes before seven o'clock.

"This one boy, Tristan, said he'd bring me back. His dad's the director."

Tomás accepted that without even a comment. Back home, Tía or Abuela would have demanded to know more about this random boy. His last name, who his parents were, whether he could be trusted to be alone with Ángela. Instead, Tomás turned back to his little brother. "So Jaime, this is where you get off the bus. Look around so you recognize it."

There was nothing to recognize. Other than the fact

that there was an open white metal gate and the dirt road that led to the homestead, there was nothing on this stretch of straight highway that made it any different than other parts. All brown and tan with small patches of snow that were sure to be gone by the afternoon. With Jaime's luck, the driver would just drive him back to where the buses parked at night and Jaime would have a slumber party on the bus all by himself.

The sound of the bus's diesel engine roared through the empty highway before it appeared over a hill. Ángela leaped out of the truck and waited by the edge of the road, hopping from one foot to the other. Any more excitement and Jaime would have thought she was awaiting the arrival of a long lost friend.

"Try Tío Daniel again, will you?" Jaime asked his brother. With the time difference, it would be almost eight o'clock in Guatemala. Tío would be at work but he was allowed to answer his phone in an emergency. The phone rang and rang as the bus neared. Tomás shook his head and hung up when the bus stopped in front of them.

"I'll try again throughout the day. I'm sure Abuela is up already and telling the doctors how to set her hip properly."

Yes, Abuela would tell everyone what to do, and she was always right. But Tomás hadn't seen her in eight years. He didn't know how her arthritis kept her from working on extra damp days; didn't know that she took naps when she thought no one was watching. And didn't remember that the nearest hospital was forty-five minutes away by bus.

"Jaime, *vamos ya*," Ángela waited at the bottom step of the bus.

Tomás motioned Jaime to go.

As soon as they walked on the school bus, a skinny boy with a mop of bleached hair on the top and short, dark hair on the sides stood up and waved from the mob of teenagers in the back. "Yo, Angela!"

He said her name the English way, making the A sound as if he was about to vomit and then choking on a sharp G. She smiled, waved, and in an instant, Jaime's cousin was swallowed by the mob. She peered over her shoulder only once to make sure Jaime had gotten on the bus behind her and gave him a slight wave before joining the older kids.

"Sit down," the driver grumbled as he waited before moving the bus.

Jaime glanced around the front of the bus where the younger kids sat. Most of the seats were taken, either by a person or a backpack. One boy about his age with blond hair and an infestation of freckles glanced up from his book with a small smile, removed his bag from the seat, and went back to his book.

Jaime slid beside him. "Tank you."

The boy ignored Jaime and turned the page of his book.

What Jaime should have done was introduce himself and ask the boy his name, but the boy didn't seem to want to be disturbed. Jaime got it. He didn't like being interrupted when he was reading either. But mostly, he just didn't want to try to speak English.

He pulled out his sketchbook and started sketching random lines. A couple of times he turned around to look at Ángela. Her group was loud and each time he glanced their way, he caught Ángela laughing along with them as if she understood everything they said.

Maybe she did. With more years of school, her English had always been better than his. And her brain had a knack for it.

He turned back to his drawing. Crazy lines and angles intersected in total chaos, making no sense as each line pushed another out of the way. A self-portrait? Or maybe it was a family photo.

When they got to school, he remembered he didn't know the way to his classroom. The boy on the bus went in a different direction, which was disappointing since Jaime had hoped they'd be in the same class. Of course, he could ask someone for directions. Except he didn't know how to ask and he'd forgotten his teacher's name. Lots of kids passed him who looked like they might speak Spanish—at least they didn't look too different from kids who had gone to school with him back home—but he couldn't get the words out quick enough before they were gone.

One mother kept saying, "*Vamos, ¡rapido!*" to her young daughter, who had dug her heels into the shiny tile and refused to budge. Jaime knew better than to bother a frantic mother with a question like directions.

The school wasn't *that* big, he could figure it out. He found his way back to the bathroom he had gotten to know very well. It was definitely the correct bathroom—he caught a glimpse of a boy entering it while unwrapping a chocolate bar. From there he recognized the science photos outside his classroom. Maybe he should have tried harder to stay lost.

Meesus Whatever looked him in the eye and greeted him by name and a handshake as soon as he entered.

"Hi," he said in English and then rushed to the desk under the window.

She did the same thing with every kid who came in. Good. It would have been weird if she only greeted him.

When everyone was present, they all stood and put their hands over their hearts like in sports with the national anthem, but instead of singing, they recited some kind of poem in bored voices. Jaime stood and put his hand on his heart along with them. Once he understood what was going on, he adapted the same bored look too, but kept his mouth shut.

"Jaime," Meesus said once they were seated. Busted. She must have realized he hadn't recited the poem. "I'd like you to ..." But then she went on and he didn't understand what she said next.

His look of complete incomprehension must have clued her in, because she changed her tactics, speaking slower and repeating her meaning with different words. After the "sign out" disaster of the other day, maybe she figured that if you get the same response with the same answers, it's time to change the questions. Or maybe she just took him for a complete dimwit.

"Say your name."

"Jaime."

"And what do you like to do? What do you like?"

Jaime understood about sixty percent of what she asked and hoped he was answering correctly.

"I like *arte*."

"Art?" Art, of course. He had to remember that some words in English were similar to Spanish, just without the last letter, like *música/music*. So would that mean the other subjects were *historia/histori*, *ciencia/cienci*, and *matemática/matematic*?

"Yes, I like art." His hand inched to his bag. Should he show her his sketchbook? Or was she asking for something else?

"Do you like drawing, painting, sculpture, pottery?"

"Yes."

A few kids snickered.

Meesus frowned, maybe thinking that he was just saying yes without understanding the question. Well, that was pretty much true. He didn't know the specific words she used, but guessed she asked him about different kinds of art, and he did like all the ones he'd tried.

Instead of asking him another question he didn't know, she pointed to the girl in front of Jaime. The girl turned to look at Jaime, introduced herself (Kaili?) and said something she liked that Jaime didn't understand. After Kaili, the rest of the class continued with the introductions. With twenty-three kids in the class, it was hard to keep track of who was who, especially when some names were strange, like Wyatt and Autumn. Other kids mumbled and didn't look at Jaime when they talked. Jaime didn't know where the mumbled name stopped and what they liked started. But his ears pricked when Diego, who had a cool design shaved on the side of his black hair, said his name and said he liked *Star Wars*. With a name like Diego, he had to speak Spanish!

And then there was Carla, who sat one row over and two desks up, with long, black hair and copper-brown skin. She reminded him a bit of the Guatemalan natives. Jaime himself was part Mayan, but her cheekbones were much more defined than his. When she pushed up her purple-framed glasses and smiled at him, he almost caught his breath. "I know Spanish. *Yo gusto gatos.*"

He bit his lip to stop an unexpected chuckle. Her Spanish was so incorrect it was funny. He wanted to correct her but then remembered how he didn't like it when people laughed at his English. The next girl started talking before he got a chance to tell Carla that he liked cats too.

Once everyone had introduced themselves, Meesus said something that made everyone groan. They put away their books and stood up to sharpen pencils. Jaime pulled one out of his new pencil case and waited to see what would happen.

Meesus handed out papers to each row to pass down. None were left when they got to Jaime. He raised his hand. Meesus looked from the extra copy in her hand to Jaime and then nodded and handed him the last one.

It was a test. And not just any test. A math test. He should have just kept his arm down and drawn more invisible desk insects with his finger.

He glanced at the numbers, expecting to be totally baffled. He didn't understand what the instructions said, but the example showed converting mixed number fractions to decimals and percentages. Was that it? It seemed a bit rudimentary; he'd done this last year with Miguel and two of Abuela's tortillas while trying to figure out six-fifths. Miguel, the engineer wannabe, had used his compass to determine that the tortillas were not perfectly round, not perfectly equal to one another, and therefore impossible to divide exactly into fractions or determine percentages. So he'd nibbled the edges to balance them out. What turned out to be impossible was nibbling two tortillas into perfect circles.

Jaime worked through the problems quickly, imagining Miguel in the quest for the perfectly round tortillas. When he got to the word problems, he stopped. He couldn't do it. None of the words made sense, except "eight" and "six." He knew those and figured they were part of the problem. Eight-sixths was consistent with the other problems. He reduced the fraction to four-thirds and didn't have to do the math to know that was 133 percent or 1.33. He picked out the numbers in the others, made them into fractions and percentages, and finished.

He walked over to Meesus's desk with the test in hand. She had a look as if she was about to say that she couldn't help him during a test, but then replaced it with surprise when she saw he had finished.

"Three minutes," she called to the class before grabbing her red pen. She ran down the problems and then turned the page to the next set. She frowned before returning to double-check the first page. Jaime held his breath. Maybe he remembered these wrong. After all, Miguel was the one who was good at math and Jaime's brain had been on tortillas during the test.

Meesus finished going through the test and put a check mark and then a plus sign at the top of the page before handing it back to Jaime. He had no idea what that meant.

"Deez, good?" he hesitated, pointing to the mark.

Meesus shushed him, warned the others they had thirty seconds left, and then whispered, "The best."

He walked back to his desk, his eyes fixed on the check plus as Meesus called time. Who would have ever thought he'd be good at math? If only he could tell his parents and Abuela. And Miguel.

At lunchtime, Jaime looked around the cafeteria for the freckled face boy from the bus, but he wasn't anywhere. A rustle of candy wrappers and the strong smell of chocolate made him recognize Choco-chico from the bathroom—round face, round body, round legs, and a perpetual lingering scent of chocolate—but since they had never actually met and their only connection was the fact that they both liked to hide out in the bathroom, Jaime didn't even wave.

Diego and two more boys from his class, Freddie and he forgot the other one, were playing with their Pokémon cards. Back home Jaime had two Pokémon cards that he had found on the ground, but he had never played the game. The few times his parents had money to spare, he preferred getting art supplies or comic books.

The boys said hi when Jaime sat down and then continued with their discussion. As far as Jaime could tell, they weren't playing any game, but rather were admiring one another's cards and bargaining to get the ones they wanted. When Diego noticed Boy Whose Name Jaime Couldn't Remember had the card he wanted, Jaime saw his chance.

"I have that card at home, Diego. I can get my parents to send it if you want," Jaime said in Spanish.

The boys looked up at him as if their bartering opportunities were now ruined. Diego's cheeks reddened.

"I don't speak Spanish!" he said as if that would be the worst thing imaginable.

"Sorree," Jaime said in English, though he didn't know why he was apologizing; he wasn't the one who had just lied. If Diego really hadn't understood, wouldn't he have said so?

They continued talking about their cards—Diego trying to negotiate for the card he wanted, the other boy saying he wanted two cards for his one.

"*Mira*," Jaime tried again to help Diego in Spanish, pointing to one of the cards the other kid wanted. "You have two of this one."

"Dude! What's your problem?" Diego gathered his cards and lunch to move to the other side of his friend. "Can you believe it? Now I've got grease marks on my cards."

Jaime didn't understand what Diego said but got the

general idea as he watched Diego make a fuss about wiping his cards clean on his shirt, even though Jaime hadn't touched any of them. This time, he didn't even bother apologizing.

He pulled out his sandwich from his Ninja Turtles bag, secretly hoping Diego would be jealous of his coolness when his lunch bag was a boring blue.

Freddie looked from Diego and his other friend to Jaime, hesitating before he spoke. "Do you, um, have Pokémon cards, Jaime?"

"No." Jaime shook his head. They were at home after all. Here he had nothing.

During library time, the librarian showed him the e-mail address that had been set up for him when he enrolled in school. He'd never had his own e-mail address; before coming here he'd never had anyone to e-mail other than Tomás, and Mamá had always taken care of that. And the best thing was the librarian spoke enough Spanish to let him know that he could spend fifteen minutes of the library time on the computer—for free!

Queridos mamá y papá, he started the note to his parents. He knew it could be weeks, maybe even months before there was enough money to splurge on a few minutes at the village's Internet café. Still, he wasn't going to leave any form of communication untried.

How is Abuela? Is she all right? I can't believe what hap-
pened to her. He kept on writing, but without accent marks
and correct punctuation because he didn't know how to
do them on this English keyboard. *It makes me sick. I wish I
could make them pay for what they've done. I feel trapped. I don't
know why Tomas likes it here. There are no neighbors except for
the cows and horses. The people who live on the ranch with us are
pretty nice though. And it snowed yesterday which was amazing.
But it's not Guatemala and the people are not you guys, not family. Please pray that the Alphas all get struck by lightning and it's
safe once more to go home. I don't belong here. Love you, Jaime.*

The day dragged on with many things Jaime didn't
understand and many kids he didn't know. At one point
Meesus paired him up with Samuel, who spoke Spanish
fine, except Samuel had never spoken Spanish in school
and didn't know the names for a lot of the stuff they were
doing and got frustrated when Jaime didn't understand his
English words for things like "stapler."

Once the final bell rang, Jaime dashed out to the bus.
He sat in the same seat as this morning, except next to
the window, and closed his eyes. He opened one when
he felt the seat indent next to him, but the freckle-faced
boy from the morning already had his book open and
his nose in it. Jaime leaned against the window and went
back to closed eyes.

A hand tapped his shoulder. His eyes regained focus

as Jaime's bus buddy pointed out the window. What? It wasn't as if there was anything to see out there. Not even a raven pecking at the roadkill. Then he realized the bus had stopped. And why. His stop.

"Tank you," he said to the boy as he gathered his things and stumbled out of the bus. The white iron gate that marked the entry to Meester George's property stood wide open, with a barbed wire fence on either side. Jaime stepped carefully on the cattle guard to cross onto the property and then shuffled his feet down the dirt road. Judging by how long it took to drive it, Jaime guessed walking to the trailer would take a good hour. He dragged his feet more. Maybe an hour and a half.

"Coo-coo!" A strange birdcall came from the west.

Jaime shaded his eyes to stare at the horizon. A figure too far away to discern stood on the far ridge. One of those striped-face antelopes that liked to frolic with the cattle? Or a mountain lion looking over Pride Rock?

Except antelopes and lions didn't make birdcalls. And he didn't see any birds.

The figure sped down the ridge as if it were floating. Jaime waved, and within minutes Don Vicente pulled his gray-spotted Appaloosa to a stop in front of him. Jaime's eyes landed on the elaborate beadwork on the horse's bridle, which matched perfectly the beaded pattern on Don Vicente's leather belt.

"I figured you wouldn't want to walk back to the house on your own," Don Vicente said from under the brim of his battered straw cowboy hat. Jaime let out a breath he hadn't known he'd been holding. What a relief to hear some normal Spanish!

"Company would be great," Jaime said.

"Hop on." The old cowboy removed his left foot from the stirrup and moved his leg forward of the saddle.

"I've never ridden a horse before," Jaime admitted. Just the idea caused his heart to race.

"Better get started then." Holding the reins in his right hand, Don Vicente reached out with his left.

Jaime licked his lips. He could do this. If he could get on a moving train with the first ladder rung higher than his head, then a horse with a chest-high stirrup and an arm reaching out to help should be nothing. Don Vicente held the gelding steady and pulled Jaime up. The act felt clumsy and it didn't help that Pimiento stepped to the side when he was half on. At last he sat on the horse's back behind the saddle.

"Sorry, Pimiento," he apologized to the horse for kicking him accidentally. He shifted a bit farther back so the edge of the saddle didn't dig into his privates. "Is it okay to sit here? Will it hurt Pimiento?"

Don Vicente leaned over to pat the horse's neck. "This old boy's used to saddlebags weighing much more than you. Just make sure you don't slide off the back end."

Jaime scooted a bit closer and adjusted his backpack straps. Don Vicente might have been teasing but that didn't make it any less possible.

"Hold on." Don Vicente nudged the horse before Jaime could ask to what. Within a couple of seconds, the gelding went from standing still to a gait much smoother than the coin-operated horse Jaime once rode when he was little. The idea that they had floated down the ridge wasn't so far-fetched now. At first Jaime clung to Don Vicente's belt loops, until one tore off, leaving Jaime with a piece of worn denim in his hand. Better hold on to the old man's waist, though he didn't want to ruin the beaded belt either. Maybe one day he wouldn't need to hold on at all. One day when he could ride as well as Don Vicente.

Instead of riding along the road, Don Vicente took to the open land. The ground under Pimiento's hooves was both rocky and sandy, but the gelding didn't stumble once. On a small hill, the cowboy pulled Pimiento to a stop and pointed with his sunbaked hand. Down in the valley, two tiny coyote pups were half chewing, half playing tug-of-war with a stick while their *mamá* kept surveillance nearby. With their young round faces and furry gray coats, the pups had to be the cutest things Jaime had ever seen. He itched to pull out his sketchbook from his backpack, but he wasn't entirely sure how to do that on horseback.

Whether through sight or scent, the *mamá* coyote

became alerted of their presence. She gave a faint yip, and the two pups dropped their stick game and stared at their *mamá* with wide eyes. She gave them another signal and before Jaime could see where they'd gone, the family had turned tail and disappeared.

"The Navajo Indians here have a lot of stories about the coyotes and how they're tricksters," Don Vicente said. "You'll never see an Indian cross a coyote's path. They think it's bad luck. They'd rather turn the car around and go several miles out of their way than drive over the place they saw the coyote cross."

And with that, Don Vicente turned Pimiento around and let him walk down a different direction.

"Are the coyotes dangerous?" Jaime turned back to the coyote. He couldn't see her, but he felt the *mamá's* eyes watching them.

"Anything is dangerous if you aggravate it, especially when it comes to protecting its family. But in all my time working on this ranch, I've only had to kill one and that was because it went after a weak calf I had spent all night trying to save."

Jaime understood that. Family was everything. The one thing he'd die protecting. That was why it was so hard not to go after the Alphas for what they had done to Abuela and Miguel.

"What about other animals? Tomás says there are bears

and mountain lions. You're not afraid they'll hurt or kill you?"

The old rancher didn't take a second to think about it. "When it's my time to go, it won't be by bear or mountain lion. I'll just leave. Ride off into the sunset and disappear. No mess, no fuss. Just my time."

"Like Luke Skywalker."

"Who?"

"He's a . . . never mind." Jaime knew Don Vicente didn't watch TV or movies. Not when he said that being out in nature was more entertaining. Jaime supposed when you were older than Jesús, you'd lived most of your life before the invention of television anyway.

"*Pero . . .*" Jaime paused to think of a tactful way of asking what he wanted to know. "You're not planning on riding into the sunset any time soon, are you?"

A grunt came out of Don Vicente. "Don't get me wrong, I love your brother like my own, but he doesn't understand the cattle like I do. Not many do."

Don Vicente's meaning couldn't have been clearer. Tomás worked hard, but at the end of the day, cattle ranching was just a job. It wasn't his passion. Not like it was for Don Vicente, not like *arte* was for him.

"Do you have kids, Don Vicente?"

"Yeah, thousands."

Jaime stared at the lean back in front of him and then grinned. "I meant kids that don't have four legs."

"Not officially." The cowboy shifted his hat to reveal a couple of wispy silver hairs on the nape of his neck. "Cici and I tried but it wasn't meant to be. Instead, I had Mr. George riding with me before he could walk; I remember his two sisters being born. When he grew up and brought home a wife, he made me godfather of their first daughter. His whole family are my kids, and quite a lot of people in the community as well. Mexicans, gringos, Indians. Family knows no race and they're all my kids, a part of me. Tomás too."

"And me and Ángela?" The words escaped before Jaime could stop them. He shouldn't have said that; they'd only known the man for a week and a half. Don Vicente would think he was disrespectful.

The old rancher twisted in the saddle with more flexibility than Jaime thought possible for anyone of any age. His dark eyes deeply set in his leathery face and half hidden by the hat brim, he stared long and hard at Jaime.

"I only take my kids out on rides."

CHAPTER SIX

Just as he had the day before, the freckle-faced boy met Jaime's eye and removed his backpack from the seat next to him as soon as Jaime and Ángela got on the bus.

"Let's sit up here." Jaime pointed to the free seat across from his bus buddy. But Ángela didn't hear him, or chose not to. She passed their seat with a flip of her long, dark hair and with a singsong voice that dragged out the three-letter word to five syllables, she greeted the older kids on the back of the bus.

"Heyyyy!"

"Angela, baby!" The same boy from yesterday who pronounced her name all gag-like pretended to swoon at the sight of her, dropping to his knees and reaching out with his hand to kiss the top of hers like some stupid sign of chivalry. Any minute Ángela would tell him off for embarrassing her. Instead she giggled. A giggle that echoed across the bus and made the driver look in the rearview mirror to check out the situation. Jaime turned away from Ángela in disgust and disappointment. The freckle-faced boy rolled his eyes and Jaime couldn't have agreed more. Xavi (Jaime couldn't bring himself to think of him as Ángela's *ex*-boyfriend) never acted like that. And as a result, Ángela had never acted so stupid.

Jaime would have to talk to Ángela. Let her know she was making a fool of herself and that Tía and Abuela would never approve of her hanging out with the likes of that guy, with his disrespect and revolting public displays of affection. Besides, it was too soon after Xavi had disappeared. At least she should show some grief and restrain herself around other boys. Jaime didn't know the custom for this kind of thing—after all, Ángela and Xavi hadn't been married—but he figured at least a couple of decades would be a respectable amount of mourning time.

Ángela didn't get on the bus after school. Jaime replayed the conversation in the truck from the first day. She definitely said Monday, Wednesday, and Friday.

Yet today was Thursday and no Ángela came running when the bus stopped outside the high school. Jaime wanted to ask the driver to wait for her. At least another five minutes. In Guatemala, he could have bribed the driver, but somehow he didn't think the drivers here worked that way. Besides, he didn't have any money.

Instead Jaime watched the town turn into a few scattered buildings until even those disappeared and the desert took over with its shrubby pines and spiny cacti, foothills, and a former volcano in the distance.

In his all-knowing way, Don Vicente rode up on Pimiento just as Jaime got off the bus. Somehow he'd known Ángela wouldn't be there because he didn't bring an extra horse. Or maybe he didn't realize that there were days Ángela *should* come home on the bus.

Back at the corral Jaime greeted Tomás and told him the news—Ángela hadn't been on the bus.

Tomás pulled off his work gloves and dug his phone out of his jeans. No messages, but also no reception. "She's probably hanging out with her friends."

"So we aren't going to look for her?"

Tomás shrugged and checked his phone again. This time it showed one bar of reception. And also that it wasn't even five o'clock. "I'm glad she's settling in." He pulled his gloves back on and continued mucking out the corral.

Tía would never have allowed it. Not without at least telling someone where she was going, Jaime thought as he made his way back to the trailer and sat on the steps to watch the dirt track for any vehicles. Pointless really, since any engine coming down the private road could be heard anywhere on the homestead.

She finally arrived in a dirty white car much too small for all the people it held. Without trying, Jaime counted six heads once Ángela poured out. It was impossible to see how she'd even fit in there in the first place.

"Bye, losers!" she said in English and laughed when they called her names in return. Names that Jaime knew from *la tele* and knew no real friends should ever call each other.

Jaime waited for the car to disappear before standing up from the steps. "Where were you? You missed the bus."

She pushed past him and opened the door he guarded. "I didn't miss it. Just didn't get on it."

"Why not?" He followed her in.

"Because I didn't want to be bombarded with these annoying questions."

He was about to retort that if she'd been on the bus he wouldn't have needed to ask these annoying questions. There would have been other questions of the annoying variety. But he went for a more convincing argument.

"I worry about you." It wasn't a lie. He worried about her hanging out with that guy on the bus, and liking him. Or worse, becoming like him. "What if something happened to you?"

She dropped her defenses and wrapped him in a quick hug. "You don't have to worry about me. I'm just making new friends and we were hanging out. Got a pizza."

"A pizza?" No one in their village in Guatemala made pizza, and even if they did, Jaime's family wouldn't have been able to afford it. The one time he had tried pizza had been when one of the ladies Mamá worked for had bought a bunch for a party and Mamá got to bring the leftovers home. They warmed up the slices on the *comal* Abuela used to make her tortillas and the taste had been like heaven on earth. He and Miguel used to tease that whichever of them got rich first would have to buy a whole pizza for the other. And here Ángela mentioned a pizza as if it were something everyone could afford to eat.

"Yeah, I was just hanging out with Tristan and the others before they dropped me off. Nothing to worry about."

Jaime scrunched up his nose and saw the perfect opportunity to discuss the reason he really had been waiting for her. "Tristan? Is that the boy who sounds like he's gagging when he calls you Ang-gel-la? I don't like him."

Ángela's defenses rocketed right back up. "You don't know him."

"I don't want to know him. He's disrespectful. Tía wouldn't let you hang out with him."

Ángela turned to him with a hard look and raised eyebrows. "She let me cross an entire country with people she didn't know."

How could he argue with that? In many ways, their parents had given them up. Had allowed them to risk their lives going through unknown terrain, be at the mercy of gangs that could have killed them for sport or abused Ángela. A rich mobster *did* lock them up in a boxcar to die. Put that way, what harm could hanging out and getting pizza do?

He should give up now. Jaime knew he had no real argument against her friends other than loud voices and bad vibes. And maybe a tiny bit of jealousy for being excluded. Still, he gave the argument one last shot, even though the idea made him cringe.

"You could hang out with them here, at the ranch."

"There's nothing to do here."

"There's all these cool desert animals to draw and . . . " He was losing her. She wasn't a visual artist. What did she care about capturing the blue-black wings of a raven in motion or experimenting with shadows to create a flying bird of prey?

"Well, the thing is," Jaime grabbed the last desperate thing he could think of, "Tomás doesn't want you to hang out with them until he's met them."

"He hasn't said anything. Besides, he's not my father. He's not even my brother. And neither are you." And she grabbed the play script from her bag before yanking the trailer door back open and stomping down the metal steps. The door crashed against the side of the trailer before bouncing shut, making the whole trailer shake.

So much for talking and hanging out with his cousin.

CHAPTER SEVEN

The sight of the freckle-faced blond boy smiling and waving when Jaime got on the bus gave him a sense of relief from the tension he hadn't known he felt. After all, it wasn't like he'd get to sit with Ángela. She'd barely spoken to him last night. But she did make a point of asking—no, telling Tomás that she would be hanging out with friends after school on a regular basis. To which Tomás replied, "Cool, it's good you're making friends." And Ángela shot Jaime a look that said "see?" That was the most they'd interacted since he confronted her.

But at least someone was happy to see him. The freckle-faced boy cleared the seat for him, as he'd done the other days. Jaime responded with a smile.

Today instead of reading a book, the boy wrote in

some kind of notebook. The boy still didn't say anything and Jaime didn't ask. Their silence felt good—no criticism, no expectations, no disappointment.

The older kids in the back were belting out songs that sounded like they should be in old movies. Tomás would have known from which movies, but Jaime didn't care. He didn't know them anyway, and apparently neither did Ángela, though that didn't stop her. He caught her singing random bits of the chorus.

He got out his sketchbook and did his best to ignore the serenade. If his bus-buddy could do it, scribbling away in his journal, so could he.

What Jaime did notice was the boy sneaking glances at the sketchbook. He shifted his arm so the page was less blocked and kept doodling—imaginary creatures with swords, cars with wings, a human with his face in the shadows. When he paused to think about what to draw next, the boy passed his own notebook over.

On a clean page, the boy had written, *What is your name?*

Jaime. And then because he knew how Spanish and English letters had different pronunciations, he wrote in parentheses *(Hi-meh),* and then *¿you?* before passing the notebook back.

Sean, and then with a grin added *(normal).* Jaime laughed. Seh-Ahn wasn't exactly a normal name but at least it was pronounceable. Jaime motioned for the notebook back. Between not being able to speak English properly and not understanding how things worked in this strange country, he felt justified to scribble, *Me not normal.* This time the boy made an odd sound in his throat, as if laughing wasn't something he was used to doing.

Cool. I'm not normal either.

Well then, cool too. And they both went back to their books, Jaime drawing and Seh-Ahn writing. Perfectly normal.

Every day after lunch, Jaime's class had a subject not taught by Meesus—the last two days had been library and Spanish. (Where Señor Borrego spent the whole time teaching the others how to answer "*¿Qué hora es?*" but allowed Jaime and Samuel, the other Spanish speaker in his class, to read Spanish books as long as they wrote a book report once they were done. Perfect. Jaime had picked up the fourth *Diario de Greg: Días de perros* and happily ignored his classmates saying the time was one minus a quarter.)

When Jaime asked about art class, Meesus said Monday and then something about a teacher and a baby. Jaime hoped that didn't mean they were only allowed to draw either a teacher or a baby. Although the idea of drawing Meesus with her cardigan and old lady shoes as a baby amused him long enough to ignore Meesus talking for a while.

Today was music, and Jaime had a horrible feeling he'd be asked to sing like the older kids had done on the bus. Except he'd have to do it by himself. In public. And in English. Because embarrassment is what always happened in movies that take place in school. And in the other *Diario de Greg* books he'd read.

Except Jaime forgot Meez Macálista taught music and she didn't seem the kind to encourage public humiliation. She gave the other kids instructions to get out their instruments and start warming up with scales before returning to Jaime with a "happy to see you" smile.

"*Hola, Jaime. ¿Cómo están las cosas?*" she asked.

"*Bien,*" Jaime answered automatically. Easier than saying things were as good as they could be considering they still hadn't heard any news about Abuela, and he didn't know what to think about Ángela acting *media loca.*

His eyes wandered the room. Everyone had an instrument and seemed to be focused on twisting mouthpieces or stuffing the insides with a rag. Three of the kids, including Carla, played larger versions of the instrument. When she caught Jaime looking at her, she puffed her cheeks like she had two *guayabas* in her mouth and crossed her magnified eyes as she played the lowest note possible. Jaime laughed and turned away as he felt his own cheeks heat up.

"*¿Sabes jugar un instrumento de música?*" Meez Macálista brought his attention back to her.

Jaime bit his lip to keep from grinning. What she had said didn't make any sense—he guessed she'd translated her words literally. But it was nice to know he wasn't the only one who made mistakes in foreign languages.

"No, I never learned to play a musical instrument," he answered with the correct verb, and Meez caught the word change with a cringe.

"*Claro*, you use '*tocar*' instead of '*jugar*.'" She reached for a box under her desk and pulled out a plastic case. "In English it's called a 'recorder.'" Jaime opened the case and pulled out a plastic black and tan rod similar to the rest of the class's. "Oh, it's a *flauta*."

"Yes, it is a kind of flute. But what we call 'flute' are usually the ones that go horizontal." She positioned her hands to the side of her right cheek in demonstration.

"This one's a *flauta dulce*, and the one you mentioned is a *flauta transversal*." Jaime gave the recorder a blow and was met with a sharp screech. The other kids turned to give him a look and Diego made a farting sound on his *flauta* back at him.

Meez gathered the music in the air with her two hands like a conductor and everyone fell quiet. Like magic. She grabbed a stack of music books and began passing them out. "Work in groups, first three songs, and listen to each other to stay on the same beat."

Jaime blew into his *flauta* again, this time softer, his

mouth more relaxed, and less like he was blowing a referee whistle. The sound came out less screechy and almost sounded like a musical note.

"It takes a real stupid person not to be able to play the recorder," Diego said to his friend. "He probably believes Ms. McAllister once played for Elvis Presley. Doofus."

"Don't say that." His friend, the boy whose name Jaime still didn't know, glanced at Meez Macálista helping Samuel, who was struggling to twist the mouthpiece on correctly.

"Why? He doesn't understand." This time Diego glared at Jaime as he spoke. Jaime could feel his eyes on him but didn't look up, didn't indicate he had understood Diego's putdown just fine. "See? Stupid."

Jaime raised his eyes to give them the death glare they deserved. He turned the recorder around, covered the bottom hole with his left thumb and top hole with his pointer finger, and blew again. The note came out lower and crisper than when he hadn't covered any holes. No screeching at all. He went on to place his middle finger and then his ring finger on the recorder, each time playing a lower note. He raised his fingers one at a time until he was back to just holding his thumb and pointer in place. With no more screeching, he had successfully played three different notes.

Meez came back to him with her hand up for a high

five. "*Perfecto.* You're a natural. Soon we'll have you playing in concerts around the world."

When Meez turned away, he caught Diego giving him an evil stare. Jaime returned the glare with one of his own. See? Not stupid.

CHAPTER EIGHT

On Sundays, Tomás's official day off, everyone slept in and then padded over to the big house for breakfast, where Doña Cici cooked up enough food for a herd of ranch hands. According to Tomás, a few times a year there were up to fifteen guys helping with the roundup and Doña Cici provided food for them all. Except now Doña forgot it was only Tomás's family and Don Vicente and still cooked too much.

"*Ustedes están muy flacos,*" Doña Cici scolded Jaime and Ángela as if it were their fault they had been close to starvation just a couple of weeks ago. At the same time, Jaime got the feeling she would always be telling them they were too skinny—she did to Don Vicente. While Doña Cici was on the plump side, Don Vicente's build leaned more to wiry. The first time they'd met them, Ángela said they looked like a number ten standing together.

"Don't you feed them anything in that trailer?" she turned to Tomás while sliding more chorizo onto all three of their plates.

"I don't know about them, but you know I live on *café y frijoles*," Tomás winked, though it wasn't too far from the truth. He did pretty much only drink coffee and eat beans. Canned beans though. Not the homemade pinto ones Doña Cici added to their plates.

Truth was, Tomás didn't have time to cook or go into town to grocery shop often. He bought food that didn't spoil quickly and that could be cooked in the microwave. So far with Jaime and Ángela living there too, at least he made an effort to have bread and cheese or meat slices on hand. Anything that Doña Cici made seemed like heaven in comparison.

A week ago, for their first Sunday breakfast in El Norte, Jaime couldn't believe all the food—flour tortillas (Abuela always made hers from corn), scrambled *and* fried eggs, pinto beans, chorizo, fried potatoes, shredded yellow cheese, crumbly goat cheese, too-spicy green chile, bananas and avocados, orange *and* grapefruit juice, ground coffee, and fresh goat milk from the two does down in the barn.

Her cooking was spicier than he was used to. Mexicans, or at least these two from Chihuahua, seemed to like their chile and they liked it hot. In Guatemala, food was always flavorful but not often *picante*. Jaime could handle the bite in the chorizo but steered clear of the green chile. Yet Don Vicente poured it on his food like it was the elixir of life.

"Green chile will save you from any ailment. Keeps you healthy and trim." Don Vicente patted his flat belly. "Never been sick a day in my life."

Ángela drizzled a little on her tortilla but when she took a bite, she ended up coughing and downing a glass of juice.

"I think I have some mild green chiles in the spare freezer for when the grandkids visit." Doña placed a kind hand on her shoulder. "I'll get some out for you next week."

Ángela shook her head, still trying to air out her mouth. "It's . . . okay. I don't think . . . ah, I like the taste."

Don Vicente dropped his fork on the plate as if Ángela had insulted him personally.

"Don't say that," Tomás hissed. "*Nuevomexicanos* are very protective about their green chile. It's like saying back home that you don't like *pepián*."

"What is *pepián*? I can make it if you like." Doña Cici got up as if she were about to start cooking the Guatemalan stew at that very moment. Tomás insisted she sit back down at the table. The older woman fussed about feeding everyone else and sometimes forgot to eat herself. It wasn't until several grumbles later that she agreed to return to the table.

Last week, the older couple had asked them about their journey to El Norte and Jaime had run back to the trailer for the other sketchbook he had filled traveling through three countries. Like going through a photo album, he showed drawings of Miguel's funeral and his family members (his one family photograph had been stolen), the bus ride to Arriaga in México, and the friends they met there—Xavi, who had rescued Vida and became Ángela's boyfriend, and little Joaquín, who traveled with a secret. When Jaime got to a drawing of a smudged calf, Don Vicente had wanted to know what kind of cattle they were. Jaime couldn't remember what they looked like. It had been near sunrise and Jaime was half asleep when he tried to draw them. The cow distraction was good though. It allowed him to skip over the part of the story where Ángela had gotten mad at him for letting their bags get stolen and he'd almost lost her for good.

While Jaime had told their story, Ángela had sat with her head down and dragged her fork through a bit of left-over egg yolk. Not once had she added to the tale, or given any indication that she had even been there too. Maybe she hadn't wanted to remember it.

Now Jaime turned the question to the older couple. "What brought you two to this ranch?"

"Horses," Don Vicente answered immediately.

"You rode a horse over the border?"

"Hmm, would have had I thought of it. Had I had a horse and known how to ride it at the time." The old rancher leaned back in his chair as he reminisced. "You two crossed a river, but a lot of the border is a desert. No civilization for hundreds of miles. In some places there's nothing more than a barbed wire fence meant only to keep cattle separated. In others, not even that. Back then there wasn't much enforcement in the desert. Probably could have ridden over without a thought."

The old rancher paused as he seemed to think about that or even regret he couldn't change the past.

"Instead, guys came to my town in Chihuahua when I was a young man," he continued. "Said there was work in California on the farms and anyone who wanted to come was welcome. Didn't have anything better to do so I loaded in the truck with the rest of them. Had never been in a vehicle before and hoped I would never have to again. We were in there for days it seemed like. People got carsick, myself included. We would stop when the driver ran out of gas and were only let out in the dark."

"You didn't have trouble crossing the boarder? *La migra* didn't search the truck?" Jaime asked. Even crossing from Guatemala into México had been a challenge. They had hidden in a truck filled with used clothes to throw off the patrol dogs, and still their driver distracted the guard with a bribe.

Don Vicente shrugged. "If they did, I don't remember and it couldn't have been a big deal. Most farmers were using us, and Chinese workers too, and many thought we'd just return home once the crops were done. Some did, though most just moved from farm to farm depending on what needed planting or harvesting next."

The country was built by immigrants, Jaime remembered Meesus saying in their social studies class. That immigrants did the work no one else wanted to do, or the work no one was willing to pay more money for others to do. Only those desperate or without other options took these jobs. It was one of the few things Meesus had taught this week that Jaime had understood. Because he knew it all too well.

"It didn't take long for me to realize I didn't like farming, probably not even a week," Don Vicente continued. "I got caught pulling a weed out of one of their horse's tails and the foreman, a nasty twerp from Sonora, gave me a lashing and docked a week's pay for laying my 'dirty' hands on the steed. Decided I wasn't going to have none of that and just left."

"Did they come looking for you to bring you back?" This time Jaime remembered the Alphas back home, and how they would have come looking for him and Ángela had they stayed in the country.

Through his weathered face, Don Vicente gave Jaime a look that said getting caught had never crossed his mind. "I wasn't a slave, and I hadn't charged anything to the company store, which lots of the others did. They hadn't paid me anything at that point so really it was them that owed me. Didn't matter. I just wanted out. Was hitchhiking back to México when I heard of a mustang roundup. They're wild horses, and as work it sounded better than planting asparagus. George Padre was there, the current George's *papá*, saw that I worked well with the horses, even though I'd never been around them before, and brought me here. Haven't wanted to leave since."

"When was that? What year?" Jaime asked.

"After the dinosaurs, I'm pretty sure. There was one time I thought I saw one but it ended up being a wooly mammoth instead." Don Vicente winked and the idea that maybe he honestly didn't know his age or the current year crossed Jaime's mind. The man never mentioned years in numbers, but rather referenced things like "the year of the forest fire" and "the season the calves were all a bit cross-eyed."

"And during all this time, you never learned to speak English?" Ángela asked the old man.

Doña Cici shook her head while scowling at her husband. Apparently Ángela had hit a sour spot between the two.

Don Vicente sat tall in his chair and looked at Ángela right in the eye as he spoke. "Here, so close to the border, there's always people that understand me, and how often do I need to talk to people? The horses and cattle, that's my job, and they don't care about my native tongue. I wasn't about to be like everyone else. I may have lived here most of my life, but that doesn't change who I am, a poor man from Chihuahua."

Jaime agreed. Why did he have to adapt and blend in? He didn't need English, just like Don Vicente didn't. Meez Macálista spoke great Spanish and Samuel in his class didn't like being a translator but he still helped when Jaime needed him. Next time someone said he should learn English, he'd reply that he was remaining true to himself. Just like Don Vicente, he didn't need English to work. His art would speak for itself.

"But being able to speak English can open so many doors," Ángela said. "You can travel almost anywhere and find someone who understands you."

"My traveling days are over. If I can't get there on horseback, it's not worth going. Besides, in all my years, I never once came across a situation where knowing English changed the outcome."

Ángela opened her mouth like she was about to argue, but the looks from both Doña Cici and Tomás said that it was useless to try to teach an old cowboy new tricks.

The tension in the room remained thick until Jaime turned to Doña Cici. "And how did you come to work here?"

The older woman stood up from the table and began to load the dishwasher. "My story isn't nearly as interesting. I came with my parents. Again, it wasn't hard to cross, just told the guard we were grocery shopping and he believed us, since we only carried the empty grocery bags and a bit of money. He didn't know we didn't have anything else, lost everything in a fire. We came up here and I met Miss Eleanor, Mr. George's mom, at church when she had her hands full with a newborn and Mr. George who was barely walking. George Padre wasn't interested in helping with his children, so she was on her own in that regard. We had never met but she just turned to me and asked if I wanted a job. I said yes, not even knowing or caring what the job was. At that time, no one worried if you had papers, just as long as they didn't have to pay you as much as a gringo."

"But people worry about that now. What if you get caught?" Jaime asked, though what he was really asking was how safe they all were here on the ranch.

Don Vicente must have read his mind because he placed a hand on top of Jaime's. "There must be close to a hundred thousand undocumented workers in just Nuevo México. We work on the farms and ranches out here, and in the cities we work in construction or restaurants or clean houses. If we're all taken, the state wouldn't be able to survive. Everyone knows we're here, but as long as we don't get into trouble, they're happy with us doing the work they don't want to do. And let me tell you, this ranch is too far away from anything for someone to come down that bumpy dirt road who shouldn't."

The worry eased. The old man had a point. Just getting to school took nearly an hour.

Jaime's family helped Doña Cici put away the food, half of which went into containers for them to take back to the trailer. Once the kitchen was spotless to the point that even Abuela wouldn't have been able to find a speck of dirt, they moved through a hallway filled with photos of Meester George's parents, children, and grandchildren. Jaime's favorite was a framed newspaper clipping of an old photo showing a group of men around a corral of wild-eyed horses. The two young men closest to the camera were blurred and unrecognizable, except that one had long, dark hair and the other short. Yet there was something about the two men that made them seem happy and at home around the wild horses.

"Is one of these men you, Don Vicente?" Jaime asked.

The old man grunted. "Yeah, the one with the bad haircut. My friend Sani is the good-looking bastard next to me." He squinted at the herd of horses and pointed to two ears barely visible in the black-and-white photograph.

"And that was Reina, my first horse. Never let anyone ride her but me."

Jaime searched the edges of the photo, looking for a date, but whoever cut it out of the newspaper hadn't preserved the year. He followed the others into the TV room, which was really more like a movie theater. The screen extended larger than Jaime's arms and lay flat against the wall. A couch the shape of a massive U covered the other side of the room. And to top it off, a popcorn machine stood in the corner. A real popcorn machine.

"You're sure Meester George won't mind if we watch something?"

Doña Cici shook her head. "He lets me watch whenever I want. He's already paying for the service so someone might as well take advantage of it."

Even though they were stuffed from brunch, they made popcorn, because how could they not, and each settled on a section of the couch. Don Vicente crossed his arms over his chest and fell asleep before 007 lit his cigarette in *Dr. No*, the first James Bond film and a movie Jaime hadn't seen since Tomás still lived in Guatemala. By the time the opening credits rolled, Don Vicente was back on his feet and heading outside.

"Just because it's Sunday doesn't mean the cattle can take care of themselves."

Jaime paused the film and turned to the man as he gathered his battered straw cowboy hat.

"You should stay and watch with us. It's a good one."

"I have my own television outside. Always changing, never the same." And with that, Don Vicente left the house.

"When we got married and they built the annex for us, the family gave us a TV. Vicente somehow strapped that bulky thing onto Reina, the horse he had back then, and gave it to a sick friend who needed the entertainment. He never did like things he didn't have a use for." Doña Cici rearranged herself on the cushions and motioned to Jaime to unpause the film. "Now let's see what use we can make of this handsome Bond man."

For a second Jaime thought about joining Don Vicente. For three days in a row, the old man had picked up Jaime from the bus stop and taken him through different parts of the ranch to get back to the homestead. Don Vicente showed him tracks of critters Jaime had never heard of, like the hoof print of a piglike creature called a javelina. Yesterday he had shown Jaime a den that housed hibernating snakes. Don Vicente even promised to teach Jaime to ride his own horse, something he couldn't wait to try. Today would be a great day for that—a brisk breeze with the sun high in the breathtakingly blue sky. While the horse grazed on the young spring grass, Jaime could sketch out the arroyos and the critters that lived in them.

But the television had James Bond, and Jaime loved watching movies with Tomás. With all his work, Jaime barely had any time to spend with his big brother. Not to mention he'd barely hung out with Ángela since the snowstorm. Learning to ride a horse could wait. It was family "Bonding" time.

CHAPTER NINE

Monday morning started with a beep from Tomás's phone. Cell reception on the ranch was spotty. Sometimes it took hours to get notice of a voice message. Text messages tended to arrive more promptly, but a one-minute call from Guatemala contained a lot more information than a single text possibly could.

Without talking, Jaime and Tomás got out of bed and walked the phone over to Ángela's bedside, where they got the best reception.

The phone said it was 4:36. The sky remained so dark it seemed impossible to think the sun would ever return.

Tomás's phone didn't say when the message had been sent, just that there was one new voice message. Jaime swallowed. The message could have been sent a few minutes ago, or several hours.

Tomás held out his phone on speaker. Jaime and Ángela crowded around it, their heads touching each other in their attempt to get as close as possible. Mamá's voice filled the trailer as she rushed to say everything in sixty seconds or less.

"*Hola mi'jos.* Your father has been promoted to supervisor at the chocolate plantation, so hopefully we'll have money to use the village computer for a Skype date soon. I'm taking care of baby Quico three days a week so Rosita can work the cash register at Armando's store—you wouldn't believe how big he's gotten! Ángela, your *mamá* said to remind you that you're a young lady and to act accordingly. Both your *mamá* and *papá* send their love and hope to add credit to the phone soon. Abuela, though, is not so good, not being able to get out of bed with her broken hip, and refusing to eat. She keeps saying she's lived a good life; she might not be with us for much longer. We'll let you know if something changes. Love you all—" and then the phone went dead. She'd paid for only one minute of phone time and Jaime guessed she didn't have the extra coins to make the call last any longer.

Tomás replayed the message to hear her voice again. Jaime knew, because he wanted the same thing.

"—she might not be with us for much longer. We'll let you know if something changes. Love you all—"

Tomás pressed the button to save the message while Jaime collapsed on Ángela's bed.

It couldn't be true. Not when so many people loved her, counted on her. If the Alphas hadn't threatened and pushed her, Abuela wouldn't have broken her hip and been left stranded in bed. If Jaime and Ángela hadn't left, they wouldn't have threatened her. However he looked at it, the blame came back to haunt him.

Tomás shook his head as if that could change the news. "If Abuela is in pain, if she's suffering, then maybe it's best if she . . ."

But he wasn't able to finish his thought. Jaime glanced at Ángela, who scrunched her covers in her arms against her chest for comfort.

"She never said good-bye," Ángela sniffed. "We never said good-bye."

The morning they had left Guatemala, Abuela had cooked them a feast. Not as elaborate as Doña Cici's, but with food they had on hand and all the love she had to offer. Considering the potential danger of their journey, when it came time for them to leave, Abuela had walked away, not wanting or not being able to see them off. Now, if it came to it, they were the ones unable to say good-bye.

Tomás put his arm around both of them as the three

cried on one another's shoulders. Vida walked across the bed to join the huddle, licking each of their arms, unable to kiss away their tears.

"She's not gone yet," Jaime reminded them. "She's so tough, she could live years. . . ."

Or minutes. Their grandmother always did what she set her mind to do, and as much as she wasn't someone to give up, Jaime had never known her to change her mind. If she couldn't get out of bed, if she didn't have anything to keep her busy, then she would feel useless. She'd never had patience for lazy people.

They tried calling Tío Daniel, Ángela's *papá*, but just as it had the millions of other times, the phone rang and rang. Tomás even tried to ring the pay phone in the village Mamá must have called from, but that one, too, received no answer. In Guatemala it was 5:58 a.m.

"There's nothing we can do but respect and accept her choice," Tomás said as he made instant coffee.

Respect and accept? Jaime heard the faltering of his brother's words and knew they were as empty as he felt. As far away as his family was, Jaime always thought they'd still be there, in the same house, in the same village. Just a phone call away, even if it took a while to get credit. But just as with Miguel, there would be no cell phone reception in heaven.

• • •

"Did Tomás receive any calls during the day?" After an endless day at school, the worry released a tiny bit as Jaime got to ask the question that had been nagging him all day.

Don Vicente pulled Pimiento to a stop where the bus had left Jaime seconds before and lifted his battered cowboy hat. "Not while we were together, and we were in the barn with the calves most of the day."

He removed his foot from the stirrup and held out his strong, weathered hand. Jaime grasped it and swung his leg over Pimiento's back. After a few days of riding, he no longer kicked the gelding when mounting, though he still wasn't able to get on the horse on his own.

"Abuela is not doing well," Jaime explained, though Don Vicente hadn't asked. "Mamá thinks she might . . . " But just as Tomás hadn't wanted to talk about it this morning, Jaime couldn't say it out loud either.

"I heard. But you have to remember this is not always a bad thing."

"Of course it's a bad thing! She'd be gone."

In his frustration, he squeezed Pimiento's sides. The gelding leaped into a gallop, which had Jaime hanging on to Don Vicente's waist for dear life. The old man gathered Pimiento up in a few strides and returned him to a walk within seconds. Jaime's ears pounded with the sound of his heartbeat. It took several deep breaths to ease his hold. A fatal equine accident might not be the best way to get to see Abuela again.

"I never had much use for church and people telling me how to think," Don Vicente said. "But I believe a body is just a vessel for the soul, and like any container, it's prone to deteriorating. A soul, however, can never die. It lives forever in the world and in the people it touched. A part of her is in you, and that part you'll keep forever, whatever happens."

As much as Jaime wanted to, he found no contradiction to Don Vicente's words. Better than, "At least she won't continue suffering," or, "She'll be in a better place." Empty words that would have left him hollow.

"I hate being here, so far away from everything and everyone I love. I just want to go home. To *mi familia*."

Don Vicente reached behind him and patted Jaime on the knee. "I left México because I had no one. I didn't think of it at the time, but I came looking for a family and found it in the people I met. You have a family in Guatemala, but that doesn't mean you can't have family here too."

Except Jaime didn't want anyone else. His family was perfect the way it was. Back when Miguel was alive and Tomás lived at home and the world seemed simple.

"I still want to see her, talk to her," Jaime grumbled at the cowboy's back.

Don Vicente pulled Pimiento to a stop on top of the

ridge that gave them a sweeping vista. The cloudless blue sky and the brown land stretched to infinity with nothing but scattered vegetation to interfere.

"From here you can see anything, talk to anyone," Don Vicente said as he took a deep breath of the dry desert air.

Jaime slid off Pimiento's back and sat on a boulder. He turned his gaze to the south and imagined he could see beyond the cacti and juniper bushes, past the Río Bravo and through México where the land changed from desert to jungle, over the Río Usumacinta and into Guatemala until he could see a patio surrounded by individual rooms. His Tío's house, where Abuela lived.

He saw into the kitchen and Abuela's hunched back as she rolled out *masa* for tortillas. She turned around, gnarled hands tossing a ball of *masa* from one to the other, her gray hair pulled into a bun at the nape of her neck, and her dark eyes bright and proud.

Hola, mi'jo. Her voice cracked as it did when she was tired but she wanted to pretend she wasn't.

Hola, Abuela, he replied to the figure in his mind.

They stood there in the kitchen for minutes, or even hours, with only the *masa* ball moving from one hand to the other.

You know it's time, right? she said. He shook his head no, trying to clear his mind. He could choose what he wanted to happen, what he wanted her to say. But Abuela always did what she wanted, even in someone else's imagination. *You can't change that.*

I won't let you go, he insisted. He forced his mind to think of her saying that she was getting better, that she was happiest staying with her family, that she wasn't going to leave him. But just as before, she wrote her own script.

You don't need to worry about me. I'm where I want to be. I love you, mi'jo. She tossed him the ball of *masa* and her image began to fade.

No, Abuela, please don't. Abuela—

"*¡Abuela!*" Jaime found himself back on the ridge clutching a small rock in his fist. He stood and flung the rock with all his might toward the house in the Guatemalan jungle. Instead it flew a bit before landing on the rocky ground, scaring a black bird into the sky to circle above his head. Once out of his hand, he realized his mistake and scrambled to get the rock back. He picked it up again and held it to his face. It didn't take too much imagination to think it smelled a bit like corn *masa*. He placed it next to his sketchbook in his backpack.

He got back on Pimiento without any help and Don Vicente nudged the gelding to walk down the other side of the ridge. Neither said anything for the rest of the ride.

They crossed over a small hill and the homestead came into view. A giant dust cloud traveled at a breakneck speed down the road and away from the ranch. Tomás in his truck. Jaime waved to his brother in the distance, silently begging him to come back, but the other continued racing along until only dust remained.

Quinto, the other ranch hand, sat on a bench outside the barn, listening to a *fútbol* game on the radio, instead of working.

"Where did Tomás go?" Jaime asked as Don Vicente steered them to the barn.

The ranch hand shrugged his shoulders and fiddled with the knobs on the dusty radio for better reception. "Who knows. Got a call and left."

A call? Jaime's breath caught in his throat. It was probably nothing. Other people called Tomás when the reception was good—Meester George, checking in to see that the calves were all healthy; the feed store saying the specially ordered shipment had come in; or kids wanting to raise a steer for the agricultural fair. But none of them made Tomás drive off like Wile E. Coyote on fire.

"Did he speak to the person in English?" Jaime asked.

"Don't know. Spanish, maybe. I wasn't paying attention. *¡Oye hombre! ¿Qué piensas?*" Quinto shouted at the radio where the referee had just given the opposing team a penalty.

Jaime tumbled off Pimiento and crumbled to the ground from weak legs. Instead of dusting himself off, he hugged his knees and tried to look at the horizon as he had from the ridge, but the hills were in the way.

Don Vicente dismounted with the grace of a feather floating to earth and handed Pimiento's reins to Quinto. "Untack him and offer him some water. Then give him a good brush and rub down before offering more water."

Quinto crossed his arms over his barrel-like chest and gave the old man a glare. "Do I look like your groom?"

"Do you have anything better to do?" Don Vicente gave him a look. Quinto took the reins with a huff, raised the radio's volume, and led the horse to the tack room.

Don Vicente watched his gelding clop away before placing a hand on Jaime's head. His old joints made it hard for him to crouch down. Jaime leaned into the bony legs and sniffed.

"You said good-bye on the ridge?"

Jaime nodded but his mouth remained dry as the desert surrounding him.

"Then she knows she was loved and cared for."

Yes, she knew. Everyone who knew Abuela loved her. Or at least respected her. Except those darn Alpha gang members. They beat a twelve-year-old boy to death as if it were nothing. They had no conscience about harassing an old lady, shoving her down the steps so that she broke her hip and was left with no life to live. Where was justice? How had God allowed these things to happen?

He stayed on the dirt with Don Vicente patting his

head and the *fútbol* match crackling on the old radio. When he finally shifted, the rancher offered a strong hand to help him up. Jaime hugged his bag to his chest. Inside, he could feel the rock from the ridge and the edges of his sketchbook, his safety blanket. It had been Abuela who had bought him his first sketchbook when he was five or six. Before that, he had scavenged for loose bits of paper, drawing on receipts and inside food boxes. A vendor at the *mercado* where Abuela sold her tortillas was about to throw away two unlined notebooks that had been damaged by the rain. In exchange for half a dozen tortillas, Abuela came home with the two books for Jaime, telling him to "draw the world." When he got back to the trailer, he decided, he would draw a portrait of her so that when he was as old as Don Vicente, he'd still remember what she looked like.

"You mentioned the other day," Jaime's voice rasped and choked as he struggled to talk to the old rancher, "that when it was your time to go, you'd ride into the sunset and disappear."

Don Vicente stopped walking and turned to Jaime with a smile. His teeth were yellow, worn down, and crooked but all remained intact. "And I told you I'm not riding away any time soon."

CHAPTER TEN

Tomás came home an hour and a half later with a bucket of fried chicken, a family portion of mashed potatoes, a big container of ice cream, and four DVDs from the rural library.

And Ángela. Who apparently had not appreciated being picked up early from the play rehearsal, even to mourn Abuela's passing.

"Grieving is best spent eating with your family." Tomás handed out forks and paper towels for napkins. "I thought of getting tortillas, but then we'd have to cook something to go with them."

"I'm glad you didn't get tortillas. No one's would compare." Jaime sighed as he bit into a drumstick. Even the chicken didn't taste as good as Abuela's, though she cooked hers differently. "Do you know how to make her tortillas, Ángela?"

"No."

Jaime waited for his cousin to say more but she just picked bits off the chicken and piled it on her paper towel.

"I thought she showed you and Rosita that time Miguel and I—"

"She didn't."

"I'm sure your tortillas would be great," Tomás said, scooping a large forkful of mashed potatoes into his mouth.

"I don't know how to make her tortillas, so just leave me alone." She removed a big chunk of chicken from the bone and shredded it bit by bit.

Tomás looked like he wanted to say something more but decided changing the topic was a better idea.

"I don't know if you know this, Jaime," Tomás said between his next bites, "but before I left, I was in love with this gorgeous girl. It didn't matter she was a few years younger than me, Marcela—"

Jaime let go of a drumstick halfway to his mouth. "I remember Marcela! Miguel and I used to argue over who'd get to marry her—"

"No way, bro, I saw her first," Tomás teased as he stole the piece of chicken Jaime had dropped on the table. "I finally got the courage to ask her out and Abuela kept telling me I had to be a gentleman. Of course, I promised I would but she didn't trust me—can you believe that? So

Abuela sent me on the date with Ángela here and Rosita. The three girls spent the whole time talking with each other. It was like I was interfering on *their* date. I told Abuela later that she'd ruined my date, but you know what that *viejita* said? Abuela said, and I still remember this, 'A family makes you who you are. If a girl doesn't like your family, she'll never like you.' Turned out Marcela and Rosita became best friends but nothing ever happened between us. Not even a kiss. Do you remember that night, Ángela?"

"Marcela disappeared a few years ago." Ángela ran her unused fork up and down the table until it scratched the surface. "They said she got kidnapped."

"*¿De verdad?*" Tomás gasped. Jaime nodded. Those were the rumors when she got separated from her brother while trying to cross México. No one had heard from her since.

"Damn, I didn't know." The table fell quiet. Jaime knew what Tomás had been trying to do. Remembering stories about Abuela—funny ones, embarrassing ones. Ones that kept her close to their minds and hearts instead of ones that focused on the loss and grief.

Jaime figured he could do the same. "One time, Abuela caught Miguel and me—"

"I'm done." Ángela scooped up all the bits of chicken she'd picked off but hadn't eaten, and gave them to Vida. "Remember not to give her the bones."

"Do you want ice cream?" Tomás asked. "Chocolate caramel nut fudge. There's no room for it in the freezer so, poor us, we're going to have to eat it all."

Tomás removed the lid and waved the container of gooey goodness in front of her face.

"I'm not hungry." She got up from the table and locked herself in the tiny bathroom.

"When Miguel died," Jaime said in a soft voice, "she didn't speak for a few days."

Tomás nodded before digging into more food. It was Abuela who thought everything could be solved with food. Abuela also said her grandchildren had to eat what they were served and not complain. Jaime took that to heart as he reached for the next drumstick. If anything would be a way to celebrate Abuela's life, it would be a full stomach.

A few pieces of chicken and a quarter of the mashed potatoes remained when Ángela finally came out of the bathroom. Jaime tried to put a plate in the microwave for her, saying it was what Abuela would have wanted, but she just shook her head and curled up on the bench to study the play script.

He sat at her side and put his arm around her, giving her shoulders a squeeze.

She shifted away, curled up smaller, and brought the script closer to her face.

Tomás made a sign with his hand to knock it off and

give her some space. The trailer was so small, you could barely be in the kitchen area without bumping into the table. But their house in Guatemala hadn't been much bigger. Papá had built it with the help of his family for Mamá as a wedding present. Just two rooms, a sleeping one and a kitchen, with no glass in the windows and a front door that hung off center, and they'd gotten along just fine.

Tomás took the remaining container of ice-cream soup into the sleeping area, and he and Jaime watched *Guardians of the Galaxy* on the TV/DVD player Tomás had rigged from the trailer's low ceiling. Every few minutes, Jaime leaned over to check on Ángela, but she remained curled tightly, nose in the script, and even maintained her distance from Vida, the world's best comforter. After Abuela.

CHAPTER ELEVEN

Tomás's truck pulled up in front of Jaime and Ángela as they exited the trailer. In the passenger seat sat Don Vicente. The lines of his face cracked deeper than normal, as if being confined in a vehicle instead of astride his horse was causing him great pain. His cowboy hat was less battered than the one he normally wore, his beaded belt cleaned, and his faded jeans had crease lines down the front; Doña Cici had probably ironed them for him. Jaime never saw a man look so out of place in a vehicle when he should be on a horse.

"Get in the back of the truck," Tomás called out from the open window. "We'll drive you to the bus stop."

"Where are you going?" Jaime asked.

"Hell," Don Vicente muttered.

Tomás sighed as if the two had already been through this a million times. "Mr. George wants us to take a look at a new bull calf on another ranch. We need to get some new blood in the herd and this calf is supposed to be top of the line."

Don Vicente spat out the window. "Manuel Vegas wouldn't know a quality bull calf if it gored him in the gut."

"Mr. George said its sire is a champion," Tomás said for Jaime and Ángela's benefit.

"A good dad don't make a good son," Don Vicente went on.

"Then you can tell that to Mr. George—after we've checked him out." Tomás sounded like he was trying to be patient.

"Waste of my time," the old rancher mumbled.

"So stay. I'll send Mr. George photos along with what I think. I know what he's looking for."

Don Vicente muttered some choice swear words but didn't get out of the truck. When it came to the cattle and the horses, nothing happened without Don Vicente's approval. Meester George might say they needed a new bull calf, but Jaime knew it would be up to the foreman to decide which bull calf they bought.

Jaime and Ángela hopped into the back. Apparently it was illegal to ride in the back of a truck on a public road here in El Norte, but since the dirt road belonged to Meester George until the highway, there was no one to get them in trouble. It was like being on top of the train cars in México—without the fear. But within a minute, Ángela banged on the truck for Tomás to stop, and climbed into the cab, claiming something about the wind messing up her hair. Girls.

At the end of the drive, Jaime got out of the back with his bag. Next time, he'd ask Tomás to go faster, take the turns a bit tighter. A few minutes remained before the bus was due and Tomás leaned out the window while Ángela exited the cab on the other side.

"We might not be back when you get home from school, so make sure you let Vida out of the house right away," Tomás said. "There's sandwich makings and some cans of beans if you're hungry, but we'll be home for dinner for sure."

"Is he going to be okay?" Jaime whispered, nodding toward Don Vicente, who sat as straight as he would in a saddle except his arms were crossed and he continued muttering curses under his breath.

Tomás leaned farther out the window to whisper in Jaime's ear. "Truth is, he's scared of driving."

"I'm not scared of driving," Don Vicente grumbled, though that did nothing to convince them it wasn't true. "I just think horses get the job done better."

Tomás retreated back into the cab. "How did you even hear that? I thought you were old," he teased. But the ancient rancher didn't even crack a smile.

"Wait just a second," Jaime said. The bus wasn't visible yet. He opened his sketchbook, grabbed a pencil, and quickly drew some rough lines on the page. He gave the completed image a good look, checked for the bus, and added a few more details before carefully tearing it out of the rings. It was far from his best, but it was still recognizable.

Jaime walked to the other side of the truck and handed the sketch to Don Vicente. The old man's grumpy face relaxed as he finally broke into his first smile of the day. In his weathered hands, Don Vicente held a picture of himself sitting astride his Appaloosa gelding. He folded the top edge into the airbag groove so the drawing remained visible and in place in front of him.

"I don't think Pimiento has ever looked so good. Maybe you can draw us a new bull calf. It's certain to be better than this live one we're looking at."

The roar of the bus's diesel engine cut short the conversation. As always, Ángela dashed to the rear of the bus with her snooty friends without looking back. Jaime climbed in after her and turned before going to sit with Seh-Ahn. From the rundown truck the two cowboys, one young, one old, waved before heading in the opposite direction. Jaime watched them retreat, wishing with all his might that he could have gone with them to check out the bull calf.

CHAPTER TWELVE

For the first time, Don Vicente wasn't waiting for him on Pimiento when Jaime got off the school bus. He searched the rocky ridge and the various hills in the direction of the homestead for any movement before scuffing his shoes down the dirt road. Tomás had said they probably wouldn't be home, but the reality of not having a ride back and having to walk home alone hadn't occurred to Jaime.

Vida greeted him with a thousand kisses before squatting in the bushes near the trailer. They shared a turkey and cheese sandwich with ketchup before setting off, Jaime with his sketchbook under his arm, to check on the livestock. The two floppy-eared dairy goats greeted him with loud cries and he told them Doña Cici would be out to milk them soon. For once, Quinto must have done his job before he left for the day because the horses in the paddock and the cows and calves in the corral all had hay and water; the rest of the cattle out in the vast parts of the ranch were used to taking care of themselves.

From the corral, a trail led into the foothills. Jaime wondered if he could find the *mamá* coyote again and another part of him hoped he wouldn't. With Vida along, he didn't want to find out what would happen if the two canines got too close to each other.

He came to a dry arroyo carved out by groundwater and skid down the sandy banks. A few meters away a jackrabbit stared at him with its peripheral vision. Next to Jaime, Vida froze. The brown and white hairs on her back rose as they stared each other down. Sketchbook in hand, Jaime drew the outline of the jackrabbit's large tan ears that looked more like feathers with their prominent veins and black edges.

Unclear who twitched first, the jackrabbit and Vida took off up the sides of the arroyo. The hare ran for a few strides and then leaped into the air like a horse jumping over a fence. No way the dog could catch it. Not that he would tell Vida that.

He sat on a rock and continued the sketch as he remembered—the bulging eyes, the long, lean body, the black and gray tail tucked under the bottom that didn't quite touch the ground because the folded-up legs were too long.

He sharpened his pencil extra sharp and used the slightest touch to add fur and texture. There, perfect. Vida returned with her tongue dragging almost to the sandy dirt and a look of pure contentment of a flat-out run, even though the jackrabbit had gotten away. The sun in the west said that it would be dark in an hour and his stomach in the present said Tomás should be home by now making something he'd call dinner.

Jaime kept his eyes on the trail as he headed back. Snakes hibernated, right? And scorpions? Were they awake for the spring yet? But mountain lions didn't hibernate, did they? And were they nocturnal? He hugged his book to his chest, made sure Vida stayed at his heels, and quickened his pace home. One thing he'd noticed about Nuevo México—as soon as the sun started to go down, it got cold. And fast.

Tomás's truck was still missing when he got back to the trailer, but headlights were coming down the hill. Jaime waited for his brother with Vida at his side. The headlights seemed closer together and lower to the ground than Jaime remembered. The dog ran to greet the dusted-up white car that definitely didn't belong to Tomás. The driver's door opened to reveal Ángela. Ángela? Driving? A mixture of nervousness and jealousy bubbled inside. Back home, only Papá and Tío Daniel knew how to drive. But then again, neither owned a car for anyone to drive.

And here was Ángela driving like she owned the road. Now that he thought about it, she had swerved continuously down the ranch track like a drunk driver. What kind of friends would let her potentially kill herself by letting her drive?

She reached for something in the seat behind her but someone held her arm as if begging her not to leave. She laughed as the person holding her kissed her hand. The car's interior light illuminated a mop of bleached blond hair. Tristan. If Abuela were here, Ángela would have never acted like that, and Tristan would never have dared.

"Ángela, *vamos*," Jaime said.

His cousin turned to him and even though it had gotten too dark to see her face in the shadows, he was sure she rolled her eyes. Her arm was magically released and she waved at the people in the car. The car beeped two times before taking off at dust-inducing speeds back to the highway.

"What is it?" she finally turned to him

"Tomás isn't back yet," Jaime said.

Ángela shrugged as if Tomás always left them home alone. Which he did, Jaime supposed, but he was always somewhere within Meester George's fifty thousand acres.

"I'm sure he'll be here soon," Ángela said.

"Should we check in with Doña Cici? Maybe she's heard something?"

"They're grown men looking at a cow—"

"—bull," Jaime corrected.

"Whatever. You know how long grown-ups talk. They're probably arguing whether black cattle produce better meat than white."

"Ours are reddish brown with white faces. Herefords." Jaime surprised himself. He had no idea he knew their cattle's breed but apparently he did. Wait til Tomás and Don Vicente heard him ask about the new Hereford bull calf!

"Which is making me even more hungry. What's for dinner?"

"There's sandwiches and beans."

"Great. Let's put beans and cheese on the bread and put them in the microwave to melt."

The worry in Jaime's stomach changed to hunger. That sounded a lot better then just beans from a can.

The microwave concoctions made the bread mushy and of course the canned beans tasted bland compared to Abuela's savory ones, but the overall result wasn't bad. Jaime had three slices, and this time didn't share with Vida. Dogs and beans didn't seem like a good idea.

They left the rest of the beans in the can, placed them in the waist-high fridge, and raised the counter to reveal the sink underneath. Everything in the trailer either served multiple functions or was nested like Russian dolls. Miguel would have enjoyed the clever engineering.

Thinking of Miguel led to Jaime remembering their

journey and the friends they had made. And how Ángela seemed to have forgotten all about them, based on how she let that Tristan boy kiss her hand like that.

"Do you remember the first time we met Xavi and Joaquín and Rafa?" Jaime asked while drying a plastic plate.

Ángela pulled the drain plug and lowered the counter over the sink. She wiped the top of the counter, but didn't answer.

Jaime tried again. "We were washing dishes then too and you were acting all weird around Xavi every time he came with buckets of water."

The trailer was tiny. There was no way Ángela couldn't hear him. He tried one last time. "Remember how you told Xavi you were sixteen? Did you ever tell him you were really only fifteen?"

Ángela went to her bed, which was currently a table, and pulled out a thick geometry textbook from her bag. "Xavi's dead. It doesn't matter what I told him."

She opened her book with such a bang that Jaime stopped bringing up their old friends. He opened his backpack and pulled out the homework folder. The spelling words he had to memorize and define blurred in front of his eyes.

Only a few weeks ago guys with machetes and baseball bats had attacked Ángela, Xavi, and him on the train. There had been nothing to do but jump off and run fast.

A blinding headlight had caused him, Ángela, and Xavi to split up. A truck had followed Jaime, but somehow he'd managed to squeeze himself halfway into an animal's den and hide. By pure luck, he had found Ángela in the morning with nothing more than a sprained ankle. Vida had returned on her own. Without Xavi.

Jaime doodled on the side of his spelling sheet.

He missed Xavi. And little Joaquín. And sometimes even big-mouthed Rafa. And it stank big time that he didn't know for sure what happened to any of them.

Inside his bag, he found the recorder Meez Macálista said he could borrow until the end of the school year. She also lent him a music book. He'd barely gone through one song when Ángela slammed her book shut.

"You have got to stop. I can't handle that noise."

It isn't noise, but he sighed and forced himself to finish the rest of his homework before getting the beginner reader book out of his bag. It took twenty minutes to read and he was pretty sure he understood about half of it. Enough to get that it was about a frog and toad, and they were friends who went on adventures, sometimes flying a kite and sometimes cleaning a house. Of course, the drawings helped a lot.

He looked outside. It was darker than any night he'd seen on the ranch with only one faint light coming from the annex of the big house. Tomás should really be back by now. He thought again about asking Doña Cici if she knew anything about them, but then her light went out and Jaime figured she must have gone to bed.

"Think Tomás is okay?" Jaime asked.

Ángela didn't even look up. She was reading from her play script by now like she was attempting to memorize the whole thing for her two-line role. "Of course, why wouldn't he be?"

"It's almost nine o'clock." He pointed to the clock on the microwave.

Ángela turned a page, keeping her eyes on the script. "They probably stopped for some food."

Jaime returned to the window. No lights anywhere. "What if the truck broke down?"

"Then Tomás is probably fixing it. He's resourceful."

Very true. Tomás called Don Vicente an animal whisperer, while the older man called Tomás a machine whisperer.

Jaime brushed his teeth, changed into the sweatpants and undershirt he slept in, and beckoned Vida to join him in the bed he normally shared with his big brother.

The dog happily curled up in his arms as he stared awake at the trailer door that didn't open.

The day was lightening when Vida's bark and a slamming truck door jerked Jaime awake. Heavy boots stomped up the metal steps and the door opened.

"What happened?" Jaime asked, sitting up in the bed.

From his angle, he saw Ángela do the same.

Black circles surrounded Tomás's eyes and his face was so pale he could have passed for a gringo. The hair on the back of Vida's neck rose and she stayed at Jaime's side, unsure in the near dark whether she knew the strange man at the door.

"Don Vicente is in a detention center. He's going to be deported." And Tomás with his big cowboy muscles rested his tired head against the thin trailer wall and began to cry.

CHAPTER THIRTEEN

Jaime jumped out of bed and rushed to his brother. "A detention center? You mean he's in jail? But he's not a criminal. What happened?"

Tomás took a few choking breaths before rubbing his eyes with his sleeves. "Officers blocked the road and demanded to see everyone's papers. Don Vicente wanted to take the side roads but I said the highway was faster. It's all my fault."

Tomás let out a sob that caused Vida to bark from her spot on the bed. Tomás tossed his car keys into a pile of dirty clothes and turned on his heel back out the door. From their trailer, Jaime watched the shadow of his brother stagger over to the big house. Part of him wanted to go too, the other part was too scared to interfere. A light came on in the kitchen and the shadow of Tomás disappeared as Doña Cici let him in.

Jaime waited by the door, watching the big house, and didn't even notice the chill in the air until he saw Ángela huddled on her bed. He draped an extra blanket over her shoulders and returned to his post against the doorjamb, clutching one of Tomás's sweaters.

The sun was up over the ridge when Tomás made his way back. With the blanket still draped over her shoulders, Ángela made them mugs of instant coffee—black and sweet for Tomás and very milky and sweet for Jaime; hers just as sweet with a color in between. She had converted her bed back to a table and benches and made a pile of toast smothered with butter.

Tomás took his coffee but didn't drink it as he sat on Ángela's former bed. Vida inched her way to him. He placed a hand on her one ear and she kissed his palm to make him feel better.

"How's Doña Cici?" Jaime asked.

"About ready to march down to the detention center and demand they deport her with him."

"She wouldn't!" Jaime gasped. Tomás shrugged his shoulders.

"So, what happened?" Ángela asked.

"Immigration control blocked up the whole highway. Everyone knows about the few fixed points within a hundred miles of the border, but this one was a pop-up. I've never encountered one there before and I've driven that road more times than I remember."

Jaime remembered the checkpoints he and Ángela went through in the southern state of Chiapas in México. Men with rifles asserting their power and scaring everyone in their path. They had witnessed a Salvadoran woman literally dragged off the bus after the officer noticed her Central American accent. His heart had gone out to her, and she'd been a complete stranger. He refused to think about Don Vicente enduring the same thing.

"At first I thought the traffic was due to an accident. By the time I knew what was really happening I couldn't turn around." Tomás said this to Vida as she continued to reassure him with her kisses. His free hand brought the coffee up to his lips but he seemed to forget what he was doing and set it back down without drinking. "They took us both in."

"What, why?" Jaime asked. It didn't make sense. Tomás had a driver's license from the state of Nuevo México and papers that said he could legally live and work here. And Don Vicente had been here forever. When Tomás had picked them up after they crossed the U.S.-México border, they had come across one of the fixed checkpoints. Maybe the guard had asked Tomás a simple question, but from Jaime's memory, it seemed like the officer had barely glanced in the truck, had seen a grown-up, two youths, and a stray dog, and waved them by like it was nothing.

Ángela placed a piece of toast in Tomás's hand and he ate it, though Jaime was sure he didn't know what he was doing.

"They said they were looking for criminals, but I think they were taking advantage of the situation to make as many arrests as possible," Tomás explained. "In English they call it DWB: Driving While Brown."

"What does that mean?" Jaime asked.

"It means if you look Latino, they bring you in," Ángela explained.

"Look Latino?" Jaime asked. There wasn't one way a Latino looked. Jaime and Ángela were brown with dark, straight hair, but their moms were closer to tan and both had curly hair. "Jennifer Lopez looks nothing like Shakira, who isn't anything like Cameron Diaz, and none of them resemble Zoe Saldana, even when she isn't blue or green. How could anyone think Latinos look the same?"

"Exactly, we're a culture, not a racc," Tomás agreed. "What they did is racial profiling and stereotyping. They took Don Vicente because he's brown, has no papers, and doesn't speak any English. They brought me in because I'm brown and had Don Vicente with me."

"But they let you go."

"After hours of questions. They were convinced my

papers were fake and spent hours interrogating me to catch me lying. When they finally let me go, I said I wasn't leaving without Don Vicente. I even lied and insisted that he was my *abuelo*, but they wouldn't budge. There was nothing I could do." Tomás rubbed his forehead and squinted his eyes shut. He stayed that way for a few minutes but no more tears rolled down his cheeks. He slammed his hand on the table and finally looked up again. "Hurry up and get dressed. I'll drop you off at school."

"But is it safe for us to go there?" Jaime asked. He didn't really like the school here and would do anything not to have to go, but this was different. Miguel had died coming home from school in Guatemala. What would prevent immigration officers from stopping his school bus? Or even coming into the school building? He knew he couldn't be the only undocumented kid at school. What then?

"Churches and schools are typically considered sanctuary spaces," Ángela responded instead. "They're safe places where a police officer can't arrest anyone unless that person is endangering people, like in bomb threats or school shootings. We talked about that in one of my classes."

Jaime turned to Tomás to see if it was true. Not that he didn't believe Ángela, but she did like school more than he did.

Tomás nodded. "I can't see immigration officers

wanting to target schools. Most kids don't carry identification, and besides, it's a lot of work to look after kids in a detention center. It's one thing to detain a whole family, because the parents can look after the kids. But if not, the government has to pay a lot more people to take care of them, including teachers, since children are required to go to school. I'm more concerned with you staying here."

"Here?" Jaime looked around the trailer. They were down a long dirt road in the middle of a cattle ranch with no visible neighbors. Just the other day Don Vicente said no one would bother coming down here.

"They know about Doña Cici; they could decide to target her," Tomás read his mind.

A breath choked in Jaime's throat. The trailer didn't have a lock, and even if it did, it wouldn't make a difference. He'd seen too many movies and cop shows where the police just barged through thick wooden doors. The trailer door was made of flimsy aluminum.

"When I mentioned this to Mr. George, he reminded me this is private property and legally, no one can trespass, not even an immigration officer, without permission. Still, don't let anyone in."

Tomás's message couldn't have been clearer: Immigration officers were like vampires; you don't invite them inside.

"I need to check on the cows and calves, feed everyone, and then we'll go." Tomás drained his coffee in one shot and shoved a whole slice of toast into his mouth.

"You need to sleep." Ángela got into her demanding mothering role with her hands on her hips. It'd been ages since she did that and it made Jaime smile. Good, the old Ángela wasn't completely gone.

But Tomás shook his head as he swallowed. "Sleep can come later. I need to stop by the local sheriff's office. The sheriff knows Don Vicente and maybe has some connections to help bring him back here. To his real home."

CHAPTER FOURTEEN

Jaime couldn't focus in school. When Meesus asked him to demonstrate on the whiteboard how to figure out 150 percent of forty-five, he said, "No tank you," which resulted in staying in during morning recess.

He'd forgotten to make his lunch and sat by himself in the cafeteria staring at a blank page of his sketchbook and doing his best to ignore Diego.

"It sucks when your mom doesn't like you enough to pack you a lunch," Diego said when he passed Jaime's table on his way to the other side of the cafeteria.

Jaime twirled the pen in his hand, wondering if he could fling it at Diego like a javelin. Instead, he drew a deep line in his sketchbook that tore the page. He liked it better when he understood less.

"Aren't you hungry?"

Jaime looked into the purple-rimmed glasses and wide black eyes of Carla. He could feel his own face matching the color of her frames.

"No food." He pointed to everyone else's lunch and shrugged, before realizing he should have lied and said he'd eaten already. He wanted Carla to think he was cool, not pitiful.

She set her tray down and pointed to the hot lunch line. "You can get some free lunch."

He looked at her in disbelief. Did "free lunch" mean what he thought it did? Why would anyone, especially in this country that hated immigrants and jailed them for no reason, give him free lunch?

Either she could read minds or he spoke his concerns aloud in perfect English without even knowing it, because she grabbed him by the arm and led him to the lunch line.

"*Hola Juanita,*" she greeted the lunch lady and then continued in English. "This is Jaime. He needs some food."

"*¿Tienes la forma?*" She walked over to a table and waved a form at him. He shook his head no. She sighed and brought the form over to him. "Have your parents fill this out so you qualify for free or reduced meals."

"I don't think I—" He stopped himself before saying anything else. Juanita seemed nice, but he couldn't go around telling everyone who spoke Spanish that he didn't have papers.

Juanita waved the form at him again. "Doesn't hurt to fill it out anyway. Anyone can do it."

Jaime read through the Spanish form she handed him. It asked how much his family (Tomás) made per year (no clue), information about food allergies (none), and basic questions like his name and school. Nothing about his immigration status.

"Now, I can't have you starving today." Juanita pointed to each of the two gray slops of food in front of her. "Do you want beef or cheesy mushrooms?"

"Go with the mushrooms," Carla motioned to the less gray one on the left. "It's actually really good with the pasta."

"*Bueno*," he shrugged at the mushrooms, though honestly, they weren't his favorite. He doubted he'd notice if he were eating brains; he already felt like a zombie.

Doña Juanita piled his tray with the mushrooms, pasta, some green vegetable, a red apple, a sugar cookie, and a carton of milk.

A group of girls had moved their lunches to the table where Jaime had been sitting, saving them both a spot in the middle. Carla jumped into their conversation as soon as they sat back down. A few times Carla or one of the other girls asked him a question and he lifted his shoulders to say he didn't know, not sure what they were asking or talking about. He ate all his food, just like Abuela had taught him, but afterwards he couldn't have said what anything tasted like. Honestly, he wasn't even sure what happened the rest of the day.

On the bus back home next to Seh-Ahn, he hugged his knees to his chest and shook his head no when Seh-Ahn placed a hand on his shoulder to ask what was wrong.

When Miguel was killed, there was nothing that could bring him back. With Abuela being attacked, the damage had already been done and he was too far away to help out. But Don Vicente was *here*. In a detention center. Not yet deported. There had to be a way to help him.

If this were a movie, Jaime would organize some kind of jailbreak that involved tools baked into cakes, blacked out security cameras, and underground tunnels. But in real life he knew none of that would work. For one thing, he didn't know how to bake a cake.

As much as he thought, he couldn't think of anything that would realistically change what the future held. Don Vicente would have to return to a country he no longer called home.

Not being able to change the past was a helpless fact of life. Not being able to change the future made the help-lessness a hundred times worse.

• • •

A wave of intense heat hit as soon as Jaime left the air-conditioned bus. Not the humid heat from back home, but a dry heat that seemed to beat down directly from the sun and cause the spring shoots to curl up in hiding. No sweat gathered on his forehead, as if it evaporated before reaching the surface of his skin. He could hardly believe that just last week snow reached his knees and his ears burned with cold.

He waited at the entrance of Meester George's ranch for a long time as he scanned the ridge and rolling hills of the property. Maybe Tomás had been lucky at the sheriff's office and the police were able to pull some strings. Maybe the detention center realized their mistake and Don Vicente didn't belong there with the criminals. Any minute a birdcall would echo over the ridge and Pimiento would come galloping across the desert, dodging cacti and rocks.

But no. Don Vicente did not ride up to meet him.

Jaime began the long walk back to the trailer. He turned with a bend in the road and the sun shone right into his eyes. He squinted and kept walking.

"Tsssssssssss!" The sound of an angry insect caused Jaime to stop. He shielded his eyes and glanced around him. Nothing. He looked around again before looking down. There, not more than two hands' length from his left foot, lay a coiled snake. Its triangular head lifted from its fat diamond-patterned body and its forked tongue flitted from its mouth.

"Tssssssssss!" the noise continued. The snake's tail shook to create the noise Jaime mistook for an insect.

Other than the snake's tail and tongue, neither moved. He couldn't. Not with his foot so close and his jeans not thick enough to prevent a bite. Snakes sensed motion and could strike faster than the eye could see. Jaime blinked and forced himself to breathe calmly. Back home he and Miguel sometimes caught snakes, held them for a few minutes (or Miguel would hold them while Jaime drew them in his sketchbook), and then set them free. Only from afar had Jaime encountered a venomous snake, and he was pretty sure this one was not the kind you picked up and relocated.

They stood there, staring at each other. The snake's glare was so intense, Jaime wondered if it could even see him or if it was compensating for its poor vision by focusing extra hard.

After a few minutes, Jaime figured the snake probably wasn't going to strike unless it felt threatened. It had had plenty of opportunity, and even if it was hungry, it had to know it couldn't swallow Jaime whole. So they'd reached a stalemate. Jaime couldn't move because the snake would misinterpret the action as a threat, and the snake wouldn't move because it was a snake and incapable of logical thinking.

The snake continued to give him an evil stare until it seemed convinced that Jaime would neither attack him nor turn into a bite-size morsel. Finally, it uncoiled its body and slithered into the bushes, marking an extra tally on its scoreboard: Snake 1,527,952, Scared Mindless Human 0.

It took several minutes for Jaime to be able to continue on his way and several more for his ears to stop pounding with the sound of his heartbeat.

He turned his gaze to the dirt road and shuffled his feet down the long track to the trailer. About halfway back, his brain buzzing with thoughts of Don Vicente fighting off snakes that came up through the plumbing of the detention center, the sound of an engine interrupted his reverie. Tomás. Except instinct told him it wasn't. Too loud. Like the roar of a diesel engine; Tomás's truck ran on gasoline.

Because of the curves in the road, no vehicle was visible, but a cloud of dust rose over the nearest hill. Jaime crouched behind a juniper bush on the side of the road. His uniform shirt was green today and his jeans were blue. He prayed that he couldn't be seen. And also prayed that señor Serpiente didn't have a spring cottage hidden nearby.

The truck was huge, white, shiny, and new with four tires on the back wheels. The driver wore a tan felted cowboy hat over his gray hair. He had a look of authority on his red face as he zoomed by. Immigration officers had found them.

Jaime took off as soon as it passed. By the time the dust settled, the truck was out of sight around the next curve. There was no way he could get to the house before the vehicle; even if he had been on Pimiento he doubted the horse could have outrun the truck. All he could do was hope that Tomás had told Doña Cici about the vampire rule of not letting immigration officers in.

With the homestead in sight, Jaime paused to catch his breath. He left the track and cut across the field to sneak up closer. He was so focused on avoiding any long twigs or coiled ropes that could be a snake, he forgot about the other natural dangers. His left sneaker collided with a barrel cactus and he bit his lip to keep from crying out. No time to pull out the spines; he limped forward with one eye on the ground and one eye on the homestead.

The truck stood in front of the kitchen door to the big house as Jaime limped behind another juniper. Could he possibly go around the side, enter through the front door, and get Doña Cici out before the officer found her? Unlikely. Doña Cici lived in the annex next to the kitchen.

A diversion then. The cows with their newborn calves were still in the corral instead of grazing with the rest of the herd throughout the vast ranch. If he could cause a stampede, then . . .

His plans stopped as two figures walked toward the fancy new truck. The red-faced officer. And Tomás.

He couldn't let them take Tomás again, except his legs refused to move. Tomás didn't look like he was in immediate danger—he walked normally beside the man, but his head hung low so Jaime couldn't read his expression.

They stopped in front the truck, the red-faced officer leaning against the hood with his arms crossed over his broad chest. The two men were talking but too far away for their voices to carry. The officer finally pushed himself upright and shook Tomás's hand before entering the kitchen of the big house as if he owned the place.

Tomás looked after the man. His shoulders slumped and then he turned, dragging his boots back to the trailer. Jaime waited in his spot for a few more minutes before bursting toward the trailer. The cactus spines poked through his shoe to prick his toes at every step but he didn't slow down. He leaped up the metal steps and threw the door open. "Who was that?"

Tomás leaned on the table, resting his head on his arms. He looked up and stared at Jaime with red, sleepless eyes. "That's Mr. George. I have to find two replacements for Don Vicente, immediately. Preferably guys with papers."

And he dropped his head back onto his arms with a thunk that made the table collapse.

CHAPTER FIFTEEN

The table fell on Tomás's knees, which made him
swear so loudly Abuela must have scolded him from heaven.
Tomás tried to raise the surface back to table level, and
continued swearing when it dropped back to bed level.

"The mechanism is busted. I can't fix it." And he threw
the cushions on the table, flopped on his back, and covered
his eyes with his arm. Vida curled up in the crook of his
arm, waiting to comfort him whenever he was ready.

Jaime stood in the middle of the trailer as helpless as a
fish in the desert. His fear of snakes now seemed frivolous.
Tomás needed him.

He thought about Abuela and what she would do. "Are
you hungry?" he asked.

"No."

Jaime raised his eyebrows. The Tomás he knew never turned down food. "Have you eaten?"

"No."

Jaime took off his shoes and pulled out the cactus spines that had gone through the synthetic leather. They left red marks on his foot but at least it didn't hurt anymore when he moved. There wasn't much on the food front. Between Abuela and now Don Vicente, grocery shopping hadn't been a priority. He stood on his toes and rummaged through the small cabinet above the sink. He found a packet of saltines in the back. In the waist high fridge, Doña Cici had left them soft goat cheese and in the door stood a half-eaten jar of homemade red jam. The letters were faded but Jaime could just make out the word "*capulín.*" He didn't know the word and figured it must be Mexican for some kind of red berry. He opened the lid and ran his pinkie along the rim to taste it. Sour but sweet at the same time. Perfect.

He fixed himself and Tomás some crackers with cheese, some with jam, and some with both. He held the plate next to Tomás so Vida wouldn't get it and bossed his older brother like their grandmother would have done.

"Eat. It'll make you feel better."

Tomás shifted the arm covering his face and glared at Jaime with one eye. But then he sighed, and took the plate out of Jaime's hands as he sat up.

"Does this mean that Meester George doesn't think Don Vicente is coming back?" Jaime asked as he nibbled on a cracker.

"It means that there's too much work for me and Quinto to finish calving season on our own, even with Mr. George here." Tomás popped a whole cracker in his mouth and pulled out his phone to check the time. With a full mouth, he made a sound like he remembered something but had to wait until he swallowed to speak. "I got you something."

A plastic bag sat by the door. Tomás leaned over from the bed and pulled out two smartphones in hard plastic boxes. "For you and Ángela."

"*Pero*, I don't need a phone." Jaime held the box, not even sure what to do with it. It wasn't as if he had any friends to contact.

"I want you to keep it with you anyway. Take it to school or when you leave the trailer. Doña Cici accidentally left the landline off the hook and it just about killed me when I couldn't contact you last night."

Jaime turned the plastic packaging over. The black screen shined and glared at him like a mini television, or a security camera. "We can't afford it."

Already Tomás had spent too much on them—when Jaime asked if they could buy a mango last time they were at the grocery store, Tomás had looked at the price and shook his head no. Such a fancy phone had to cost millions more than a mango. And any extra money they had should go to Guatemala.

Tomás tilted his head from one side to the other like he didn't want to admit that Jaime was right. "I opened a family plan. It is a bit more than what I was already paying, but it'll give me the peace of mind that we can reach each other when we need to. Here, I'll set the language to Spanish and program our numbers into it."

Tomás showed him how to use it with taps and swipes. Once Tomás finished, he handed the phone over to Jaime, who threw it in his school bag like a hot potato. If he couldn't even get in contact with his family in Guatemala then what was the point?

Ángela's reaction to a phone when she got home was completely different. She clutched it to her chest and stared at Tomás like he was some kind of god.

"You got me an iPhone?"

Tomás shook his head. "No, it's the free phone they gave me with the plan."

Ángela looked it over carefully before turning it on. The fact that it wasn't worth several hundreds of dollars didn't seem to bother her. "How many minutes can I use?"

"Call and text as much as you want to people here. Guatemala of course costs extra. But there's only five hundred megabytes of data per month, so save that for e-mails or Skyping your parents and don't download music or anything unless you're at a Wi-Fi hot spot."

Ángela didn't seem to have heard anything beyond "as much as you want." She squealed like Cinderella getting to go to the ball, before lunging at Tomás for a huge hug. Once she released him, she dug through the front pocket of her bag and pulled out a sheet with phone numbers. Like an old pro, she started adding numbers to the phone without having to be shown how. Within minutes, her phone beeped with the arrival of new messages from her friends. Show off.

Maybe Jaime should ask Seh-Ahn if he has a number. Or Carla, though calling a girl on the phone required more nerve than he thought he had. Then he'd have to talk to her. In English. He wasn't ready for that.

And he and Seh-Ahn seemed to do just fine without talking.

By the time he got on the bus the next day, Jaime didn't even want to think about phones. Ángela's kept beeping with messages all night until Tomás threatened to throw it in a cow pie. Except Tomás had used more explicit words. Ángela silenced it then, but a few times while Jaime lay awake, he caught the glare of the phone reflecting against the wall. And all through breakfast (burnt eggs and toast, Tomás had "cooked"), the phone had flashed continuously as if it were breathing.

Pulling out his sketchbook once he sat next to

Seh-Ahn, he turned to the back side and the last page. He pushed thoughts of flashing and buzzing out of his mind and tried to shut his ears to ignore Ángela's rowdy friends in the back.

He drew a creature of his own creation—four arms, four stalk eyes, human body (complete with belly button), but then wheels like an army tank for legs. Behind the creature, he drew a cactus. He drew the creature again, this time next to the cactus to show that while the cholla wasn't a tall cactus, the creature wasn't much taller. Then he drew a close-up of the creature's face, its mouth open with sharp teeth and all four eyes staring at the sky. He couldn't decide on a nose or ears, so he left the creature without but did add a few whiskers around its open mouth.

Next to him, Seh-Ahn pointed at the drawing and then pointed at himself. Jaime passed the sketchbook over with a shrug. Seh-Ahn didn't ask what the creature was, and not for the first time, Jaime was glad his bus friend never asked Jaime to explain himself. Seh-Ahn pulled a pencil from his bag and before Jaime realized it, the other boy had scribbled some words on the sketch. Criticism? Praise? But when Seh-Ahn returned the sketchbook, Jaime saw they were speech bubbles like in a comic strip.

Above the first image, Seh-Ahn had written, "I'm so hungry! There's nothing to eat." Jaime smiled. Not only had he understood Seh-Ahn's words (at least he hoped he did), but the idea of his creature being hungry hadn't even crossed his mind.

Over the second drawing with the creature near the cactus, the caption read, "At last! Food!"

Ay no, Jaime could see where this was going, and liked it. His eyes shifted over to the final, close-up drawing. "Ouch, it hurts! Save me, Mommy!"

Jaime laughed. He gave Seh-Ahn a thumbs-up, who returned it with a grin and thumbs-up of his own. Jaime flipped to the other side of the page and began the next comic strip panel. Like a manga, they worked the story from the back of the book and by the time they got to school, Jaime had drawn and Seh-Ahn had written two full pages of their comic.

What do you want to call our story? Seh-Ahn wrote on the sketchbook.

Jaime looked out the window. The bus had just pulled into the parking lot, leaving about fifteen seconds before they stopped and had to get off.

The aventurs ov Seme Jaime wrote quickly.

Seh-Ahn started correcting his spelling, but then wrote back, *What is Seme?*

The bus slowed down. How could Jaime explain? And in only a few seconds before it stopped and they had to get out?

Sean + Jaime = Seme

Jaime presented it like a math problem just as the bus hissed to a stop, and said the word out load. "Seh-Meh. Yes?"

Seh-Ahn read his formula and gave him another thumbs-up.

After school, Jaime had the sketchbook out by the time Seh-Ahn sat next to him. He drew the next installment on the right page and then balanced the book between them before moving to the left side while Seh-Ahn added the text to the pictures on the right. The collaboration worked well—Jaime being left-handed and Seh-Ahn right, they were able to draw and write simultaneously, frequently pausing to see what the other had done to influence what they would do themselves. By the time the bus stopped in front of Meester George's ranch road, the creature (Seme) still hadn't learned how to eat cactus, hadn't scared off the deadliest rattlesnake (though Jaime already had plans to bring the rattler back for a rematch), and Seme's greatest wish was to learn to ride a stallion even though his wheels prevented him from sitting astride anything.

With Jaime's mind preoccupied with Seme's further adventures, the walk to the trailer went by in an instant. He barely noticed he was back until a voice called out to him in English.

"Hi there, son."

The red-faced cowboy loomed in front of him in a way that made Jaime feel extra short. The gray felt hat cast a shadow over the cowboy's face. Broad shoulders turned into a bigger belly, accented by narrow hips with a massive, shiny silver belt buckle holding up his jeans. His small flip phone was clipped onto his belt next to a revolver. Jaime forced his eyes off the gun and focused on the rancher's boots, which were not only the size of Vida's body but were made from some scaly leather that could very well have been rattlesnake.

Jaime took a couple of steps back.

"Do you have a name?" Meester George asked in his loud, booming voice.

"Jaime," he said in a whisper.

"Well, Jaime, when someone says hi to you, the polite thing is to say hi back."

Jaime scanned the area for Tomás but couldn't see him. He hadn't understood a word Meester George had said but it couldn't have been good. He heard the scolding tone of the man's voice and knew he was in trouble.

"Sorree," he apologized without knowing what he was apologizing for (he had learned people up here liked that word), and then retreated as fast as his legs could carry him into the trailer.

He glanced out the window. No Meester George. And

still no Tomás. Jaime could only hope that whatever he'd done wrong wouldn't cost Tomás his job. According to the request Meester George made to Tomás yesterday, he obviously thought Don Vicente was replaceable, even after centuries of working for him. Which meant that Tomás, having worked for the rancher only eight years, could likewise be replaced.

Heavy boots stomped up the metal steps and Jaime was sure Meester George would burst into the trailer. But when the door swung open, it was Tomás with Vida.

"Come, Mr. George wants to meet you." Tomás stood in the doorframe and motioned outside with a jerk of his head.

Jaime crouched down to greet Vida. At least she didn't think he'd done anything wrong. "I don't like him. He scares me."

"Doesn't matter, you still have to treat him with respect. He's my boss and has been very kind to let you and Ángela live here."

"He hates me."

"No, he just thought you were rude for staring at him and not saying hi back."

Really? That was it? Jaime straightened up and brushed off his school uniform, making sure there was no dust from the walk to the trailer and that his shirt was tucked in nicely.

The cowboy leaned against the corral fence. He turned at the sound of their steps and Jaime had to stop himself from running away again. The rancher looked even bigger and more intimidating than he had minutes before with the sun now shining on his large red face. He let his hand hang for another reassurance from Vida, but the dog had trotted off to socialize with the ranch dogs.

Jaime took a deep breath, squared his narrow shoulders, and held out a hand instead to the rancher.

"'Ello, Meester George. My name ees Jaime."

Meester George nodded slightly before swallowing Jaime's hand with his own beefy paw.

"Hello, Jaime. Nice to meet you, son."

Okay, now what? There wasn't much more he knew how to say in English, and even if he did, he had no idea what to say. What did grown-ups talk about anyway? He looked over at Tomás for help but his brother was just staring at the cows. That could work.

"Cows nice?" Jaime wanted to ask if the cows were healthy but that sentence would have been too complicated. "Cow babies good?"

That was apparently the right thing to ask. Meester George responded at length about how pleased he was with the herd this year and a bunch of other stuff Jaime didn't understand. When Tomás responded, he spoke in perfect English that also didn't help. At some point the men switched the conversation from the cows to the new ranch hands. Jaime only understood that because Tomás pulled out his phone and showed the owner e-mails with the subject "RE: Ranch hand wanted/*Se busca ranchero*."

"*¿Pero solamente hasta que regrese Don Vicente, verdad?*" Jaime asked his brother, but it was Meester George who answered with a stern look.

"You're in the United States, son. Speak English here."

Jaime felt himself shrinking even smaller than his regular short height.

"Sorree."

Meester George shook his head. "Don't be sorry, just learn what's right."

His words pricked like cactus needles embedded up and down his spine. Who's to say that English was right and Spanish wasn't? Had he misunderstood when Meesus said Spanish was the second official language of Nuevo México? At any rate, he remembered his teacher back in Guatemala saying that Spanish was the second most popular language in the world after Chinese. If there was anything that wasn't right, it was everyone thinking that people who didn't speak English were inferior.

Meester George's stern face muscles relaxed a fraction, but just a fraction. "If I visit your country, I'll try to speak to you in your language. But here, I want you to speak mine. Understand?"

"Yes," Jaime lied. He hadn't gotten half of the words. Instead, what he understood was that Meester George liked things done his way and his way was in English. Part of him wanted to forget what he had asked and just return to the trailer, where he could try calling home for the millionth time. But what he had to ask was more important. "Don Vicente—"

Meester George interrupted with the answer to the question he thought Jaime had tried to ask. "Cente never would learn English, no matter how hard my father and I tried. And now look where it got him. Old bastard."

Again Jaime didn't understand Meester George's meaning. The words indicated that Don Vicente was detained for not speaking English. At the same time, the tone implied that the rancher cared, but didn't know how to show it.

Even more reason Jaime had to ask his question. Make Meester George understand his concern. "*Rancheros,* uh, ranchers no stay. Leave. Don Vicente come . . . ?" He waved his arm as if beckoning someone closer.

Under his breath Tomás muttered, "Back."

"Ranchers leave when Don Vicente come back?" Jaime finally asked what should have been answered ages ago if Meester George hadn't been such a snob.

Meester George removed his hat and wiped his brow even though it wasn't hot enough today for him to sweat. He explained the situation in a sad tone, but his words were too complicated for Jaime to understand.

A blank gaze on Jaime's face must have told the rancher Jaime didn't understand, because he sighed and nodded at Tomás to translate.

"We don't know how long the new ranch hands will stay. Mr. George hired an immigration lawyer for Don Vicente. They have a trial date set in three weeks."

"¡Fantástico!" Jaime couldn't believe the great news. "So why is he upset?"

Tomás turned away but not enough to hide his sad face. "I haven't met her, but the lawyer isn't optimistic of his chances. A couple of years ago it wouldn't have been a problem, but now she says everything has changed and judges are almost impossible to persuade."

"But she's still going to try, right?"

"That's what he's paying her to do." Tomás nodded over to Meester George, who nodded back as if he understood what Tomás said. Maybe he did. Jaime's respect for the red-faced cowboy rose a little. Maybe he wasn't as pompous as he came across.

Jaime turned back to Meester George and searched his brain for the right words. "I go see Don Vicente?"

But it was Tomás who shook his head, replying in English. "No way. You're illegal. I don't want you anywhere near there."

Jaime caught the word "illegal" like a stab to his heart. Sure, he entered this country without permission, swimming across the Río Bravo that separated México from El Norte. The act might have been illegal, but as a person, he was no different than any other human. How could anyone actually be "illegal?" How could his brother say that? But in front of the boss man wasn't the time to debate that with Tomás.

He tried a different plan. "I write he—"

"Him," Tomás corrected automatically.

"I write him . . . paper?"

"You mean a letter?" Meester George raised his thick gray eyebrows.

"Yes," except Jaime thought "letter" meant letters of the alphabet. Well, he was going to write alphabet letters on a piece of paper so he guessed it made sense. So then why was Tomás shaking his head slightly no?

Meester George didn't notice and placed his beefy hand on Jaime's shoulder. For the first time the rancher's defenses came down. "I think he'd like that."

Meester George told Tomás to contact a couple of the guys who'd e-mailed about the job, and then walked to the big house, where scents from Doña Cici's open kitchen window were making even the cows hungry.

"So he's not even going to wait to see what happens in

court?" Jaime asked once he knew the rancher was too far away to scold him for speaking in Spanish.

Tomás turned to head back to the trailer with Vida now at his heels. The lines around his eyes deepened with worry and lack of sleep. "The court date is not for another three weeks and we still have a couple hundred cows ready to pop. Each calf has to be tagged, dehorned, and castrated if they're boys. Don Vicente did the work of two men, and even then, whoever we hire won't do half as good a job. Let's keep praying for a miracle and that the new hands are temporary."

"I can help."

Tomás draped an arm around his shoulders and drew him close, half affectionately, half teasing. "Sure, but you still have to keep going to school."

Oh well, it was worth a shot. "Why did you shake your head when I mentioned writing Don Vicente a letter? I know my English is bad but I didn't say anything wrong, did I?"

The sad look returned to Tomás's eyes as he opened the trailer door for them. "Of course not. It's a very sweet and thoughtful idea. Except that Don Vicente doesn't know how to read. He never went to school."

Jaime should have guessed—that was often the case for older people in Guatemala as well; Abuela had only attended school until she was nine. Still, a smile crossed

Jaime's face. He reached into his backpack, remembering the bus rides with Seh-Ahn and the story they had created without saying a thing to each other, and pulled out his sketchbook. "Then it's a good thing I know how to write him a letter without any words."

CHAPTER SIXTEEN

Sunday breakfast wasn't Sunday breakfast without Don Vicente. And having Meester George sitting at the head of the table while on the kitchen phone with his wife, who was still visiting their new grandchild, made things even more awkward.

Doña Cici hid her worry by fussing over Meester George, Tomás, Jaime, and Ángela more than usual. She outdid herself by adding thick pancakes, fresh strawberries, poached eggs, and steak (actual steak!) to her already enormous buffet of tortillas, chorizo, beans, cheese, fruit, and other kinds of eggs.

"Eat some more, Ángela," Doña Cici whispered so as not to interrupt Meester George's phone call. "You've only had a tortilla and one egg."

"It's delicious, but I'm not very hungry." She forced a smile and took another bite of egg.

"How can you not be hungry?" Jaime asked between a mouthful of pancake, eggs, and chorizo. "We barely ate anything last night."

"You're out of food?" Doña Cici exclaimed loud enough to cause Meester George to give her the stern "I'm on the phone" look.

Tomás gave Jaime a look of his own that said "don't go there" before reassuring the chef. "Of course we have food. Jaime's just exaggerating."

What had really transpired was that Tomás had come in late, crashed on the bed, and told them to scrounge. The only thing Jaime had found was a packet of microwave popcorn and some goat milk Doña Cici had left. Even Tomás's trusty cans of beans were all gone.

Meester George hung the phone up back in the kitchen and spent the rest of the meal talking with Tomás about the cows and the status of the new ranch hand applications. Everyone else chewed their food without comment. Except for Ángela, who stopped eating completely. On her plate remained half a tortilla and some egg. Abuela would have never allowed it.

"You don't have to starve yourself to prove Tomás wasn't lying about no food," Jaime whispered as he helped clear the table.

"What do you know?" She left through the kitchen door without scraping off her plate or putting it in the dishwasher. The men left to get back to work (so much for Tomás's day off) and only Jaime helped clean up.

"Are we watching another movie with that handsome Bond man?" Doña Cici asked once everything looked clean enough to serve a king.

Jaime shook his head. Without Tomás and Ángela, and even Don Vicente sleeping through the opening credits, movie day had lost its appeal. "I have homework to do."

Not completely a lie. He still needed to practice the recorder and come up with a topic for a research project he would have to write in English. Meesus insisted.

Doña Cici nodded her understanding and proceeded to fill two large canvas shopping bags with leftovers. Jaime knew he should refuse and not betray Tomás. But last week he had accepted the leftovers gladly, and they really didn't have anything to eat in the trailer. Besides, Doña Cici wouldn't take no for an answer. "I'll carry them over myself if I have to."

"*Gracias.*" The bags threatened to pull his arms out of their sockets.

"Your brother is not used to caring for people other than himself. You being here is good for him." She opened the kitchen door and watched Jaime waddle under the weight of the bags.

"No matter what, this kitchen door is always unlocked."

immigrants continued to infiltrate the country despite all the border surveillance and guards.

"I no understand," he muttered. Freddie entered the room, smiled at Jaime, and shook Meesus's hand in greeting.

When Freddie sat down, Meesus returned to Jaime as if they hadn't been interrupted. "The correct phrase is, 'I don't understand.'"

"I don't understand," Jaime repeated and he still didn't. He knew Meesus wasn't really a secret agent. For one thing, he didn't think secret agents took the time to correct poor English.

"You know we've been talking about the impact of immigration on our country, and I'd like to move on to discussing real refugees and immigrants," Meesus explained.

Jaime shifted. He could still make a run for it. Except his sketchbook with *The Adventures of Seme* and his other drawings sat on his desk in the opposite direction from the door.

"Whether you're here legally or not is none of my business. Understand?"

He nodded. Okay, maybe he should believe her. Then why did he still have a bad feeling about this?

"But if you'd like to share what it's like to immigrate or be an immigrant, I think it would be great for the class to learn from you."

• • •

Jaime had just set his backpack and lunch (a feast of le
over egg, steak, and cheese in a tortilla with strawberr
for dessert) in his cubby and sketchbook and homewo
folder on his desk, when Meesus looked up from writi
on the whiteboard.

"Jaime, come here for a second, please."

Something about her determined and no-nonsei
face put Jaime on guard. He went through a mental che
He'd said good morning to her just a minute ago witl
shake of her hand, as she liked, and he'd done all his hon
work (math, which he continued to be surprisingly go
at; reading for fifteen minutes a book Meesus had ch
sen, *The Magic School Bus,* which was for little kids but s
interesting; and had chosen manga for his research proje

So why did she have that look that said he wasn't goi
to like what she had to say?

Meesus set down the marker she was holding to lo
at him above her thick glasses. "Would you be interested
sharing a little bit about your immigration story in so
studies today?"

Jaime gulped as he reached for her desk to stea
himself. His legs began to shake. Why didn't he realize
before? With her stern face and her passion for order a
rule following, maybe Meesus had a secret life as a *m*
officer. She'd been sent to schools to find out exactly h

immigrants continued to infiltrate the country despite all the border surveillance and guards.

"I no understand," he muttered. Freddie entered the room, smiled at Jaime, and shook Meesus's hand in greeting.

When Freddie sat down, Meesus returned to Jaime as if they hadn't been interrupted. "The correct phrase is, 'I don't understand.'"

"I don't understand," Jaime repeated and he still didn't. He knew Meesus wasn't really a secret agent. For one thing, he didn't think secret agents took the time to correct poor English.

"You know we've been talking about the impact of immigration on our country, and I'd like to move on to discussing real refugees and immigrants," Meesus explained.

Jaime shifted. He could still make a run for it. Except his sketchbook with *The Adventures of Seme* and his other drawings sat on his desk in the opposite direction from the door.

"Whether you're here legally or not is none of my business. Understand?"

He nodded. Okay, maybe he should believe her. Then why did he still have a bad feeling about this?

"But if you'd like to share what it's like to immigrate or be an immigrant, I think it would be great for the class to learn from you."

. . .

Jaime had just set his backpack and lunch (a feast of left-over egg, steak, and cheese in a tortilla with strawberries for dessert) in his cubby and sketchbook and homework folder on his desk, when Meesus looked up from writing on the whiteboard.

"Jaime, come here for a second, please."

Something about her determined and no-nonsense face put Jaime on guard. He went through a mental check. He'd said good morning to her just a minute ago with a shake of her hand, as she liked, and he'd done all his homework (math, which he continued to be surprisingly good at; reading for fifteen minutes a book Meesus had chosen, *The Magic School Bus,* which was for little kids but still interesting; and had chosen manga for his research project).

So why did she have that look that said he wasn't going to like what she had to say?

Meesus set down the marker she was holding to look at him above her thick glasses. "Would you be interested in sharing a little bit about your immigration story in social studies today?"

Jaime gulped as he reached for her desk to steady himself. His legs began to shake. Why didn't he realize it before? With her stern face and her passion for order and rule following, maybe Meesus had a secret life as a *migra* officer. She'd been sent to schools to find out exactly how

"No."

"No?"

"No, tank you."

Even worse than Meesus being an undercover immigration agent or being forced to speak English in front of his class was what he'd actually have to tell them. He'd relived the horrors too many times in his head; saying them out loud to people who wouldn't understand would be impossible. Sharing with Don Vicente and Doña Cici over breakfast was one thing. They knew the hardships, they understood the emotions, they were immigrants themselves. His classmates would never understand. They might even think he'd made things up just for the attention.

"It could just be one or two details," Meesus tried to reassure him.

The bell rang and Meesus waved him to his seat. Jaime folded his arms across his chest with his sketchbook sandwiched in the middle. Not happening. Not at all.

Meesus introduced the day's lesson and began the discussion of the differences between immigrants, refugees, migrants, and pioneers.

"Doesn't matter what you call them." Diego muttered. "They're all here to take away our jobs."

Freddie raised his hand as he gave Diego a look. "An immigrant is someone who moves to a new place, usually looking for a better life. Like more money or to be closer to family. A refugee is someone who has to leave their country because there's a war or because their life is in danger or something."

"Well said." Meesus wrote Freddie's explanation on the whiteboard. "An immigrant leaves because they want to, a refugee because they have to. What about migrants and pioneers?"

Jaime ignored the discussion as a new thought crossed his mind. People kept saying he and Ángela were immigrants. He thought of himself as an immigrant too. But Freddie seemed to say that immigrants left their home because they wanted to, because they hoped things would be better.

Only part of that rang true for Jaime. He wasn't just a person settling into a new place to seek a better life. He was more than that: a refugee, a person who left his country because of danger. Coming here hadn't been his choice, or even his parents' choice. The choice to leave had been made for him. Had he stayed, he would have died.

A weight seemed to lift from his shoulders and was replaced with self-assurance. He raised his hand without thinking and then quickly lowered it. Except Meesus caught his movement and called on him.

"Jaime, do you have something to share?"

The whole class turned to look at him. He started to shake his head no. That he was just stretching. Except he now thought about Diego's words that Meesus hadn't heard, that people from other countries were just here to take away jobs. How some people thought he and others like him were all criminals. If he didn't speak up, no one would know the truth.

"I am refugee," he said with more pride and assurance than he thought possible when a few seconds ago he dreaded this conversation. "I leave Guatemala to live. Bad people with drugs, *pandilleros*—"

"Gang members," Samuel interrupted even though he didn't like translating for Jaime.

"Yes, gang members. They say *unir* with them or die."

"They would kill you if you didn't join their gang? They'd really do that?" Carla asked. Jaime could feel his face paling. The memory of Miguel's murder haunted him daily. He knew his classmates wouldn't understand, would be incapable in their safe worlds to get that in other parts of the world, bad things really did happened. But at the same time, and he hated himself for it, he liked that Carla seemed impressed with his past life.

"Yes. Gang members kill people. Kill cousin. Parents say, 'Go to El Norte. Live with brother.' Me and Ángela, other cousin, we go."

"His parents must have been glad to get rid of him," Diego said in his low voice, but Jaime heard it just fine. And understood more than he would have liked.

Freddie turned to Diego. "Don't be mean."

Diego shrugged and maintained the low voice. "Just telling it like it is. Parents that love you don't send you away."

Jaime waited for Meesus to tell Diego off, make him stay in during recess for being so rude and completely incorrect. Except she hadn't heard him.

At any rate, what did Diego know? Jaime's parents did love him. His whole family loved him and Ángela so much that they were willing to send them on a dangerous journey, choosing between definitely dying and possibly dying. They did it to keep them safe, because they loved them.

"They didn't have a choice," Freddie insisted in a voice that Meesus definitely heard, though he had been talking to Diego.

"Exactly, they didn't have a choice," Meesus said. "Their lives were in danger and leaving was the only chance of survival. I definitely think that marks you as a refugee, not an immigrant. Thank you for sharing, Jaime. So what do you think is a good example of someone who is an immigrant? Samuel?"

Samuel lowered his hand and began to share his family's immigration story—something about not finding enough work and not being able to earn what they needed to feed the family. But Jaime stopped paying attention as Diego's words continued to gnaw at his brain. If his family had really loved him, they would have done more to keep him and Ángela safe. They knew people who hadn't completed the journey. Marcela, Tomás's old crush, who was kidnapped and sold as a slave. Other people from his village had left and were never heard from again. That could have been him or Ángela. Their parents knew of the dangers, which meant their parents could have sent them to their death. And what parent who loved their child would do that?

CHAPTER SEVENTEEN

Goat milk squirted out of Jaime's nose when Ángela exited the tiny trailer bathroom. Her eyes and lips were covered in black makeup and her cheeks had gone a pale color instead of her usual bronzed brown. She looked like *muerte*, and not in that intriguing, undead, vampire way.

"Why do you look like that?" Jaime asked.

"It's for the play. It's called stage makeup."

"But aren't you a nun?"

She sent a death glare at him over her blackened eyes.

"You don't know anything," she said. In English. And then left the trailer without breakfast.

Jaime downed the rest of the milk and grabbed a banana along with his backpack and hoodie before dashing after her.

"*¿Qué te pasa?*" he asked when he caught up with his cousin.

"Nothing." Again, in English.

"*¿Por qué estás de mal humor?*"

"I'm not in a bad mood." She groaned and shook her head like she couldn't believe what she had to deal with. She walked faster up the hill even though they had plenty of time to make it to the bus.

Jaime lengthened his stride to keep up with her. Every few steps he turned to look at her, started to ask another question, and then changed his mind. Each time he looked, her blackened eyes remained focused ahead.

"Do you want the banana?" he offered her his break-fast as a peace offering.

"No, it's too ripe." At least this time she said it in Spanish.

"*¿Y?*" He waved the banana in her face, waiting for her to accept it. "You need to eat something."

"No, what I need is for you to leave me alone. Gaaawd." And she was back to the English, and back to walking faster than necessary.

The bus took forever to arrive, and while they waited Ángela did an award-winning performance of ignoring Jaime. Except had he not been there, he doubted she would have maintained the emo stare at the highway. She also wouldn't have stepped in front of him to deliberately get on the bus first. Or flicked her hair over her shoulder and strutted (yes, strutted) to the back of the bus where, instead of sitting on the seat that awful Tristan always saved for her, she wrapped her arms around his neck and plopped down on his lap.

"Hey, babe. Loving the Goth look." Tristan draped an arm over her thigh. Jaime stopped watching. Hopefully, Abuela wasn't watching either.

"You gotta sit on your own seat," the driver shouted as he glared at Ángela through his rearview mirror. "I ain't moving til you do."

Jaime turned just enough to catch Ángela slide off Tristan's lap, redness threatening to burst through her pale makeup. He shifted his gaze to the roof of the bus as it rolled back on the highway. *Gracias, Abuela.*

When he finally turned to say hi to Seh-Ahn, his friend had a note for him.

Your sister is acting really weird.

No me digas, Jaime wanted to write, but didn't know how to translate that he was in full agreement. Instead, he copied Seh-Ahn's words. *Yes really weird.*

It also would have been too hard to explain that Ángela wasn't his sister. And that for the first time in his life he was glad she wasn't.

"Jaime, do you have a minute?" Meez Macálista called out to him in Spanish as his class finished their music lesson.

"Ooh, you're in trouble," Diego muttered as he knocked into him as he left the room.

Jaime rearranged the recorder in his bag, making sure he hadn't scratched it. What was it with teachers and their ability to always want to talk when you least wanted to?

He watched the rest of his class leave to return to Meesus's room. Carla hung back to wait for him, her head tilted curiously to the side, causing her black hair to fall over her purple glasses.

"I have to go," he told the music teacher.

Meez glanced at the clock. "There's still forty-five minutes before the final bell and I already told Mrs. Threadworth I wanted to talk with you. How are you doing?"

Carla tucked the strand of hair behind her ear and sent Jaime a small smile before following the rest of her class out. Jaime wished he could join her, maybe ask her a casual question on their way back to class (she liked cats, right?).

"*Bien.*" Jaime sighed.

"You look distracted today."

Jaime shook his head. Now was not the time to talk about Abuela. About Ángela who continued to become more distant with every day. About Don Vicente and his inevitable deportation. About the fact that just like Miguel's murder, he couldn't think of anything to do to help. And above all, he didn't want to talk about his desperation to return home, and hope Diego was wrong about his family not wanting him.

"I'm fine."

Meez didn't let it rest. "Have you made some friends?"

"Sort of."

Meez gave him that look that said as a teacher she expected a better answer and wasn't going to let him go until he complied.

Jaime let out a breath. "Freddie and Carla are nice, but I like Seh-Ahn best."

"Who?"

"Seh-Ahn. He's on the bus but not in my class."

Meez still pretended she didn't know who he was talking about. Annoyance grew inside Jaime. He knew Meez knew everyone in the school, from the littlest kindergarteners to the burly eighth graders who looked old enough to vote. She just wanted him to keep talking and he was not in the mood.

"Seh-Ahn," he said quickly. "Blond hair and freckles. Reads a lot. Seh-Ahn." He flopped his arms to his sides to emphasize how tired he was of her stupid game.

"Oh, you mean Sean?"

Jaime's shoulders slumped as his annoyance grew. "He said his name was Seh-Ahn."

"He . . . *said* that?"

"Well, no. He wrote it." Like he wrote the text for *The*

Adventures of Seme, like he and Jaime always wrote things to each other. Suddenly Jaime wondered if this boy had been playing a joke on him. Was their whole friendship just some stupid game to see how gullible he was? Jaime could see Ángela's friend Tristan playing a trick like this, but Seh-Ahn? Who always waved and saved him a seat but never pestered him with questions when he wanted to be left alone? Jaime couldn't believe it. Didn't want to believe it.

Jaime hid his head in his hands. No wonder Jaime never saw him in school; his cover would have been blown. But why would he do such a thing? "I hate him and I hate it here."

"Jaime." Meez kept a hand on his shoulder even when he tried to shake it off. "Sean is an Irish name. It's pronounced Shawn but in this case it's spelled S-E-A-N, which is pretty normal. Have you ever heard of the actor Sean Connery?"

"James Bond," Jaime replied without thinking about it.

"Exactly," Meez smiled kindly. "Your friend and the actor have the same name."

"So why didn't Seh-Ahn, I mean Sean, correct me?" But Jaime answered the question for himself as soon as he asked it. Because he never spoke to Sean, and Sean never spoke back. Maybe Jaime said hi and a few other words but besides that, they never talked. That was one of the things

Jaime liked best about Sean. They understood each other without speaking.

"Sean is . . . ," Meez paused as she tried to remember her Spanish. "I don't know the word. In English it's 'deaf.'"

"'Death'? Like *muerte*?" He clutched his schoolbag to his side. She couldn't mean he was a killer. Then, that he was dead? What happened? Sean was alive this morning. He—

Meez waved her arms to calm Jaime down. "Oh no, different word. This one means he can't hear. His ears don't work."

"He hears nothing?"

"Nothing."

"And he can't talk?"

"He makes sounds sometimes and laughs, but it's hard to learn words when you can't hear. He talks with his hands and has a special hearing teacher who helps him learn to communicate like that."

It all made sense now. Jaime could see Sean in his mind making gestures with his hands and had never given them a second thought. Most of his family used their hands in addition to verbal communication. The more passionate the topic, the bigger the gestures. He never thought Sean's signs were actual words.

He planted himself on a chair in front of Meez's desk, strewn with instrument parts and sheet music. "Show me."

"I only know very basic signs and how to spell my

name." Meez glanced at the clock. Jaime followed her gaze. Music class had finished ten minutes ago and now there were only thirty-five minutes left until the final bell. Meesus might wonder where he was. Or she might be glad that for once she didn't have to overexplain things.

"*Por fa*, Meez," Jaime pleaded. She bit her lip and Jaime could almost see her mind debating the situation—she had work to do and Meesus would get upset that she was keeping him so long. On the other hand, poor Jaime, all alone from a different country and unable to speak the grueling English language, finally made a friend. Jaime noticed her weakening and went on. "On Fridays after *música*, Meesus lets us have a free period to read or start homework as long as we're quiet. I'm not missing anything."

"*Bueno*, I do think learning different ways to communicate is a good thing." She sighed before motioning him to the other side of her desk to view her computer. "Let's look it up on YouTube."

Meez accidentally loaded a British Sign Language video instead, and after a few seconds of her saying, "That's not what I learned," she figured out her mistake. Apparently, different countries had different signs for the same letters. Weird. Even among deaf communities, someone from one country wouldn't be able to understand someone from a different country. It didn't seem right, but at the same time, who should decide that their country's signs were the "correct" signs? The same as with spoken languages, one wasn't better than another.

They watched the American Sign Language alphabet video three times before Jaime remembered all the letters. He had to think before each one but after that third time, he could spell his name using his hand. And A-N-G-E-L-A and T-O-M-A-S. Because it was a basic American Sign Language video it didn't show how to add accent marks to letters, but a lot of people didn't write Spanish names with accents, so maybe it didn't really matter.

Then they watched the video that showed them how to say basic signs like "hi" (simple, just a wave), "my name is" (placing a hand on your chest for "my" then tapping the pointer and middle fingers of each hand against each other to create an X while palms faced your chest for the word "name"), "thank you" (tapping your chin with fingertips and then extending the palm out), and a few others.

"Jaime, you have to go." Meez stopped the video and closed the browser. "The bell will ring in a minute."

He couldn't miss the bus, but for the first time ever, he didn't want to leave school. Not with so much left to learn.

"Can we do this again? On Monday?"

Meez laughed. "I'm the music teacher, I have my own classes to teach. But I'll ask Mrs. Threadworth and Mr. Mike, Sean's teacher, and maybe they can arrange something."

"Cool," he said in English just as the bell rang. He

tapped his chin with his fingertips before bringing his palm out in front of him in thanks. Meez waved "bye" in return.

He wove his way as quickly as he could through the herd of kids and bulging backpacks to his class. Meesus stood on the toes of her leather granny shoes cleaning the whiteboard when Jaime returned to the classroom.

"Jaime, where have you been? Is everything alright?" she asked.

"I'm perfect," he said in English as he gathered his hoodie and lunch bag before holding out his hand the way she liked. "Bye, Meesus."

She blinked behind her glasses before shaking his hand. "Good-bye, Jaime."

Then he dashed out of the room like Vida after a rabbit. The driver of bus thirty-six gave him a "you're late" look and closed the door behind him. Jaime dropped onto the seat next to Sean as he caught his breath. He shoved his stuff under the seat in front and turned to his friend, who held his head at an angle as if to ask what happened.

"Hi, Sean." Except Jaime said it with a wave and finger spelling S-E-A-N. Sean's eyes widened and his mouth opened into a grin so huge he could have been an anime character. A second later Sean's right hand flashed in a series of signs. This time Jaime's eyes widened and mouth dropped. Too fast, too new. His brain raced as he tried to figure out what Sean had said. No clue.

Sean's smile turned into a kind and understanding one as he repeated his spelling signs slow enough for a turtle to get it. H-O-L-A, J-A-I-M-E.

Jaime's dropped mouth turned to a smile. His friend "spoke" Spanish! Or at least he knew how to spell "*hola*" correctly. Jaime dug into his backpack for his sketchbook and drew the two of them—Sean with blond hair and lots of freckles and himself with black hair and no freckles. Underneath he wrote "*amigos*" because "friends" was too hard to spell. Sean pointed to the word and then linked his pointer fingers one on top of the other, and then switched which finger was on top to do it again. Then he pointed to Jaime before tapping his own chest and did the finger linking sign again. Jaime nodded and repeated Sean's sign. *Yes, we're friends.*

With nothing left to say, Sean eagerly tapped the back of the sketchbook. Maybe it was time to introduce a new character in *The Adventures of Seme*.

CHAPTER EIGHTEEN

Legs stuck out from under the table when Jaime entered the trailer after school.

"Good, you're home," Tomás's legs said while the rest of his body seemed to be swallowed by the table. "Hold the table up so I can fix this."

Jaime dropped his bag and braced the table, glad that after a week of eating on their laps, Tomás finally had the mechanism to fix it. He wanted to tell Tomás about Sean "speaking" sign language. How even though they didn't talk, they understood each other perfectly. And how he wished other people would be so easy to understand. Diego. Immigration officers.

Ángela.

"I have potential good news and potential bad news,"

Tomás said before Jaime could tell him about his day. Jaime took a deep breath. Nothing good ever came from such a line.

"Don Vicente stole a horse and escaped out of the detention center?" he asked in an attempt to keep the tone light.

It worked.

"You're like me. You watch too much *tele*," Tomás said, laughing.

Jaime wanted to say it wasn't *televisión*, it's what happened in an episode of *The Adventures of Seme*. Except Seme still couldn't ride on a horse with his tank wheels so he'd held onto the horse's tail while making a rattler noise to scare the horse into running off.

"But it does have to do with Don Vicente," Tomás continued.

Jaime grasped the table extra tight to make sure it didn't pinch his brother's fingers. "Okay."

"So, I misunderstood. The lawyer has set up a trial, which is good, but it's only to get him out of jail. It doesn't mean that he won't still get deported later on. It's called a bail bond hearing." Tomás pressed against the table to tighten a screw.

"Basically," Tomás continued, "if the judge thinks Don Vicente is an honorable man and won't disappear, they will release him from the detention center and he can come back to the ranch until he gets summoned for another trial, and *then* they will decide whether he gets to stay permanently or not. Chances are not good that he'll get to stay, but they're so backed up, and deporting actual criminals is much more important, so it could be a couple of years before the deportation trial takes place."

Tomás was right. Definite potential for things to go in many ways. Don Vicente might still get deported, but in years. Years. Jaime's own life had changed the moment Miguel had been murdered. So much could change in years. "But he gets to come home in the meantime?"

"If the judge thinks he's trustworthy," Tomás repeated. "If not, then he stays in jail, but would most likely be moved to a different facility, maybe thousands of miles away, where they have more space."

We can't let that happen. But how do you prove someone is trustworthy? Jaime wondered. It wasn't like Don Vicente went around with a camera recording his every move like in reality shows (and everyone knew those weren't "real" anyway). Still, there had to be a way. "So he'll only get moved if this hearing doesn't go well. That means we just have to convince the judge to let him go."

"And then a lot of money has to be paid to make sure Don Vicente attends his deportation trial. See if the table holds."

Jaime let go of the table. It stayed upright, but that hardly seemed important.

"I can help raise the money. I've sold my art before," Jaime reminded his brother. Of course that had been to gringo tourists in Ciudad Juárez, and out here in the middle of ranchland, there were no tourists but . . . "And at school we have these things called 'bake sales' which all the kids love. I'm sure Doña Cici will make—"

Tomás slithered out from under the table and put his arm around his little brother, giving him a playful shove. "A bond is usually set at several thousand dollars. That's a lot of cookies and sketches. But don't worry about that. Mr. George may be a lot of things I don't like, but he's always been fair where money is concerned. He'll take care of covering the bond."

"*¡Perfecto!*" What was the problem then with all this "potential" business? This sounded fantastic. Sure, there was still the deportation trial, but they had years to figure something out.

Tomás dropped his arm from around Jaime. "We need to get him out of jail first, and there's no guarantee they'll let him go, even with a good lawyer and the money. Especially if he's been talking to other inmates about riding off into the sunset."

"You know about that?"

"Don Vicente has been saying that for as long as I've known him. A guard might interpret that as him running away."

Jaime shook his head. He couldn't blame the old man. Riding into the sunset did seem a better option than being in a detention center.

Somehow, Jaime would have to prove that Don Vicente wasn't riding off anytime soon. That he was an important and valued member of the community, that he loved the ranch and had no reason to leave it. But how could he convince a judge of that? Jaime's English was no good, and even in Spanish he doubted he could make a compelling case.

He pulled out his sketchbook and began doodling sketches of Don Vicente on Pimiento to help him think—the old man picking him up at the bus stop so he wouldn't have to walk back alone and waiting on the ridge while he mourned Abuela. There had to be a way to show the judge what a great person Don Vicente was.

An idea began to form in his mind, based on stories Don Vicente had told him when they rode home together. But it would require a lot of work.

CHAPTER NINETEEN

Meez Macálista kept her promise. After the mid-morning break on Monday, there were special guests in Jaime's classroom.

"Hi S-E-A-N!" Jaime signed to his friend. "What are you doing?"

He'd learned that sign almost by accident: It was what Sean had asked that morning when Jaime had passed him on the bus to tell that Tristan jerk to leave Ángela alone because he'd been holding Ángela's hands in his as if he were about to propose. But Jaime could only tell him off in Spanish and Ángela had told Jaime to mind his own business. In English.

Jaime supposed the sign could have meant, "Where are you going?" instead, since that could have fit in with the context as well, but Sean didn't give him a strange look now. Instead, the other boy signed back his greeting but then shrugged like he had a secret and wasn't going to tell.

Cool, Jaime could wait. He pulled out his sketchbook from his desk and flipped it to the back side where they were creating *The Adventures of Seme*. He'd just sketched out Seme when Meesus called the class's attention. Jaime closed the book, but kept his pencil inside to mark the page.

"Class, we have two guests with us today." Meesus stood in front of the room with her arms crossed as if challenging anyone to misbehave and make her look bad. "Some of you might know Sean. He's in seventh grade and is here with his teacher and sign language interpreter, Mr. Mike."

During all of this, the interpreter signed to Sean all the words Meesus said. This Meester Mike, a round man who seemed young even though his dark brown hair was thinning, moved his hands and made facial expressions as if he were acting or dancing. Jaime would much rather watch Meester Mike's signs than listen to boring Meesus whom he didn't understand half the time anyway. With sign language at least, it seemed like he didn't have to know each sign to get the meaning.

"Because Sean goes to our school," Meesus continued, alternating between looking at Sean, Meester Mike, and her class, "we thought it would be good for you to know how to communicate with a deaf person."

Sean began signing to his interpreter, who in turn spoke to the class as if he were Sean.

"Hi everyone, I'm Sean. Next time you pass me in the hall and want to say 'hi,' that'd be nice. Just make sure I know you're there. If I can't see you, it's okay to tap my shoulder to get my attention. That's not rude. Just like I'm not being rude if I do the same to get your attention." Sean tapped Meesus on the shoulder and preceded to shake her hand in greeting, just like she made everyone in her class do at the beginning and end of every day. Meesus smiled and then gave her class a look that said she wished they were all so polite.

"I don't want him touching me. What if deafness is contagious?" Diego mumbled. Jaime gave him a dirty look, but said nothing. Learning comebacks in English had not been on the top of Meesus's vocabulary list. Besides, something about the acoustics in the room seemed to allow Diego to say things from his desk that Meesus never heard. Jaime wasn't sure it worked the same from his location by the window.

"We're going to show you the alphabet, which is the most basic thing in American Sign Language, and very useful. Even if you don't know the sign for something, you can spell it out," Meester Mike continued to translate Sean's signs.

"Assuming you know how to spell," Diego muttered and again Meesus didn't hear. Though somehow Sean did, or else he just randomly turned to give Diego a well-deserved dirty look.

"It's okay if you can't spell well," Meester Mike spoke and signed at the same time so everyone would understand. "Even in the deaf community, we often skip letters deliberately to sign faster. Just like some people text words that aren't spelled correctly."

Sean and Meester Mike proceeded to show everyone the alphabet. Jaime paid attention to the first round, just to make sure he remembered the video he'd seen with Meez Macálista, and watched everyone else. He noticed Carla, who had immediately moved on to spelling her name, C-S-R-L-S. Without thinking about it, Jaime went to her desk and showed her a fist with his fingers flat against his palm and thumb up.

"Letter Ah ees like deez." He then changed his hand to a fist with his fingers curled in and the thumb across the fingers for an S. "Deez ees letter Eh-seh."

"Like this?" Carla showed him her letter A. He moved her thumb a fraction (though he had no idea if it mattered) and then nodded.

"*Perfecto*," he said as if he hadn't learned the alphabet himself just a few days ago. He waved his hand in the air to get Sean's attention. Once his friend was looking at him, he pointed at Carla and then raised his eyebrows in question and did a thumbs-up. Carla spelled her name for Sean and got a thumbs-up from the master. As her teacher, Jaime took partial credit for her success.

"Thanks," Carla said.

Jaime tapped his fingers on his chin and extended his hand out in gratitude too before returning to his seat.

Sean and Meester Mike went around the room helping people with their signs while Meesus tried to print out the American Sign Language alphabet for them to take home. Jaime didn't need to guess too hard to know she planned on quizzing them on the alphabet tomorrow—she liked her quizzes. He opened up his sketchbook again to finish the panel of Seme cornered by a huge blob-like creature who stared at Seme in stupefied wonder.

Sean came over, as Jaime knew he would, but before he began to write the comic's dialogue, he pointed to Carla and then wrote on a small reporter-type notebook he pulled out of his pocket, *She's pretty.*

Jaime blushed and wrote back, *Yes.*

She likes you too.

¿Yes? He looked over at her. Carla turned her head and signed, Hi J-A-I-M-E, correctly this time. He gave her another thumbs-up and quickly dropped his head back to his sketchbook while Sean nudged him in the ribs.

Sean tapped him to look up and motioned for the sketchbook. Jaime slid it over for Sean to add the dialogue while peering over his friend's shoulder. Carla was now signing hi to the girl next to her while Meesus tried to remove the paper jammed in the printer. He returned his eyes to the sketchbook but didn't get a chance to read what Sean had written.

"Look, it's Dumb and Dumber," Diego said just loud enough so a few kids heard.

"*Cállate*," Jaime said under his breath and gave Diego an evil look. But he couldn't say any more. He was right about the audio imbalance in the room. Meesus looked up from the printer right at him even though Jaime thought he'd been extra quiet. The printer beeped and the teacher's attention went back to the job at hand.

When Jaime tried to read the comic for a second time, Sean had his notebook on top of the drawing with different words instead. *What did he say?*

Jaime shook his head. He didn't want to exclude Sean, but didn't want to hurt his feelings either. Besides, he didn't know how to spell it. Instead he wrote, *It bad. He bad boy.*

Sean stood and leaned over his notebook to scribble his message before walking away with it in hand. *Don't look,* it had said.

Which of course meant Jaime had to watch. Sean headed over to Diego all smiles, pointed at Diego, snapped his fingers, and then touched his chin with one hand before lowering it face down. Diego's eyes shifted uneasily around the room, not knowing if he was being told off or complimented. Sean smiled wider and repeated his signs before writing the meaning in his notebook.

Diego read it out loud, "'You're good with signs.' Yeah, I guess I am." He repeated the signs Sean had done a few times, but changed "you're" to "I'm" by tapping his chest so that his signs became "I'm good with signs."

Except all the finger snapping caught Meester Mike's attention and he waved his arms to stop. "Careful, you're signing that you're a bad dog. What were you trying to say?"

Jaime drew his attention back to his sketchbook and pretended to add a shadow under Seme's wheels. His skin prickled with the glare Diego sent him, as if it had been his idea for Sean to call him a bad dog.

"Nothing," Diego said to Meester Mike. "I was just repeating something I saw on TV."

The hairs on Jaime's neck rose as he felt Diego stare at him again.

Twenty-four copies of the American Sign Language alphabet finally in hand, Meesus passed out the sheets and told them there'd be a quiz tomorrow. Yup, Jaime knew it.

"Now class, when you pass Sean at school or even around town, you can say hi. Does anyone have any questions for Sean before he returns to his class?"

"How old are you?" asked this girl Autumn who Jaime never spoke to but seemed nice enough.

Meester Mike signed the question to Sean and then again spoke Sean's response as if he were the boy. "I'm twelve. My birthday is at the end of the summer."

Freddie then raised his hand and waited for Sean to point to him. "How long did it take you to learn ASL?"

"I knew basic signs before most people learn to speak. Things like 'milk,' 'more,' and 'all done.' My parents are hearing people and we all learned together. When Mr. Mike started teaching me, I learned more. But just like you don't know all the words in English, I don't know all the signs in ASL."

Without waiting to be called on, Diego leaned back with his arms across his chest. "What's it like not being able to hear anything?"

Of course he would ask that.

Sean made some kind of sign that involved putting his hand to his head. Meester Mike signed something back with a slight shake of his head, like he didn't want to verbalize what Sean had expressed. The two had a quick debate, hands flying in every direction and Sean frowning until the boy sighed and signed something else.

"Sorry, I got confused with a sign that looks similar but means something completely different," Meester Mike covered up and then returned to interpreting. "Now talking for Sean, I've never been able to hear so I don't know what I'm missing."

But that had not been what Sean said the first time; the signs were completely different. Jaime wondered if (or rather hoped) Sean had signed some clever comeback like, "What's it like not being able to think anything?"

Perhaps sensing that the questions might get more insensitive, Meesus started to wave both hands by the side of her head, the deaf sign for applause, and encouraged everyone to do the same.

"Thank you, S-E-A-N," Meesus spoke and signed at the same time. Sean waved at the class, and Jaime could have sworn he let out a sigh of relief as he left the room.

Meesus closed the door behind Sean and Meester Mike before beginning a lecture about sensitivity and being respectful to people who are different. Too many words Jaime didn't understand. Besides, sneaking a look at his sketchbook to finally read Sean's dialogue for Seme in the land of the bug-eyed blob was more interesting.

"No sign of evolution, no sign of intelligent life forms."

The bell rang for lunch.

He snapped his sketchbook closed and stashed it in his desk before joining his classmates. He wasn't sure what "sign" meant in this context, but he had a feeling the comment described Diego perfectly.

CHAPTER TWENTY

Jaime ate his lunch quickly and joined a game of capture the flag. Some of the kids in his class were inspired by the sign language lesson and tried to sign messages to their teammates. Except none of them knew more than one or two words and the alphabet, so they were prone to making up hand movements that made sense to no one but the signer. Still, it added extra fun to the game. The bell rang before anyone captured the flag (two T-shirts that should have been in the lost and found).

Back in the classroom, Jaime stashed his lunch bag in his cubby and reached into his desk for his sketchbook. He had the best idea for the next image of Seme and it couldn't wait for the bus. Besides, today's after-lunch "special" class was art. The district hadn't found a replacement while the art teacher was on early maternity leave, so Meesus allowed them to paint or draw while she reviewed quizzes and papers.

It was one of the best parts of school. Or would be if he could find his sketchbook. He checked his desk, sure he had placed it in there before lunch, and didn't see it. He must have put it in his backpack. Only he didn't.

He definitely had it while Sean had been in the class. Did he put it in his cubby? No, he would have seen it there when he stashed his Ninja Turtles bag, but it was worth checking again.

Diego leaned against the cubbies with his arms crossed menacingly over his chest. "I think I saw your sketchbook in the bathroom. Do you pee sitting down so you can draw on the pot?"

But Jaime only heard two words—"sketchbook" and "bathroom."

He raced to the door, ignoring Meesus's reminder to please sign out, and in half a second got to the bathroom, the one he'd hid in that first day.

Torn-up paper shreds littered the bathroom floor like some gruesome art installation. He stepped closer, gulping and gasping for air. No, it couldn't be. Not his work, not Seme, not his family. Images of cacti, four stalk eyes, and hands catching a ball of tortilla *masa*—the portrait he'd made of Abuela—all torn into nothingness.

There would be no way to tape them back together. Impossible to know which piece belonged to which drawing, impossible to reconstruct any of the drawings. Even if they had been dry. Which they weren't. Each piece lay drenched in ammonia-smelling yellow liquid.

He gagged, unable to breathe. His hand reached over to a stall to brace himself. Except there lay the cover of his sketchbook, draped over one of the doors. It hung empty and gutted, with only the spiral ring holding it together. On the back cover facing him was a black marker drawing of a horrible stick figure peeing and the words "Diary of a Pee-Pee Kid."

He didn't understand. The words, yes, but why? How? What had he done to have anyone hate him so much?

"Now that's what I call art."

Jaime turned to see Diego had followed him into the bathroom and held his hands in front of his face in a box like a photographer judging a shot.

"What the hell, man?" Jaime said in Spanish, except he used one of Tomás's more colorful words. He turned and shoved Diego in the chest. "Why did you ruin my sketchbook? *My* sketchbook!"

Diego crossed his arms and smiled. "I don't understand Spanish. And you can't say anything to anyone about it or I'll have you deported."

Jaime balled his fist and threw his whole weight into a

punch at Diego's face. Except Jaime had never been good at fighting, and Diego turned his head so Jaime connected with the side of his hard skull instead of the eye he'd been aiming for. They both cried out, but Jaime must have been hurt more because Diego immediately swung his own fist. Jaime screamed again. Pain like he'd never felt split open his head and his vision blurred to darkness.

Slowly, light started to take over the darkness and shapes regained a more realistic form—urinals, washbasins, random bits of paper. He blinked a couple of times and found himself in the heap of wet, shredded art.

A gasp came from the door. From his spot on the floor, Jaime caught sight of a round face and round body. A scent of sweet chocolate mixed with the sharp ammonia: his old bathroom buddy he called Choco-chico. Diego dashed for the door but before he could make his escape, Choco-chico screamed so loudly that the whole school must have heard.

"Mis-ter Tru-ji-llo!"

Seconds later, Choco-chico's fourth grade teacher entered the bathroom. "What's going on here?" The teacher took in Jaime, Diego, and the giant mess before turning to Choco-chico. "Nate, go get Mrs. Threadworth."

"He hit me first," Diego said but the teacher ignored him to reach out a hand to help Jaime up instead.

"Are you okay? What is this stuff on the floor?"

My life. Except Jaime couldn't say that. Just thinking it made him want to cry, and he'd rather be deported than let Diego see him cry. He accepted the teacher's hand and slowly stood up. His head throbbed. Meester Trujillo held him steady as he blinked a few times and then cautiously touched his face. He could almost feel his nose swelling by the second and his eyes found it hard to focus. Gently he wiped his upper lip and discovered blood.

"Leave it." The teacher demanded. Jaime thought he was telling him not to touch his nose. But then he saw Diego reaching up to remove the sketchbook cover from its display on the bathroom stall.

The teacher gave Diego a look that said he better not move, before turning to examine Jaime's nose.

"I don't think it's broken, but you should go to the nurse," the teacher said in accented Spanish.

Choco-chico returned to the bathroom with Meesus.

"My students? Fighting? This is unacceptable." Her nostrils flared and her lips were so tight it seemed a miracle she could talk. Jaime had never seen his teacher so angry.

"It's not my fault. I was just defending myself," Diego insisted while rubbing his skull with an exaggerated moan. "He hit me first on the side of my head."

Meesus turned to Jaime with her hands on her hips. "Is that true?"

Jaime's right hand traced over his left fist. He'd forgotten about that. "Yes, I hit him."

"Principal's office. Both of you. Now." Meesus pointed to the door.

"But my head really hurts," Diego whined. "I need to get some ice."

Meesus looked like she would agree to a detour when her shoe stepped on a wet paper strip and she skidded. Meester Trujillo caught her before she hit the floor. She regained her footing as her eyes focused on the paper mess and the draped sketchbook cover.

"It'snotmine," Diego said in one syllable. Meesus placed each foot carefully on the sections of clean tile and removed the cover from the bathroom stall. On the inside cover, Sean had written in his best penmanship, "The Adventures of Seme, by Jaime Rivera and Sean Gallagher."

Meesus bent down to peer at the shreds on the floor. Her nose scrunched.

"Is that—did you *urinate* on this?" Her eyes bugged out of her head.

Diego retreated against the wall. "I thought—it was just a joke."

Meesus contorted her face into an ugly mess. She breathed deeply, once, twice, three times.

"Mr. Trujillo, can you please look in on my class while

I sort this out?" she said in her calmest voice before turning to her two students. "Come. We'll get you two some ice and then I'm leaving you with the principal."

The nurse gave them plastic bags of ice (though Diego placed his much lower than the place Jaime had hit him) and then Meesus talked to the principal by herself while the boys waited in chairs outside the office.

Jaime kept himself in blank zombie mode, refusing to think about anything. Any other emotion would have him crying and he refused to let Diego see him like that.

"I've called your parents," the principal's receptionist said. "They need to come in to take you home."

For one tiny moment Jaime thought the receptionist had called Mamá and Papá in Guatemala and that they really would take him home. Home to their kitchen and bedroom house where he could sleep outside in a hammock under the mango tree to the sound of crickets.

Then he remembered the emergency contact number the school had was for Tomás; he'd seen his older brother fill it out when they registered.

"Where is he? Where's my son?" A man burst into the office about twenty minutes later. Jaime was sure he was going to scream at the school staff for unjust treatment, but instead he grabbed Diego by the arm and practically lifted him off the ground. When he spoke, he scolded Diego in Spanish.

"I get a call from work to say that *mi hijo desgraciado* has destroyed a book, peed on it, and then broke the kid's nose?"

"His nose isn't broken—" Diego said in Spanish. So much for not speaking it.

"*Cállate, desgraciado.* Broken nose, bloody nose, same difference. I can't take this. You're staying at your mother's house from now on."

Diego hung his head. Diego's dad dropped his arm and began pacing around the office. After the second lap, he seemed to notice Jaime's presence.

"Is this your fault?" he said first in English and then repeated himself in Spanish. "*¿Es por tu culpa?*"

"*No,* I didn't punch myself in the nose," Jaime admitted.

The dad's cheeks reddened a bit and he seemed about to answer back when the receptionist stood up from behind her computer.

"Sir, you have to calm down," she said in English.

Diego's dad paced a few more laps before collapsing on the remaining empty chair. He jiggled his keys and fidgeted. Diego fidgeted too and kept sending sideways looks at his dad.

The principal finally called them in. Jaime had seen the man around school before—he had a shaved head to hide the fact that he was bald and skin that was neither white nor brown—but Jaime never knew he was the boss because he often fixed things himself. Jaime once saw him

with a mop bucket to clean up spilled milk in the cafeteria because it was quicker for him to do it than find a
custodian in the middle of lunch.

The principal watched the three of them enter the
office and called out to the receptionist. "Do we have a
guardian for Jaime?"

The receptionist shook her head. "I left a message, but
no one's called back."

The principal nodded and then shut the door to his
office.

"Jaime, where do you live?" The principal sat on his
chair and asked in Spanish.

Jaime glanced at Diego and his dad. The last thing he
wanted was for them to know the answer. Diego's threat of
getting him deported rang in his ears.

"On a cattle ranch. Far away." Jaime kept his answer
vague. "Phone reception isn't good and my brother works
all the time with the foreman gone."

The principal accepted that without question. Everyone
knew phone reception in rural Nuevo México was a novelty.

"Your foreman is gone?" Diego's father demanded.
"Are you talking about Vicente Delgado?"

"No." Jaime's voice came out as a squeak. Why had
he mentioned a foreman? He'd forgotten one of the basic
survival rules—never say more than you have to. All he
wanted was to justify why Tomás might not have gotten

the message. "No, no, different foreman, different person," he tried again.

Either Diego's dad excelled at lie detection or selective hearing, because he continued in Spanish. "Vicente Delgado once saved my life. I skidded off the road in a bad snowstorm. Would have frozen to death if Vicente hadn't ridden up. Said he and the horse were both feeling restless and needed to get out. He rode me fifteen miles to my house, and then turned right back around to go home. In the snow."

And then Diego's father rose, walked the two steps to Jaime's chair, and reached out his hand. Surprised, Jaime accepted it. "I heard what happened and I'm sorry the old man's been detained. If there's anything I can do, you let me know."

The man still scared Jaime, but he had said something that might help Don Vicente. . . .

An awkward silence hung in the office until the principal cleared his throat.

"*Pues.*" He pressed some buttons on his computer before saying, "I'll continue this talk in Spanish and record it so there are no complaints." His Spanish pronunciation was good but he spoke slowly as if he had to confirm each word.

"I heard Mr. Trujillo and Mrs. Threadworth's reports, and I saw the mess in the bathroom. Jaime, Diego, what happened?"

Jaime shifted in his seat and glanced at Diego. Neither boy said anything.

"*Bueno.* I will have to draw my own conclusions. You

are both responsible and will have consequences. Diego, you're suspended for the rest of the week."

"Suspended?" Diego's dad blurt out. "What're we going to do with him for the rest of the week? His mother and I work."

The principal gave him a stern look for interrupting. "Also, Diego, I want three letters of apology, explaining why what you did was wrong, one hundred words each. One to Jaime for destroying his book and hitting him."

"*No puedo escribir en español*," Diego whispered without looking up.

"Then you can write them in English," the principal replied, but kept speaking in Spanish. "The second letter goes to Mrs. Threadworth, apologizing for causing her to almost fall and hurt herself. And the last letter is for the custodian who has to clean up your mess. All three letters in my hand on Monday before you can enter the school. Understand?"

"Can't you just give him fifty lashes and be done with it?" Diego's father said in a tone that made Jaime think was more serious than kidding.

The principal lifted his thin eyebrows. "He destroyed property, vandalized school grounds, and gave someone a bloody nose. This punishment seems reasonable to me. If Diego tells me a different version of the events, then I'll consider altering the punishment."

Jaime waited for Diego to say that it was self-defense, that Jaime was asking for it, but he kept his mouth shut.

The principal moved on to Jaime, still speaking in Spanish. "You hit him first when you saw he destroyed your art book, yes?"

Jaime nodded.

"We don't hit in this school."

Jaime shifted the melted ice bag on his face and nodded again.

"Fighting never makes things better. You're suspended for a day and will give me a letter for Diego on Wednesday. Explain why you hit him and why that was bad. ¿Sí?"

"Sí," Jaime said, but more to indicate that he understood, not that he was in agreement. The letter would not be easy. How could he explain that he hit Diego because he wanted to cause him as much pain as he'd caused Jaime?

"Diego and Mr. Ramirez, you two are dismissed. I'll see you and your letters on Monday."

They left, but not before his dad gave Diego a strong shove out the office door, which the principal didn't see due to his attention on his computer screen.

"Your family only speaks Spanish?" He looked over the computer at Jaime.

"I live with my brother and he speaks perfect English."

"That is easier. I'm not good at writing in Spanish." The principal's fingers flew over the keyboard and in a matter of seconds, the printer hummed. He pulled the paper out, folded it into an envelope, and signed his name across the seal. "Give this to your brother and have him write his name and return it to my receptionist when he picks you up."

"I take the bus," Jaime said.

The principal shook his head and pointed to the clock on the wall: 3:27. "Buses left. Your brother has to pick you up. You can wait in the chair outside my door."

Any other day, Jaime would have spent the time waiting for Tomás with his nose buried deep in his sketchbook. Except his nose still hurt and his heart still ached.

Someone, maybe Meesus, had delivered his bag that no longer held a sketchbook to the office. He left his homework folder zipped away. Meesus didn't like when he doodled on his homework assignments, even on the blank back side.

He noticed the receptionist print something, review the document, then put it in the blue recycling bin next to her. She turned to her computer to make corrections before printing again.

"I have paper?" he pointed to the recycling bin as he asked.

She waved her hand as if to say "have at it."

He picked through and found several pieces with printing on only one side. Still not knowing the English word for "*grapadora,*" he helped himself to the stapler without asking to make the sheets into a book. But the sheets remained blank; he didn't know what to draw, or if he'd ever be able to draw again.

"I left another message for your brother," the secretary said in English after a while. "It's four-thirty and I lock up at five. Can you check that I have the right number?"

The mantra he had created to remember Tomás's number while traveling through México rang in his ears. He compared the number the secretary had with the one he knew by heart. Both were the same.

"When you call, phone go ring, ring?" Jaime asked.

"No, went straight to voicemail."

"Reception very bad. He no get message." What had Tomás said his plans were for the day? Interviewing people to cover for Don Vicente, that's right. Which meant they could be anywhere on the ranch, especially if they were looking at the herd.

Jaime supposed he could walk home. It'd take all night and the desert would turn cold as soon as the sun went down. But he'd been through worse.

No, better wait. Tomás would notice if Jaime didn't come home soon. Jaime just didn't know if that would happen before or after the school locked him in for the night.

CHAPTER TWENTY-ONE

"Jaime, *¿qué haces aquí?*" a voice asked.

Jaime looked up from the pages he had stapled together. Every time he had tried to draw something, the memory of his massacred sketchbook on the bathroom floor came back to haunt him.

"Do you need a ride home?" Meez Macálista pulled out her phone from her jeans pocket. "It's almost five. Is your brother coming?"

His brain clicked back to reality. "I don't know. He might not know he needs to pick me up."

Meez checked her phone again before glancing around the office. "Teachers aren't legally allowed to drive students without permission. . . ."

"Tomás won't mind, I promise." Jaime grabbed his

things and stood by her side. "He lets Ángela ride home with boys he doesn't know."

"Good enough." Then she turned to the receptionist and spoke in English. "Jaime just got a text from his brother that asked if I could take him home. I don't mind."

The receptionist didn't even challenge the statement. "Thank goodness. I didn't want to stay late."

Meez waved to the receptionist and led the way to her car as she whispered, "Please text your brother to tell him I'm bringing you home. I don't want to be a complete liar."

Right. Jaime had forgotten he had a phone and that texts went through better than calls at the ranch. He had also forgotten he didn't really know how to use a phone. It took several tries to get the correct screen up for messages, then a few more to insert Tomás's name from the address book. When he finally got to the body of the text, they were at Meez's car, a green hatchback with bumper stickers covering the rear—KEEP CALM AND ROCK ON, LISTEN AND THE WORLD SINGS and one he didn't understand that said TREBLE MAKER. He got in and fastened his seat belt before composing the text. Thankfully, Tomás had also set the phone with Spanish text prediction.

The music teacher (he didn't know how to spell Meez's name) is bringing me home. See you soon. It took a few more seconds to figure out how to send it. The phone buzzed and beeped a few seconds later, causing him to jump in place. He opened the message.

great see you soon

The school's voice messages obviously hadn't gone through yet. Just as well. If he told Tomás in person what had happened, while Meez remained next to him, he hoped his brother wouldn't be too mad.

"Can you give me directions?" Meez asked as she flipped through her phone's playlists to find a Latin jazzy one.

"I think so."

They might have missed the turn if a white car covered in dirt and dust hadn't been pulling out of a ranch road. Ángela's friends. For once they had made themselves useful.

"Turn here." Jaime pointed.

As they drove down the track, Jaime squeezed his sweaty palms. By now, Tomás must have gotten the school's message.

Sure enough, Tomás exited the trailer with Ángela and Vida as the car rolled up. Jaime half expected Meester George and Doña Cici to come out and scold him too.

"So, how's my little delinquent brother?" Tomás teased. Or pretended to tease. Jaime couldn't tell.

Tomás gave Meez a big smile as she got out of the car. "We've met. Is it Ms. McAllister?"

He said this in Spanish, which Jaime saw as a good sign.

If Tomás had wanted to talk about him, he would have addressed Meez in English.

Meez shook Tomás's hand with a smile back. "Outside of school you can call me Gen."

"Like Jennifer Lopez?" Ángela's eyes widened as she sent a sly look over at Tomás.

"No, like Genevieve McAllister." The music teacher reached down to pet Vida, who immediately covered her hand in kisses. The dog always knew who to trust. "My family is Scottish, not Hispanic."

"There were a few Scottish settlers in Guatemala," Jaime said, making his teacher back home proud for having paid attention. "And your Spanish is perfect so you could be Latina."

Meez laughed. "Thank you. I'm glad you think so. And you're Ángela? Jaime talks about you all the time. And Tomás was it?"

"*Por supuesto*," Tomás grinned wider. Jaime grinned at his teacher too. She knew his brother's real name, even though when they had met on the first day of school Tomás had introduced himself as "Tom."

"So," Tomás continued after a few seconds of awkward silence. "Tell me exactly what my brother did. Were you there?"

"No, I just found him in the office and felt bad for him."

"He does look pretty pitiful. Especially with that purple nose." Tomás turned to him and waited. At least Tomás seemed to be in a good mood. Since Don Vicente was detained, Tomás had spent most of the time overworked and stressed.

Jaime sighed and told the story in one breath. "A boy in my class stole my sketchbook and destroyed it. When I found it in the bathroom, I tried to hit him. I got the side of his head and he got my nose." He left out the other, more devastating details. Like the condition in which he had found his sketchbook.

"I never thought you'd hit anyone, but I know how much your sketchbook meant to you. I'm sorry that happened." Tomás put his hand on his brother's shoulder. If he'd been mad, even if he were hiding it, he never would have done that.

"I have a form for you to sign and they're making me stay home from school tomorrow," Jaime admitted. Best let the rest out. "I got one day, the other boy got the whole week."

"Which boy was this?" Meez asked.

Jaime shook his head. As much as he hated Diego, he wasn't going to rat him out.

Meez crossed her arms and gave him her "I'm a teacher and I expect an answer" look. "We have regular teacher meetings where we discuss problems we're having with our students. I'm going to find out anyway. Was it Diego?"

Jaime nodded. He might not rat him out, but he wasn't going to lie to protect the jerk either.

"I've heard the things he says about you when he thinks I'm not listening. As a music teacher, I'm good at picking up voices people don't think I can hear. I don't blame you for hitting him. If someone deliberately destroyed my music, I'd probably be in prison."

The dreaded P word brought on another awkward silence, and this time it was Ángela who changed the subject. In English. Of course.

"What musical instruments do you play?"

Jaime gave her a look but Meez replied in Spanish.

"*De todo, piano, guitarra, flauta.* Drums too. Pretty much anything. Except maybe the didgeridoo."

They all laughed except Jaime.

"What's that?" he asked.

"It's a joke," Ángela explained.

"But what is it?" he demanded. Why was Ángela being so annoying and superior?

Meez placed a hand on his shoulder. "A didgeridoo is an instrument Australian aborigines play, made from an empty tree. Historically, women weren't allowed to play it."

"I didn't know that part," Tomás said. "I just thought the name was funny."

"Yes, it is funny," Ángela agreed, but at least she was

sticking to Spanish now. "I'm in *The Sound of Music* at the high school and we're looking for a person to play that Austrian horn. Could that be you?"

Meez raised her eyebrows. "The alpenhorn? I've never tried, but I can play the trumpet so it can't be too different. Is Louis Padilla directing that?"

"Mr. Padilla? Yes, he's my friend Tristan's dad." Ángela jumped up and down as if she just realized that Meez could be the bridesmaid for her and Tristan's wedding. Gag.

"If you're in the play as well, maybe we should get your autograph now. Before you're famous and all." Tomás winked and pulled out his phone to give Meez.

Meez played along and used her finger to autograph the screen. "Who says I'm not famous right now?"

"She once played with Elvis Presley." Jaime repeated a rumor he remembered hearing.

Meez groaned and shook her head. "Is that *chisme* still going around?"

Tomás raised an eyebrow as he looked her up and down. "I admit you look really good for your age."

Meez set her pink leopard-spotted shoes in a wide stance and held her arms out in presentation. "I know, right?"

"Elvis Presley died, like, over forty years ago," Ángela explained.

"But the kids at school said . . . " Once again Jaime didn't get the joke.

Meez set a hand on Jaime's shoulder. "I made up that rumor when I started teaching. I looked very young—some kids even thought I was an overgrown eighth grader. So I said I used to play with Elvis so kids would think I was older."

"Well, in that case, Ms. Presley, I think we'll have to ask you to stay for dinner." Tomás bowed and pointed over to the trailer.

"Are you a good cook?" she asked with her own raised eyebrow.

Tomás rolled his eyes. "*¡No qué va!* But the microwave is."

Meez Macálista laughed again. "Sure, why not?"

"We have food?" Jaime muttered to his brother, and received a sharp poke in the ribs in return.

Ángela's eyes suddenly widened as she grabbed his hand and lunged them toward the trailer door. "Jaime, quick."

"What's up?" he asked as Ángela pulled him up the steps and inside.

"I just realized we've got about fifteen seconds to clean this place before she comes in."

Jaime looked at the unmade bed, the dishes in the sink, and the dog hair covering the floor. "Why? It's just Meez Macálista."

"You're so clueless. Take the bedroom. Ten seconds now."

When Ángela got into these moods, it was always best to do what she said. Jaime gathered up the dirty shirts, socks, and underwear on the floor and lifted the spring to shove them under the bed. He gave the blanket a good shake and draped it over the pillows. He pushed Tomás's belt out of sight with a nudge of his foot just as the door opened.

Ángela leaped into the tiny bathroom and latched the door, leaving a whiff of cleaning products in the kitchen. In ten seconds she had put the dishes away, cleared the table of schoolbooks, and propped two decorative pillows on the bench where they would eat. The dog hair, though, remained at their feet.

Meez Macálista ducked through the doorway after Tomás, even though she wasn't that tall. From where she stood, she could see the whole trailer—the kitchen area in front, the bedroom to the right, and the main area to the left. Ángela came out of the bathroom next to the door, trying to hide the cleaning products behind her back.

"I'm impressed." Meez smiled.

"So," Tomás clapped his hands, "what do you like? Meat, beans, rice, potatoes, salad?"

Meez shrugged. "I eat everything."

"Good, because we don't allow picky eaters in this house." Tomás repeated what Abuela always said.

"Can I help?" Meez asked.

"There's not really enough room." Tomás waved her to sit on the bench and even then the trailer felt cramped. He lifted the counter that covered the stove, which left only the counter over the sink for prep.

Tomás put a couple of packets of instant rice in a bowl and was about to put it in the microwave when Ángela grabbed it from his hands and added two cubes of chicken bullion to the water.

There wasn't any salad—Tomás said that was rabbit food—but in some secret corner he discovered a can of mixed peas, green beans, carrots, and corn that, judging by the dust on the lid, had probably been in the trailer before he moved in. On the stove, which Tomás only used when they wanted burned food, Tomás placed ground beef patties in a frying pan and shook Goya Adobo seasoning over the tops. The smell actually made Jaime's mouth water. Why had Tomás never made them burgers before?

"He asked Doña Cici for cooking tips when you said the music teacher was bringing you home," Ángela whispered in his ear, as if she'd read his mind. "Bet he wishes we weren't here, ruining his date."

"What date?" Jaime asked. Ángela used her chin to point at his brother.

"Tecate okay?" Tomás offered Meez a beer, which she gladly accepted.

Jaime still didn't get it.

They ate overdone but still tasty burgers without buns,

chicken-flavored rice, and canned vegetables. For dessert, Tomás found mystery-flavored lollipops in his truck that he'd gotten free from the bank.

After dinner, upon Tomás's request, Meez pulled a clarinet from her car and played. (Ángela insisted, rather forcefully, that Jaime not join her on the recorder. Not that he could have in a million years.) Jaime had never heard her play other than to demo bars of a song during class, but it turned out she should be in an orchestra in a big fancy city. Without sheet music, she could play the melody of *Star Wars*, "Edelweiss" (a weird slow song Ángela picked), and as a tribute to her "former bandmate" and Vida, "Hound Dog" by Elvis Presley.

"I better get going," Meez said after playing six or seven songs. "Unlike some people here, I have to go to school tomorrow."

"Thanks for bringing me home, Meez," Jaime said.

"Yes, thank you," Tomás said. "Jaime would have gotten scared if he'd had to sleep in the school."

Jaime gave his brother a shove. He'd once slept underneath an abandoned car; the school couldn't have been nearly as bad.

Meez tucked the clarinet back in its case and pulled out her phone. "Why don't you give me your number so the next time Jaime gets into trouble, I know who to blame."

"*¡Oye!*" Jaime complained, and then complained some more when Ángela gave his ribs a hard nudge. Still, the adults exchanged numbers as if they really did expect Jaime to get into trouble again.

Though he supposed if he did get into trouble, it would be good to have Meez around. Just in case.

CHAPTER TWENTY-TWO

"Wake up, *bello durmiente,"* Tomás called from the trailer door just a meter and a half away. "Come meet our new ranch hands."

"I don't want to meet them," Jaime grumbled.

"Just because you're suspended from school doesn't mean you have the day off."

Suspended. He'd forgotten about that part. He hid his head under the pillow but that didn't stop his ears from working just fine.

"I think you'll like these new people. *Una familia mexicana.* They've been here for generations and they speak Spanish."

"A family?" It was worse than he thought. It would harder to move out a family when Don Vicente came back than two random guys going from one job to the next.

"Mother and son."

Jaime bolted up on the bed, dropping the pillow to the ground, and glared at Tomás still at the door. "You didn't say anything about replacing Doña Cici! After everything, to let her go—"

Tomás shook his head. "We're not letting her go. What're you talking about? Doña Cici isn't going anywhere."

"But you said one of the ranch hands is a Mexican lady. . . ."

Tomás laughed. A good, strong laugh. One that seemed strange among all the worry. "Women make great cowgirls. Come see for yourself."

Jaime supposed he should meet these new people. Just so he'd know they weren't *migra* officers if he saw them driving down the track. But it wasn't like he had to be friends with them or anything.

Tomás sprinted back to the cow and calf corral, where dust rose in a cloud. As he got closer, Jaime noticed the cloud seemed more like a continuous trail of rising dirt. Two riders on unfamiliar horses worked together to break one calf away from its mom's side. Once culled from the herd, the person on the rose-colored horse (they moved too fast for Jaime to tell them apart) swung a rope over their head and the calf seemed to run into its own noose. The jerk caused the calf to land on its flank and less than a second later, the rider was next to the calf on the ground with a knee on its neck so it wouldn't move and the horse kept the rope taut. Within another second, a yellow tag hung from the calf's ear, the rope and knee were removed from its neck, and the calf went running back to its *mami* to drink away its sorrows. All in about ten seconds or less. Caught between awestruck and pity for the calf, Jaime had never seen anything like that in his life.

Leaning on one of the corral's wooden posts, Meester George nodded his head in greeting. Quinto stood by the horse paddock with a pitchfork and empty wheelbarrow, while Pimiento lifted his tail to add to the multiple horse apple piles.

"If you ever want to learn to be a cowboy, son, these are the people to teach you," Meester George said as Jaime joined him against the fence.

Jaime turned back to the couple. Now closer up, he noticed the two riders taking turns roping and tagging the calves, but other than calling out numbers and genders to Tomás, they didn't appear to communicate. Like a perfect team, they anticipated each other's moves and worked together seamlessly.

Once all the calves were tagged, they rode their horses lazily toward the spectators. Jaime had to stop himself from clapping.

"*Mel, Lucas, mi hermano, Jaime,*" Tomás introduced him to the riders as he finished entering the information on his clipboard.

"*Hola, soy Mel.*" The lady on the rose-colored horse lifted her hat in greeting. She seemed too young to have a son around Tomás's age. Except for the fact that she wore her onyx-black hair in a ponytail, they looked exactly alike—slightly slanted eyes on oval shaped, tan-brown faces, and narrow straight noses. They even had the same smiles, wide and happy.

"Lucas." The man tipped his own hat just like cowboys did in movies.

As much as Jaime hated to admit it, he did like these new ranch hands. He glanced at the boss man, but they hadn't been scolded for speaking Spanish, so hopefully neither would he.

"You guys are incredible. I could never learn to do that."

"Sure you could. Why don't you saddle up a horse and join us while we drive the cows and their calves back to the rest of the herd?" Lucas nodded to the horses in their paddock.

Jaime wished he could say yes. "I've never ridden a horse by myself," he admitted.

"When we come back and finish with our chores, we'll teach you how," the woman said. "In no time at all, you'll be cutting calves and herding cows like nobody's business."

They tipped their hats again and with a turn on their horses' hindquarters, they headed back to the herd. Tomás ran over to open the gate at the far side of the corral. The ranch dogs dashed in blurs of black and white to either side of the gate and crouched in place, ready to prevent any stray cow or calf from veering toward the homestead. Vida watched the others work with interest but preferred to stay with her humans. As far as she was concerned, her job was not letting her family out of her sight, and Jaime loved her for that.

"I think those two are going to work out just fine, Tom," Meester George said once Tomás returned from closing the gate.

"Yes, sir."

"I feel bad for them. Their ranch had been in the family for hundreds of years, originally in Mexico and then became part of New Mexico in the Hidalgo Treaty. But a bad investment by Mel's brother and they lost it all. Mel said she'd work as hard as it took to get her old place back."

"She told me the same thing," Tomás replied.

Meester George wiped the sweat from underneath his gray felt hat. "Assuming first impressions last, I think it'll be in our best interest to keep them as permanent hands. They've got their own mounts, know their cows, and have some good ideas for improving and marketing the herd. I hope they want to stay on for a few years."

Jaime listened intently to Meester George. Many words still didn't make sense, but he understood the last line perfectly. Jaime hadn't finalized his plan to save the old foreman, but it didn't seem fair to give up yet. He knew with a bit more thought he could make the plan work.

"You no think Don Vicente come out," he said to the boss man. Didn't even phrase it as a question.

Meester George hiked up his jeans but his belly prevented them from rising more than a centimeter. "This has nothing to do with Cente. This is the man's home and he deserves to be here. His arrest has made me realize how much he's needed. Good help is hard to find and I want people who I trust and will stay on for a long time."

The rancher looked over at Quinto, who stood near the barn with a cigarette and a bored expression now that the rodeo show was over. The wheelbarrow remained empty and the horse paddock contained at least two additional piles.

"Walk with me, boys." Meester George waved his hand and they shuffled along the corral with the pretense of checking the fence. Vida strolled with them, her nose to the ground and her tail ready to wag.

"Tom, how many years have you been with me?"

Tomás's shoulders tensed up. He shifted his weight and took a deep breath before answering. "Eight this summer, sir."

Meester George gave a fence post a good shake and it wobbled a bit from side to side. "Let's reinforce this post here. Tell me, when does your work visa run out?"

Tomás stopped dead and Jaime noticed his eyes widen. Even Vida sensed the fear and trotted back to her humans' side.

Work visa. The documents Tomás had to live and work here in El Norte legally. As long as those papers remained valid, Tomás could stay as long as he wanted. Or as long as he was wanted. Jaime seemed to understand more English than he desired.

The Adam's apple on Tomás's throat moved up and down a few times before he finally answered Meester George's question. "It expires at the end of the summer."

"And what are your plans for the future?"

Again Tomás swallowed. Jaime glanced at the horizon. The dust hadn't settled from the cattle herded by the cowgirl and cowboy. People who Meester George said had lived here for generations. People who didn't need visas because they had been born here. The realization hit Jaime like a punch in the gut. Mel and Lucas weren't replacing Don Vicente. They were replacing someone who wasn't born in this country, and wasn't born a cowboy. They were replacing Tomás.

"I, uh, was hoping to renew the visa and stay here. If you'll have me, sir," Tomás choked out.

The boss man kept his focus on the fence and the needed repairs. "But do you like being a rancher? Working with cattle? Be honest with me Tom, I know this is not your dream job."

Tomás rubbed his scruffy cheeks while he considered his answer. Jaime leaned over to get some comfort from Vida. The dog rubbed her one-eared head against his leg and gave his hand a reassuring kiss. If Tomás stopped working for Meester George, they'd all have to leave the ranch. Jaime didn't need a lawyer to tell him that without a job, Tomás wouldn't be able to renew his visa. All of them, including Vida, would be left with nowhere to go.

Tomás opened his mouth to say something, closed it, and finally said what was on his mind. "I once thought it'd be fun to work in the movies. Not as an actor, but in the crew, building sets or repairing machinery, anything really. But that was a silly boy's dream and not realistic. I am happy here, working with cattle, working for you. I would like to stay, sir."

Now was Meester George's turn to say nothing. He stopped checking the fence to stare in the distance at the mountain that once had been a volcano. "I've been talking to my lawyer about Cente and you came up."

Jaime stopped breathing.

"I want to help you get your green card. And legal status for the two kids." Meester George turned away from the mountain to look Tomás in the eye. "The lawyer said there's a program the kids can apply for called Special Immigrant Juvenile Status. The process can take a few years to go through but the chances of getting deported are very low during the application time."

Jaime looked from his brother to the rancher. Too many words, too many possibilities of what they could mean. Maybe he didn't understand as much as he thought. Meester George seemed happy about what he was saying, but Tomás still had that tense and stupid, mouth-open look.

"The world is too unstable right now," the rancher continued. "After they took Cente, I realized I didn't want to risk losing you too. If you agree to work for me another eight years, just like you have been with your usual salary, I'll cover all the costs of making permanent residency happen for you three. What do you say?"

Tomás blinked two more times before snapping out of his stupor. "That would be fantastic! Yes, of course. Thank you, sir!"

They shook hands, making it a done deal. Jaime's eyes shifted from one to the other, still not 100 percent clear what had transpired, and whether he should be excited too.

Something about many years and money, and did "permanent residency" mean *ciudadanía*?

They continued surveying the corral, though now Tomás's shoulders were relaxed and a lopsided smile brightened his face.

"Are you serious about wanting to work in the movies?" Meester George asked once they'd made it back to the barn. Jaime noticed Quinto still hadn't done any work.

This time Tomás's face reddened. "I love movies and I thought it might be fun to work on them, but it's no big deal."

"Let's look into that once Cente is back." He pulled out his wallet from his sagging back pocket and began thumbing through business cards he'd acquired. "There's a big film industry here in New Mexico. I've got a buddy who's rented out his ranch for movies. He once told me you can make big bucks having your cattle on the screen, but I never had the time. Maybe we can get you in, be the wrangler. Haul the cattle out to location and care for them on set. Earn us both a bit of extra money."

"Definitely! I would love that."

The men shook hands again and Meester George nodded over to Quinto standing by the barn wall as bored as ever. "Have him help you reinforce those loose posts on the corral and let him know he needs to start working harder if he wants to stay with us."

Meester George released the flip phone clipped to his belt to check the time and reception, then headed to the big house.

Tomás waited until he was gone before letting out his breath. "With good news comes the bad," he said to Jaime in Spanish. "If there's one thing I hate about working here, it's having to tell people their job is on the line, and worse is having to let people go. Wait here."

Jaime crouched down to pet Vida, who immediately flopped over on her back to have her belly rubbed. She had been found half drowned, half starved, and almost completely dead. It was great to feel that her ribs were filling in and belly had gotten quite round. A little bit more and some would say she'd need to go on a diet. Some, but not Jaime. Bellies (when they weren't full of worms) were a sign of good health and he was proud that he himself had put on some weight too.

Swearing came from the barn and when Jaime looked over, Quinto stood with his feet wide apart and a demanding open hand in front of Tomás's face. Tomás went into the barn office while Quinto yelled, "I'm out of here! My cousin earns three times as much and he doesn't have anyone nagging him all day long."

Tomás came back with some money, which Quinto yanked out of his hand and made a show of counting. Without another word, he scuffed out of the barn and into his car.

Tomás came back from the barn with a couple of shovels and poles to replace the rotted ones on the fence and two gallons of water clipped to a rope around his waist.

"All I said is that Mr. George wants to see a stronger work ethic from him and he demanded his pay. Can't say I'm sorry to see him go."

The cloud of dust from his car had already settled as if Quinto had never been there. "Don Vicente didn't like him either."

Tomás put his arm around his brother and led him to the work zone. "So I guess it's up to you, my young delinquent, to help me fix the corral. You keep saying you want to help, right? My guess is that you'll be begging to go back to school tomorrow."

Not likely, Jaime thought. Though not having Diego there for a few days would be an improvement.

"What was Meester George saying about being a permanent resident? Is that the same as citizenship?" Jaime asked. A chill in the desert air caused him to shiver despite the hot sun.

"Permanent residency is a step toward citizenship. He said he'll pay all the legal fees for the three of us if I agree to work for him for eight more years. It's a good deal. Lawyers are very expensive and from what I hear, it could easily take that long to get everything finalized."

"But if you do that, you'd be like an—" Jaime tried to remember the word Meesus had used in social studies when talking about different ways people immigrated into a country, and the ways the immigrants were often taken advantage of. "*¿Cómo se dice?* 'Intent servant?'"

"Indentured servant," Tomás corrected as he removed the fencing from the first post they had to replace. "We call that *trabajador sin remuneración*. That isn't what I'm doing. Indentured servants aren't paid for any of the work they do. It all goes to paying back what is owed to their boss for the person's passage into the country. Bosses often keep the indentured servants working much longer than the original agreement. I've heard of people whose children or even grandchildren had to keep working to pay off the debt."

Jaime remembered Meesus saying something about that. As much as he loved his brother and owed him his life, he didn't think he'd be happy being forced to stay on the ranch forever. "What about me and Ángela?"

"This is an agreement between Mr. George and myself," Tomás reassured him. "You two are free to come and go as you like. University, art school. Marriage even, though I'd recommend you wait until you can at least shave for that one."

Jaime forced a smile, though his mind continued repeating clippings of the boss's conversation—legal status, citizenship, eight years. His feet felt heavy, as if held by invisible iron manacles. "I don't think I want to become a citizen of los Estados Unidos. I don't want to belong to a place that locks away men because they look a certain way; I don't want to live in a place that thinks it's better than everywhere else. I want to stay Guatemalan."

For several minutes Tomás dug into the dry, hard dirt around the wobbly post. He unfastened one of the jugs from his waist and poured water into the shallow hole to loosen the dirt.

"There's no place in this world that's perfect," Tomás said as he watched the pool of browning water. "You say you don't want to belong to a place that sends innocent men to jail, but what about a place that murders twelve-year-old boys and abuses *abuelitas*?"

Jaime picked up the extra shovel and drove it into the hole. Dirty water splashed against his jeans. He did it a few more times until the water had been absorbed by the dry dirt and the legs of his jeans were speckled in mud. "But if I stay here, I have to give up who I am and become like everyone else."

"Citizenship doesn't change who you are. It's just a piece of paper." Tomás took his turn to shovel. "It doesn't say anything about what kind of person you choose to be."

"What if I forget Spanish?" Jaime said in almost a whisper. "What if I grow up and can't talk with my family anymore? Look at Ángela. Half of what she says around us is in English."

"Ángela is trying to figure out who she is in this new place. Maybe that's the easiest way for her to accept what she's been through. Your way of deciding who you are is different and how to keep on living is different. But that doesn't mean you have to choose between Spanish and English, Guatemalan and *estadounidense*. Mel and Lucas for example. Their family has been here for generations, but they still speak Spanish and have maintained their Mexican heritage." Tomás gave the rotting post a good shake. It splintered and fell to the ground.

"But why would Meester George pay for us to get our papers? Ángela and I don't work for him." Jaime got on his hands and knees to free the remaining bits of post wedged into the hard dirt.

"He sees this as an investment. He knows if something happens to you two, I would take off in an instant." Tomás fitted the new post into the now empty hole and held it straight as Jaime packed down the mud and dirt around it. Tomás continued, "But if I stay for eight years, getting paid like normal, then he doesn't have to find a replacement until then, maybe longer if the green card takes a while or I decide to stay. Besides, I do like it here, and I like working for him. Back in Guatemala, I never thought I'd be a cowboy, but it's worked out. And can you imagine me being a wrangler for movies? That would be the perfect life."

Jaime straightened up and wiped his muddy hands on his jeans. "Maybe. Except that Jennifer Lopez doesn't do Westerns."

Tomás grabbed him in a headlock and hugged him before moving on to the next post.

CHAPTER TWENTY-THREE

Jaime had mixed feelings about having Mel give him riding lessons. He always thought it would be Don Vicente who'd teach him. Learning from someone else felt like a betrayal. On the other hand, he wasn't about to pass up the opportunity.

"First thing, you always get on a horse on the left side," Mel said as she eyed the length of his legs to adjust the stirrups. She had tacked up a brown, black, and white piebald named Picasso that Tomás had said would be a good horse for Jaime to learn on. "It's from the days that knights carried swords on their left side so they could draw them with their right hand."

"I'm left handed so I would carry my sword on the right," Jaime teased.

Mel squinted her eyes and gave him a scolding look, but the slight smile said she could tease back. "Until you're actually riding a horse with a sword, you're going to get on the left side."

Mental check—find out how hard it would be to wield a sword. If Meester George went around carrying a gun, why couldn't he ride with a sword? How cool would that be!

"Some people mount using a stump or a leg up from a friend, but I think it's important to learn to get on from the ground because something or someone isn't always going to be around to help," Mel said.

Jaime put his left foot into the stirrup as he'd done when Don Vicente had picked him up at the bus stop. With one hand on the saddle horn and the other on the back of the saddle (which Mel called the cantle), he hopped on his right foot before swinging it over. He landed squarely in the saddle, surprising himself.

"Perfect," Mel said. "Now, feet out of the stirrups, dismount, and do it again. Except this time, I won't be holding onto Picasso's reins as you get on, so you'll have to do that on your own."

Jaime repeated what he'd done before, except this time held the reins in the same hand that held the horn. Picasso moved as Jaime swung his leg over but stopped once Jaime sat astride and pulled the reins. At least he hadn't fallen off the other side.

Mel walked him though correct posture, foot location in the stirrups, and hand placement on the reins. If anything, that felt the weirdest. He wanted to hold on with his left hand, his dominant hand, but Mel reminded him if he ever wanted to learn to rope, or ride with a sword, he needed his dominant hand free.

He nudged Picasso with his heels, and they moved from a walk to a trot. He winced as he bounced hard in the saddle, but didn't complain. He raised himself a bit on the stirrups. There, better. And completely incorrect.

"Press those heels down, and sit tall and deep in the saddle," Mel called out.

Jaime listened to her suggestions. At the same time it seemed Picasso trotted too fast to do everything at once. For a few seconds he'd get it and would be able to sit through several steps. Then his focus disappeared and he'd flop all over the place again.

"Pull the reins back gently and sit. A big part of your control comes from your seat."

Picasso settled back into a walk. Jaime breathed out and relaxed into a slouch. A second later, Mel nagged him to keep his shoulders back and stay alert and in control even if they were just walking.

"You never know when a rabbit is going to jump out under a horse's hooves and startle him, or he suddenly gets it in his head that he wants to return home."

They went from walk to trot to walk a few more times and then changed directions around the corral and did the same thing over again. By the end of the lesson, Jaime's whole body ached and he wondered if he'd ever be able to walk again. Still, he couldn't wait until Mel let him go faster and he and Picasso could dodge cacti and chase rabbits with Vida at their side.

"Good job!" Mel said. "Let's call it a day."

"Can we do this again tomorrow?" Jaime asked.

Mel held the reins as he dismounted. "School and work first. Then we'll see if there's time to play."

"And can we ride outside the corral?"

"Once you prove you can handle a horse, you can go anywhere."

You can go anywhere. Suddenly, the missing link in his plan to help Don Vicente clicked into place. So obvious, he mentally kicked himself for not having thought of it sooner.

"How long before I prove I can handle a horse?" Jaime took the reins back from Mel.

Mel walked by his side. With her hat she seemed taller than him, but he noticed her brown eyes were just below his as she smiled at him. "Depends how much you want it."

Oh, he wanted it. Now the question was, how would he draw Seme, with his robotic tank wheels, on top of a horse? Because even though Seme's first adventure had ended up botched at the hands of Diego, it wasn't enough to keep a good creature down.

They exited the corral, with Mel latching the gate behind them, as Meester George headed their way. A nervous pain gripped Jaime in the stomach. When Mel offered to teach him how to ride, he never thought of asking Meester George for permission. The setting sun cast a shadow on the owner's face. Picasso and all the tack belonged to the rancher. He might not want Jaime to use any of it. Jaime stopped the horse and gripped the reins tighter.

"That the first time you ride by yourself?" the rancher asked.

"First time with no Don Vicente," Jaime agreed. "Eez okay I ride horse?"

"No one else is riding him and you did all right," Meester George said as he ran a hand down Picasso's legs as if making sure he was sound. "If you practice every day, I can see you riding out to check on the cattle on your own in a few months."

"No." Jaime shook his head. "No months. Saturday."

Meester George turned away from his gelding to stare down at Jaime. "What's happening on Saturday?"

Jaime took a step back and crashed into Picasso's neck. He could do this. Be brave. "That day I go to Don Vicente's family."

Meester George shifted his hat to have a better line of

vision at Jaime. "What are you talking about? The old man doesn't have kids."

Jaime explained his plan as clearly as he could. A couple of times Meester George interrupted, saying Jaime's idea didn't make sense and Jaime searched for new words to explain. When Mel offered to translate, Meester George shook his head. "If the boy wants something, he has to learn to ask for it himself."

Once Jaime finished, he waited to hear Meester George's response.

"Not happening." The boss man shook his head.

"But sir," he remembered to address him as Tomás did, and as the rancher preferred, "eez good *idea*. It work. It get Don Vicente out and he come home."

"The plan is a good one. But it's the part about you going around on horseback that won't fly."

Jaime shook his head in bewilderment. "No fly. On horse." He patted Picasso's neck, as he'd seen Don Vicente do so many times with Pimiento.

"I mean that you can't do it on a horse."

"Why?"

The rancher shifted into a wide stance that made him seem even bigger than normal. "For one thing, you can't ride by yourself. You can barely stay on at a trot, and I can't spare a rider to go with you for a whole day. Second, the places you want to go to are much farther away than you think. It would take days to visit them all on horseback. And lastly, you don't even know where to go."

Jaime's shoulders slumped against Picasso's neck. A few minutes ago, the plan seemed perfect and horses were the miracle to make them work. Now he was back where he started.

"But I still think the basis of your idea is a good one. You'll just have to find someone who can drive that's not your brother or the others, since I need them here." Meester George tipped his hat and headed to the barn office.

A sigh that sounded more like a horse snort came out of Jaime as he led Picasso to the barn. He had a good plan, a great plan even. A plan that would convince the judge that Don Vicente was a reliable man who could be let out on parole.

Mel showed him how to remove the cinch from the straps and lift the saddle off the horse's back. She then brought out the brushes, teaching Jaime how one brush worked in a circular motion to loosen the sweat and hair and the other to sweep off the excess.

He supposed he could try to work his plan by calling people; then it wouldn't matter that he didn't have a driver. Except he didn't really get along with phones, and wondered how many people would even answer. No, there had to be another way. Another driver he hadn't thought about.

Once Mel said Picasso could return to the horse

paddock, Jaime walked him back. The wind shifted to reveal the scent of something delicious cooking in the big house. That was it!

Doña Cici smiled at him when he entered through the kitchen door without knocking. "You got a nose like Vicente. I only just finished."

She handed him a spoon of still hot, sweet *cajeta*, similar to dulce de leche but made with goat milk.

Jaime held the spoon over his hand to ask his question first. "Can you drive a car?"

She paused her canning to nod out the window where the sky began to darken. "Not at night, my eyesight isn't good enough anymore."

"But during the day you're fine?"

"Sure, my license is still valid."

He told her his plan to help get Don Vicente out of prison. Unlike Meester George, she didn't interrupt or insist that he express himself in English. "So can you do it? Will Meester George let you drive one of the trucks and have the time off?"

He finished the question by finally sampling the spoonful of *cajeta*. Sweet and deliciously flavorful.

Doña Cici dropped the lid of one of the jars with a clatter before turning to Jaime with a stern look. "*El señor* does not tell me what I can do. When his wife's not here, I run the house. *Yo soy la que manda.*"

Jaime grinned. He knew she'd be on board. He crept a finger to one of the jars for another taste but got slapped away like a bug. Doña Cici gave him a scolding look, but then prepared a handful of saltine crackers with a dollop of *cajeta* on each one and handed them to him. "No more, or you'll spoil your dinner."

"Please let me spoil my appetite for Tomás's cooking," Jaime begged, only half kidding.

Doña Cici laughed as she returned to her canning. "Let me seal these jars and we'll go over the plan."

CHAPTER TWENTY-FOUR

Mr. Mike told me what happened, Sean wrote in his notebook the next day on the bus. *Diego is such a jerk. I know it's not the same, but I got you this.*

The notebook Sean handed Jaime wasn't anything fancy. A blue cover made from cheap cardboard and spiral rings holding the unlined pages together. It looked exactly like the one Tomás had bought him when he first arrived. Like the one that had been massacred in the bathroom.

Sean turned the notebook to the back cover. In robotic font, he'd written *The Adventures of Seme: Seme Rolls Again.*

Jaime signed his thanks by touching his chin and extending his hand out, following it with a thumbs-up.

He began drawing the story on the last page, in true manga fashion. He thought of redrawing their original stories, maybe even improving them. The first image had Seme with a cactus…?

His hand streaked ink across the page as a shrill laugh came from the back of the bus. Jaime cringed and didn't have to look to see who made the noise. He'd have to tear out the page and start on a fresh one, but just the thought of losing a page because of a mistake pained him.

No, better work with the streak and start something new. New book, new stories, new Seme.

Classmates cheered as they walked into the classroom to find the window blinds drawn. Jaime looked up from his desk where he'd been studying a road map Doña Cici gave him. She'd marked the locations of Don Vicente's friends, and he wanted to spend the remaining minutes before class figuring out their route. But that wasn't easy with everyone bursting into song and dance every time they entered the room.

"Why people happy?" he asked Freddie, who was leaning back on his chair as if to get comfortable.

"Mrs. Threadworth only closes the blinds when we're going to watch a movie."

"A movie?" He folded away the map just as the bell rang. Yes, that would definitely be a reason to celebrate. And even better with Diego still suspended.

"As you have figured out, we're going to have some

screen time." Meesus turned off the classroom light and sat by the laptop. "I found video clips of immigrants and refugees around the world sharing their stories."

Jaime sank low in his chair. He felt as if he'd be sick. He didn't want to see what others had lived through any more than he wanted to relive the experience himself.

"After we have finished watching the videos," Meesus continued, "I want you to write a story about one of the people you witnessed, imagine what their life was like before, or what happened after. How did their experiences change their lives?"

The class groaned and a few people voiced their complaints.

Now Jaime really felt sick. He didn't have to imagine what happened, he already knew. And having to write it in English would only be worse. What could he write? *It bad. Boy scared. Family says love him. They still says good-bye.*

But when the videos started, Jaime couldn't turn away from the faces on the screen. Old men with sunken eyes, women with hollow cheekbones and worry lines on their foreheads. One man with a bushy black beard kept talking about a boat. Another, a woman in a headscarf, went on about her feet. Their accented words were sometimes hard to understand, but Jaime felt he knew them. Had met one under a bridge near Ciudad México; another on a bus near the border between Guatemala and México. They all shared the same unsettled look: Even though things were better now, the soul remembered too much to ever truly be okay. The next video showed a Honduran girl with short black hair and wide, half-scared eyes staring at him from the screen.

"Mah-ee name ees Jessica—"

Jaime lunged from his desk along the wall to the screen at the front of the room before realizing it was the white-board and not the real person. A real person he knew. "Dat's Joaquín!"

He turned from the screen to Meesus's desk and slammed the space bar on her computer to pause the video. A couple of kids protested but he ignored them as he stared at the person in front of him. It was impossible. The last time he'd seen the eleven-year-old kid was on top of a freight train heading to Mexicali. They had traveled together for days before that. The kid had helped save Vida's life and had latched onto Ángela's side like an extra limb. No matter what gringos said about Latinos all looking alike, Jaime knew this was no doppelganger. This was his friend Joaquín. Alive!

"What's going on? Jaime, are you okay?" Meesus asked in a half-worried, half-annoyed voice.

"Dat's Joaquín!" he repeated. "He, she, eez my friend."

"I think you're confused. This girl is called Jessica."

"No. Eez Joaquín!" He waved his arms in the air. "I know him, her."

Meesus shook her head. "I don't think so, Jaime. I got this off the Internet. It's streaming from YouTube."

"But eez true! She dress like boy. I know. She friend."

"Okay, Jaime, she's your friend," Meesus said, even though it didn't sound like she believed him. She placed a hand on his shoulder and tried to lead him back to his seat. "Now, please sit down."

He shrugged off her hand and leaned in closer to the computer. He dragged the timeline bubble back two seconds to start the video from the very beginning.

"Mah-ee name ees Jessica—"

"See, Jessica," someone shouted in the dark.

"Shh!" Jaime moved the bubble back a second. Meesus made some comment that Jaime didn't try to understand.

"I come to deez country *de* Honduras," the girl continued. Jaime's nose almost touched the computer screen and his eyes crossed, distorting the familiar face. She sounded different from the boy he knew, and at the same time identical. As Joaquín, the boy was shy, scared, and barely talked. Now as a girl, this Jessica said many words, but in English. He'd heard that sometimes, shy people found it easier to talk to a camera than to other humans. "I no have good life in Honduras. My *mamá* and me we leave. Go live with Tía in El Norte. But my *mamá* she die. Bad men kill her. I see all."

The girl looked away as she wiped her eyes on her

shoulder. Jaime's heart pounded. He had guessed that her mother had died, but had no idea she had witnessed the murder. He'd imagined Miguel's murder many times, but it couldn't compare to being there, seeing it all, and knowing there was nothing that could be done to stop it.

The girl in the video took a couple of seconds to recover. "I dress like boy. Boys more safe. Friends tink am boy."

"'Friends'! Dat's us!" Jaime exclaimed, which caused him to need to drag the bubble back again. Half the class groaned and Meesus tried another attempt to get him to sit down. Didn't work.

"—Friends tink am boy. Friends help, then I leave friends and go alone. Ees hard. I go on trains top. Ees cold. I let go. I land on dirt. I walk long time. I eat plants."

Jaime longed for more details about what happened after they separated. He wanted to hear everything—how she survived the train, *la Bestia*. If anyone discovered along the way that she was a girl. If anyone dared hurt her.

"I find phone and call Tía. She says I muss cross *frontera*. I muss get caught in El Norte. She says only way."

She took another deep breath and Jaime did the same. Why would her aunt tell her to deliberately get caught? Who would want to be in a detention center? It didn't make any sense.

"Tía says people die in desert. *Centro de inmigrantes* in El Norte is better."

Joaquín/Jessica stopped again and when she continued, Jaime noticed she skipped over the part about how she crossed the border, and how she managed to get caught. He knew why she did that—too painful. Plus, you didn't reveal immigration secrets on YouTube so *la migra* would prevent others from doing the same.

"*Centro* have many people. Many sick. Babies cry. Too many people. *Migra* says I leave with Tía, need space for more people. Tía only family, Mamá died, no family in Honduras. Now I live with Tía. I go to school. I learn Eengleesh. In *futuro*, I go to *universidad* and get job. But today, I need money. Money for lawyer of *inmigración* so I stay. I good person. I not want be scared."

And then she started singing the national anthem. Jaime recognized it from movies even though he didn't know the words. But more surprising than that was her voice. Rich and pure and able to hit all the notes without ever cracking. She could sing any song in the world and make it sound beautiful.

The video ended with a website for her crowd funding campaign. Jaime grabbed a pen and paper and wrote down the URL, and the video's URL.

"Dat eez my friend," Jaime insisted again and Meesus didn't have the energy to argue with him. "How I make *contacto* with her?"

Freddie raised his hand as if Jaime were a teacher and

he had the answer. "YouTube lets you add comments to videos. You can put your e-mail address there and maybe she'll see it."

Brilliant! Jaime supposed he couldn't blame Freddie for having bad taste in Pokémon friends.

"Can you please?" The words were barely out of Jaime's mouth when Freddie was at his side on Meesus's computer.

"Now, boys . . . " Meesus made another attempt to regain control but they didn't listen.

"What's your school e-mail address and password to log you in?" Freddie motioned to the screen.

Jaime typed in his information. A few seconds later Freddie pointed to the comment box. "Type what you want here."

Jaime started punching keys with two fingers. He didn't know how to add Spanish accents and forgot about capital letters and most punctuation, but that hardly mattered.

joaquin soy jaime! you're alive! me and angela miss you e-mail me when you get this, and he included his school e-mail address.

"She see it?"

Freddie shrugged and nodded at the same time. "I think YouTube sends comment notifications. Even if they don't, if I posted a video to raise money, I'd check the comments. But you might also get some junk mail."

Didn't matter. He never thought he'd see Joaquín again and now that he knew she was out there. When they traveled together, hadn't she said something about San Diego? Where was San Diego? He'd do whatever he could to be in touch.

Back at his desk, he pulled out his phone and hid it under his desk to text Ángela. It didn't matter that they'd barely spoken in ages, and when she did, it was in English. He didn't care that she had been acting weird. Maybe the good news about their lost friend would make her smile again and return to her normal self. Because if it didn't, then he knew there would be no hope of finding his cousin again.

CHAPTER TWENTY-FIVE

¡Joaquín está vivo! Just saw her on video! The Spanish text prediction on his phone let Jaime write to Ángela quickly and with accent marks. Once finished, he made sure the phone was on silent before looking at Meesus innocently.

A light flashed in Jaime's lap. Except it wasn't a reply from Ángela. It was an e-mail. Tomás must have linked it when he configured Jaime's phone.

The e-mail came from a JJ Morales, subject *Hola*. Probably spam. Still, Jaime opened it.

¡¡JAIME!! Is that really you? How's Ángela? Are Xavi and Vida still with you? Can we talk after school?

¡Sí! Jaime typed back.

Just as he pressed send for his message, the phone

levitated out of his hand and into Meesus's. "No phones during school, you know that."

"But Meesus, dat was Joaquín!"

"You can get it back at the end of the day. Now class, books away for your math quiz."

Jaime stared after Meesus, unable to believe it. How could she? Just after he'd been reunited with his friend. He focused on all the things he wanted to say, things he wanted to tell his friend, things he wanted to ask. Then he thought about Xavi. He didn't want to be the one to tell her that Vida had returned without him.

The final bell rang and Meesus stood in her usual spot by the door to shake everyone's hands as they left. When Jaime got to her, she pulled his phone out of her cardigan pocket and waved it as a warning.

"Tomorrow, do not use your phone during class."

"Yes, Meesus."

She placed it in his hand then her face softened from the usual stern glare. "I'm glad your friend is alive. It gives me hope for other immigrants and refugees."

"Yes, Meesus." Jaime nodded. It gave him hope too.

Jaime buried his nose in the phone and almost crashed into other kids a few times as he walked to the bus. There were more emails from Joaquín.

What is your number? Here's mine. Or do you have Skype on your phone?

I forgot I have swimming lessons after school. Dinnertime?

I'm so glad you contacted me! Can't wait to talk to you!

Once on the bus, Jaime asked Sean to wait while he replied.

The teacher took my phone. I don't know if I have Skype, I'll have to ask Tomás. Call me when you're free. The reception where I live is not always good but keep trying. See you then!

It was only once he'd sent the e-mail that he realized Ángela still hadn't replied to his text.

Fine, she could ignore him, but to take it out on sweet Joaquín? Not cool. He sent her another text in case she never received the first one.

Joaquín has been emailing me all day. We're going to talk at dinnertime. Try to be home by then! Por fa.

He included the plea Ángela often used when she was desperate for something. While it always worked on Jaime, his begging didn't have the same effect on her.

Ángela didn't reply and she didn't come home on time.

Tomás set Jaime up with his own Skype account on Jaime's phone, but reminded him that without Wi-Fi they had limited data usage per month, so to keep the call to fifteen minutes or less.

"We don't want to miss out on a Skype call to our parents whenever they can afford it," Tomás reminded him. His own phone beeped with a message. He opened it with a smile and quickly responded before putting the phone back in his pocket.

Jaime shifted himself at the table, checked the volume on the phone, and then made sure it had reception. Two bars. Tomás said that was as good as it got.

"When do you think Joaquín will call?" Jaime's friend had just said dinnertime, and when he sent the information about his Skype address, Jaime hadn't gotten a reply back.

Tomás checked his phone again and sent another quick text before answering. "You said you think Joaquín is in San Diego. If that's the case, they're an hour behind."

So he'd have to wait even longer? Jaime didn't know if he could bear it.

Tomás's phone buzzed a third time. Jaime checked his own phone. Bars still present, but no incoming Skype calls.

"Who keeps texting you?" Jaime asked.

"Gen."

"Meez Macálista? But I didn't do anything wrong." Had Meesus mentioned the phone in class at a teachers' meeting? Or that he had ignored her when she wanted him to sit back down during Joaquín's video?

"It's all good, *hermanito*." And Tomás took his phone and Vida outside with him. Weird.

Jaime pulled out his new sketchbook that Sean had given him so they could continue their comic. He erased Seme's tank wheels from the last drawing he'd made on the bus, only to draw them again in the exact same place they had been. He did that in a few more places, making only the slightest changes, when at last his phone chimed with an incoming Skype call. He dropped the pencil on the table and tapped the video icon on the phone the way Tomás had showed him, careful not to move from the one spot he knew they had good reception.

And then there he—she was. Not quite flesh and blood, but in real-time screen and technology. Black short hair—that no longer looked like it had been cut in the dark—fastened by a pink clip, probably to look more girlish. Wide, half scared eyes that had looked at Ángela like a long lost mother.

"*¡Hola!*"

"*¡Hola!*"

For a few seconds they just stared, smiled, and waved.

Finally Jaime broke the silence. "So, uh, how are you?"

"Good, how are you?"

"Good."

More silence. Jaime looked at the time. They'd already wasted three minutes saying nothing. He had to say something. "In the video, you said your name is Jessica. But to me you're Joaquín."

She had a shy, pretty smile. A smile he only remembered

seeing after Vida had found him and Ángela sleeping under an abandoned car. In their short time together, there had been little to smile about. "Both are right. My full name is Jessica Joaquín Morales Ortega, after my father who died before I was born. You can call still me Joaquín if you'd like."

She fiddled with the pink hair clip and a question came out of Jaime's mouth before he realized it.

"So, are you really a girl or are you a boy or . . . I mean, it doesn't matter, I just—" He stopped before he continued to shove his foot farther into his mouth. Some people, he knew, were different genders than the one they were assigned to at birth and preferred going by "he" instead of "she," or vice versa. That was fine. He could call someone whatever they wanted and it wasn't his business to know the details. Joaquín was his friend, and that's all that mattered.

His friend once again smiled shyly. "It's okay. Yes, I am a girl. I pretended to be a boy to stay safe on the journey after my *mamá* died. When you're a boy, people have more confidence in your abilities, they don't question you as much. As a girl, some people are nicer, but others think they can take advantage of you. I don't like how people treat me differently. Whether I'm a boy or girl, I'm still me."

What she said made sense. Hadn't he automatically assumed that Mel, as a woman, would work in the kitchen and not as a cowgirl?

"How's Ángela?" Joaquin asked.

Jaime rolled his eyes and explained how Ángela ignored him and had all these new friends and was always showing off with them.

"And Xavi and Vida? Are they still with you?"

Jaime looked out the window. The dog was nowhere in sight but that didn't mean she was gone. Was there any chance the same could be said about Xavi? He took a deep breath.

"We got attacked and separated. Vida came back. She's with us, learning how to herd cows, and sleeps with Ángela every night. She's outside with Tomás right now. But Xavi . . . " Jaime just shook his head, unable to say more. Even after so many weeks, he didn't want to think about what happened to their friend.

"Do you think it would have been different if Xavi had come with me?" The voice was quiet and more like the Joaquín Jaime remembered.

"I don't know," Jaime said. "But I miss him."

"Me too."

"Ángela doesn't though."

"I'm sure she does."

"No. She never wants to talk about him or—" Jaime was about to add that she never wanted to talk about anyone from their journey, but didn't want to hurt Joaquín's feelings. "She has a new boyfriend. She sat on his lap the other day on a bus. In my family, you only do that with a boyfriend. And even then, only if you're old, like twenty, and engaged."

"Maybe it's easier for her to forget everything that's happened."

Jaime shook his head. "I can't forget."

"No, me neither." Joaquín rested her chin on her arms perched on the desk. "But other than that, are you okay?"

"Sometimes," Jaime admitted. "And then I remember I'm not home."

"*¡Ángela!*" Jaime rushed to the driver's door with Vida at his heels and tried to pull his cousin out of her friends' car. "*Acabo de hablar con Joaquín.*"

"Who's Joaquín?" Tristan leaned over from the passenger side.

Jaime gave him a dirty look. "*Ángela, vamos.*"

"I need to say good-bye to my friends," she replied in English.

"No," Jaime insisted, still pulling her arm and talking to her in Spanish. "There's so much to tell you."

"Alright, let go, I'm coming," she said, still in English. She gathered her things and then made a huge puckering sound at Tristan.

He blew her a kiss back. "Loves you, babe."

Jaime considered reaching into the car to throttle Tristan, but managed to restrain himself.

"Loves you too. Bye guys!" Ángela closed the door as the new driver took over. As soon as music could be heard thumping from within the car and it started driving away, Ángela turned to Jaime, her face right in his. In the fading sunlight, her expression shone red.

"What is your problem? Why are you so determined to make me look bad in front of my friends and ruin the one thing I have going for me?" she shouted at him. In Spanish. At last!

Jaime stood his ground. "Those kids are not your friends. They're disrespectful to you and others."

"You're the one being disrespectful."

"Me? I tell you that Joaquín, *nuestra amiga*, is alive and I've talked to her and you don't even ask about her. You're there all the time kissing Tristan. It's like you don't even care any more. Everything we went through on the way here, the people we met, Joaquín, Xavi. No one and nothing matters to you."

"How can you say that?" Ángela said low and menacing.

Jaime threw his hands in the air. "Because it's the truth. You don't even talk to me anymore. And when you do, it's in English."

Ángela gave him a look that said he was crazy and stormed into the trailer, slamming the door so hard it bounced and reopened. Vida stayed with him looking from the trailer to him as if she didn't understand what was happening either.

Ángela came out a second later with something in her hand. She waved it around in front of his face before slapping it in his hand.

"What's this?" Jaime started to ask but stopped short. It was a letter with a Salvadoran stamp. There was only one person they knew from El Salvador.

His hand shook as he pulled out the letter. It was written in fancy, loopy cursive that took some getting used to before he was able to read what it said.

Mi querida Ángela,

I can't tell you what a pleasure it was to receive your letter. I get very little correspondence and it was only by some miracle that your letter came to me—I have treated the postman for ailments before and therefore he knows where I live. The fact that you made the effort to find me shows what a caring person you are and it's no wonder you befriended my grandson, Xavier.

Xavier has always had everyone's best intentions at heart and is very protective of those he cares about. He left to keep me safe and the fact that he wanted to save the dog doesn't

surprise me at all. The two of you sound like a
great pair. I hope that some day I may meet you
in person.

I have not heard from Xavier since the day
he left. I know his journey has not been an easy
one. But I also know he is not lost to this world.
No black birds have circled my house, the sure
sign of death in the family. That boy has a strong
and long lifeline on his palm and there are a great
many things left for him to accomplish. Some day
he'll send word of his safety.

In the meantime, keep positive and keep in
touch. An old lady like me doesn't get many letters
and it would be nice to hear more stories about the
time you and my grandson were together.

Love and blessings,
Encarnación Alfaro

Jaime read the letter twice and then read sections a
third time. *Not lost to this world. Strong and long lifeline.*

It took a few more minutes before he found his voice.
"Why didn't you tell me?"

Ángela folded the letter carefully and replaced it into
the envelope. "Tomás gave it to me yesterday. I didn't want
to get your hopes up."

"Do you think she's right? That Xavi's still alive?" Jaime remembered the gang members chasing them in trucks while swinging baseball bats and machetes. He remembered how Xavi had saved Vida's life and how Vida loved that boy. The dog wouldn't have come back if Xavi weren't gone.

But maybe "gone" meant "taken away" in one of those trucks. . . .

"I don't know." Ángela sighed. "'No black birds have circled my house'? That doesn't mean anything."

Maybe, but maybe not. Who were they to know what anything meant? And hadn't he seen a black bird take flight when Abuela died? "She's a *curandera*. She has powers like a *bruja*."

"So she thinks."

"You don't think so?"

"I don't know what to think. I just know it will be harder to believe her, and then have it turn out she's wrong." Tears ran down Ángela's cheeks.

Jaime grasped at the first thought to try and cheer her up. "Maybe one day he'll come riding over the ridge on a white horse and—"

"Really? A white horse?" Ángela rolled her eyes at him. "Though that would be amazing." A small smile crept onto her teary face.

Jaime returned her grin before turning back to the letter. "Tell me everything. How did you find her?"

"Remember how we went to the library the first few days we were here? You and Tomás—"

"Looked at DVDs," Jaime remembered. He'd been in awe that the rural library let you borrow up to six DVDs (and endless books), and didn't ask you to pay anything.

"Well, I spent the whole time Googling her. I knew she was the *curandera* and Xavi once mentioned the name of his village. I didn't find much, not even her name, so I wrote a letter, addressing it to 'La Curandera,' and sent it to the village without any street address. I never thought it would get to her, much less that she would write back." Ángela stroked the envelope.

"Are you going to write her again?"

"Yes, but in a while. It's too hard at the moment."

He imagined an old woman with long tangled gray hair clutching Ángela's letter with a cup of tea while seeing no signs of black birds in the sky. Just that thought comforted him and he hoped it comforted Xavi's *abuela* too. "So you do care."

"It's easier to pretend I don't. To not get my hopes up. I'm so glad Joaquín is alive, but Miguel and Abuela aren't. And who knows about Xavi? It just seems so unfair."

Jaime put his arm around his cousin and she rested her head on his shoulder. He held her for several moments until the sleeve of his school uniform became damp. "Do you think Miguel and Abuela blame us for their deaths? Or Xavi for whatever happened to him?"

Several minutes passed before Ángela finally shook her head. "Honestly, I don't think so. Miguel and Abuela fought to protect their family. They wouldn't have had it any other way. And Xavi looked out for everyone. I don't think we could have changed any of their minds. So, no. I don't think they blame us."

"They were too stubborn," Jaime admitted.

Ángela pushed away from his shoulder. "Abuela was. But Miguel would nag relentlessly until he got his way. Kind of like you, *jodón.*"

Jaime grinned. Sure he could be a pain, but if it meant getting Ángela out of her slump, he'd be the biggest pain he could be. He did learn from Miguel, after all.

"So, what did Joaquín say? Or I guess she has another name?" Ángela asked.

"Come inside." Jaime grabbed her hand and hurried them back to the trailer, desperate to show her Joaquin's YouTube video. "Doña Cici brought over a tray of green chile chicken cheese enchiladas that smell amazing. And don't you dare say you won't like it. She made sure to use mild green chiles."

Ángela stopped resisting. "That does sound good. And for the record, Tristan and I are not together. He likes boys."

CHAPTER TWENTY-SIX

Diego stood in the school parking lot with his arms crossed when Jaime's bus pulled in.

Sean tugged Jaime's shirt and pointed, though a shiver had already run down Jaime's spine.

"It's about time you got here," Diego said in English.

"I thought you were suspended," Jaime answered in Spanish.

"I am."

Jaime braced himself for the insults. The snide remarks about no one caring about him and not having a real home. The comments he'd come to realize pinpointed his deepest fears.

But Diego said none of that now. He glanced at a few

teachers standing by the front doors and then at Sean, who stood next to Jaime like a bodyguard.

"Can you go away?" Diego said to Sean in English and then blushed a deep red when Sean only shifted his weight from one foot to the other.

"What do you want?" Jaime asked in Spanish, feeling braver with his friend at his side.

Diego twisted his face in a scowl and then held out a notebook. The cover was made of a purple, green, and blue striped cloth instead of thin cardboard. Even without opening it, Jaime could tell the paper was thick and able to hold paints without it seeping through.

"*Para ti.*"

Jaime shook his head. "*No lo quiero.*"

"Oh, come on," Diego switched back to English. "I paid thirty-five dollars for it from my Lego Death Star savings. It's a real artist's sketchbook. Not like that three-dollar one you got at Walmart."

Jaime stared at him with his mouth slightly open, and not because he hadn't understood. He got every single word of the so-called apology.

"You don't get it," Jaime said in Spanish. "I can't replace those drawings. I drew a picture of my *abuela* on the day she died so I would remember her. Sean and I spent days working on a project together. None of that can come back."

"I'm sorry. I didn't know." Diego looked down as if he

were sorry, but Jaime didn't expect him to get it. "Did your *abuela* really die?"

"Yes. A few weeks ago."

Lights flashed on Sean's watch and a second later the bell rang. From an old boat-size car, Carla and two family members burst out. The others dashed to the glass doors but Carla headed over to the three boys, who hadn't moved.

Diego shifted from one foot to the other as he thrust the sketchbook under Jaime's nose. "Well, take this anyway. My dad will kill me if you don't. I know it doesn't change anything but, um, your drawings were really good."

The sketchbook seemed to call out to Jaime, begging him to run his hands over the striped cover. Would it be soft or rough? The book pleaded with him to leaf through it and take in the smell of the pages. When he finally caved and reached for the new book, he did it only because he didn't want Diego's dad to lash out. Then he'd be responsible for someone else's murder.

Jaime petted the cover (soft) and felt the thick texture of the pages inside. He passed it over to Sean and Carla for their approval.

"I still don't forgive you," Jaime said

"And I still don't like you." Diego snapped a photo with his phone of the sketchbook back in Jaime's hands. Probably to prove to his dad he'd delivered it.

Then he walked away.

CHAPTER TWENTY-SEVEN

On the day Jaime intended to activate his plan, Tomás and Ángela decided to take off first thing in the morning. In Tomás's truck. How could he? Tomás knew how important this was. It could be what made the difference between Don Vicente getting out of jail and rotting there. Jaime texted his brother to see where they were and when they'd get back, and got no reply.

"Do you think Meester George will let you drive his truck?" Jaime asked Doña Cici as she placed a bowl of hot farina cereal with cinnamon sugar and toasted pecans in front of him.

"No, and I wouldn't want to. That thing is huge and I'd be scared to dent it."

"Is there another car we can use?" Mel and Lucas had a car but Jaime hadn't seen it parked at the side of the barn where their trailer was. The only other vehicle Jaime knew about was the tractor, and he doubted Doña Cici wanted to drive that down the highway.

"Be patient. We'll go when they come back. Now eat, you're still too skinny."

He had just washed his bowl (after two helpings) when the sound of the truck through the open kitchen window got his attention. Jaime ran out to meet the old farm truck Tomás used, except it was Ángela behind the wheel.

She turned to look at Jaime, lips pressed in determination, and because of her short height seemed to have more hair than eyes looking over the steering wheel.

"I'm driving," she said.

"Good for you," Jaime responded. "Now get out so we can use the truck."

"No, I mean I'm driving you and Doña Cici."

Jaime gasped. "You can't. You're not old enough—"

"Driving age is fifteen in Nuevo México."

"You're not allowed."

Ángela waved a card in front of his face. "Tomás and I just got my instructional permit. I can drive with a licensed adult in the car."

Jaime stared at the card in her hand in disbelief. "But you don't have papers."

"A driver's authorization card doesn't require legal status but still allows legal driving."

"You don't know how," Jaime insisted.

Ángela folded her arms over her chest. "I've been taking driver's education since I started school."

"You never said that!"

"You never asked."

They glared at each other for several minutes until Ángela rolled her eyes and sighed. "*Mira*, I want to help Don Vicente too. Please let me do this."

How could he refuse that? He'd forgotten how nice it was having her on his side.

"Fine, just don't kill us."

Ten minutes later, Jaime, Ángela, and Doña Cici piled into Tomás's truck, with Ángela almost hugging the wheel.

"Can't you come with us?" Ángela asked Tomás.

He shook his head as he leaned over through the window.

"What if we get stopped and asked for papers?" Jaime asked.

A heavy cloud came over Tomás's face. Jaime could see he still blamed himself for Don Vicente. "That mostly happens within a hundred miles of the border. You're not going anywhere near that mark. Ángela has her instructional permit, Doña Cici has her license. You'll be fine."

Ángela nodded and carefully checked her mirrors. "Seat belts."

"They're already on." Jaime tugged the strap around his lap.

Ángela let out a breath. "Okay, where are we going first?"

"To visit Sani." Doña Cici waved her arm to the left. "He's Vicente's oldest friend."

When they got to the highway, Ángela continued as slow as she had on the bumpy dirt track.

"You know, I can ride a horse faster than this," Jaime pointed out.

"*Cállate.*" But Ángela sped up and eventually drove faster than a horse.

They made a few turns down various roads until Doña Cici pointed at a rutted driveway. The truck bumped and rattled as the passengers knocked into one another. They finally pulled up to an area with five houses made from adobe bricks and wood. A pack of dogs rushed out to greet them, barking and snapping their teeth at the wheels. Ángela gripped the steering wheel again and didn't turn off the engine, as if she were afraid of being attacked.

"I'm nervous," Jaime said, though it had nothing to do with the barking dogs. He clutched the sketchbook Diego had given him to his chest. He knew what he wanted to draw in it and had worked all last night on the first image. It seemed fitting that Diego's dad unknowingly helped his plan. "I really hope this works."

"It will," Doña Cici assured him, but then she leaned over to the canvas shopping bag at her feet and recounted her jars of jam and *cajeta*.

"I'm staying here," Ángela said. Jaime didn't even try to convince her. Before they had rescued Vida, Ángela had hated dogs.

Jaime had to admit that these dogs didn't seem like the nicest bunch. Doña Cici, though, had it all planned out. From her shopping bag, she extracted marrow bones and made sure each dog had one to gnaw on before exiting the truck herself, with Jaime right behind her.

A man with long black hair came out of one of the houses and waved upon seeing them.

"Cici, what a surprise. We'll put some tea on. Are you here to see Sani?"

"Yes, and all of you, of course," she said in accented but correct English. Groups of twos and threes came out of the various houses. Some hugged her for minutes at a time while others greeted her with a smile. Doña Cici presented each person with a canned good of their choice.

"You don't have to bring us gifts when you come." A woman with a long gray braid hugged the jar of jam to her chest. "Just having you visit is a gift. It's been too long."

"My *mamá* always said it was rude to visit without bringing something." Doña Cici smiled. "And I have too much for us to eat so you're doing me a favor."

"Did you bring some *cajeta*?" a familiar voice asked. Jaime turned and found himself looking straight into brown eyes framed by purple glasses.

"Carla! Your house?" Jaime waved to the cluster of buildings in front of them.

"Yes, Sani is my great-grandfather. Come, I'll introduce you." She took a jar of *cajeta* and led the way to the oldest looking house, made from adobe bricks. In front of the door, a gray tabby cat cried as it rubbed against the doorjamb. Carla scooped up the cat and draped him over her shoulder like a scarf. The cat purred so loud, Jaime wondered how it didn't hurt her ears.

"No animals inside the house, Carla!" the woman with the gray braid still talking with Doña Cici called out. Carla pretended she didn't hear.

Inside the house the temperature instantly cooled from the hot outdoors. A man with long white hair and a wrinkled face sat on the couch in front of a box TV that seemed to belong in a museum for the 1950s.

"Sani, this is Jaime. He's in my class and he came here with Cici," Carla said with her head inclined slightly so her hair partially covered her feline accessory.

The old man turned and Jaime took a step back, feeling

his intense glare. He had to do this. He couldn't back down now.

"'ello, Meester Sani. I friend with Don Vicente and I—"

The old man waved a hand to stop. He pushed himself off the couch and hobbled to the TV to turn it off by hand. When he spoke, it was in perfect Spanish. "You sound like you're trying to sell me something and I hate people thinking they know what I want to buy."

Jaime gulped. "*Perdón, don Sani.*"

"Sani is already a name of respect, you don't need to call me 'don' or 'señor.' Now, what's this I hear about Vicente getting himself in jail? How did those bastards catch him on a horse?"

Jaime told the story of Don Vicente's arrest and what he wanted to do to help. He handed the man the sketchbook and showed him the first drawing he had made and how he hoped to use it in the trial.

Sani listened intently as he studied Jaime's drawing. "I like your plan and I'm glad to help. I met Vicente at a mustang roundup, did he tell you that?"

Jaime nodded. "He told me that's what got him interested in horses."

"We were both young and stupid and agreed to work the roundup in exchange for a horse. Vicente didn't care that he didn't have a home or any way to support himself.

He just wanted a horse, any horse. I worried what the elders would say if I came home with two horses and a new brother." Sani readjusted himself on the couch. "Instead, he found a home with that gringo and came to visit us, his other family, every weekend. Different times then. Less roads and fences. Less people thinking they know how to run the world."

Sani went on with stories about Don Vicente, things the two of them did together. As he listened, Jaime sketched Sani's words with quick lines and artistic notes that he would develop later into full drawings.

Before he knew it, the truck horn blared. The clock said they'd been there for almost two hours and they still had others to visit.

Jaime gave Sani his thanks and stepped outside just as Ángela sounded the horn again. Doña Cici exited one of the other dwellings, where she'd been talking with her friends.

"*Ya sé que eres la que manda,*" he grumbled about Ángela's demanding personality as he opened the truck door.

Carla's family saw them off with fry bread—a thick, deep-fried flour tortilla—that dripped with honey, before they left to visit the others Doña Cici said could help with Jaime's plan. Some people weren't home but the ones who were happily told Jaime what he wanted to know and sent their best wishes to Don Vicente. The sun was beginning to set when they finally returned to the ranch, Ángela complaining that her neck and leg were stiff from driving and Doña Cici lightly snoring on the other side of the cab.

Once back in the trailer, Jaime dove into his sketchbook, transforming the sketches into actual drawings and adding details he hadn't had time to draw. With each stroke, he wondered if this would be enough and whether he'd ever see his friend again.

CHAPTER TWENTY-EIGHT

"What time are we going tomorrow?" Jaime asked Tomás as he and Ángela dried the dishes after their dinner of instant rice, canned garbanzo beans, and turkey slices.

"We're not going anywhere tomorrow."

Jaime blinked. How could he not remember? "For the hearing. May sixteenth. That's tomorrow. What time?"

"*We*," Tomás emphasized and repeated, "are not going anywhere."

What was he talking about? "Meester George won't let you go?"

"No. *I'm* not letting *you* go."

"*¿Qué?*" He dropped the dish cloth on the floor in protest. Since when did Tomás play the strict guardian card? "Is this about missing school? I already told Meesus

I would be absent. She gave me the extra homework and I've already done it. It's okay."

Tomás shook his head. "No, it's not okay."

"But I have to go, I've worked so hard. I have testimonies to present."

"And Don Vicente thanks you for that. I can present them if you'd like, but you're still not going. Even Doña Cici knows better than to go with us to a detention center."

"You don't get it—" Jaime begged, but Tomás grabbed the plastic plate from his hands and threw it across the trailer like a Frisbee. It bumped against the wall and dropped face down on the cushion that became Ángela's bed.

Tomás pointed a finger in his brother's face. "No, you don't get it. The hearing is held at the detention center. The same place they've been holding Don Vicente for three weeks and the same place they keep every other undocumented individual they find. You go in there without any papers and you might as well be turning yourself in."

This couldn't be happening. Not after everything he'd done. "Meester George said with that Special Immigrant thing I won't get deported."

"But we haven't even filed that yet. I need to become your legal guardian first and we're going to do all that after the hearing."

Jaime planted his feet on the floor and crossed his arms.

"Well, since you're not my legal guardian, then you can't tell me what to do, and I want to go."

· Tomás grabbed the collar of Jaime's shirt and pulled him so close he could smell the turkey and garbanzo beans on his breath. "Absolutely not! That's just a one-way ticket to getting you sent back to Guatemala and murdered the second you arrive."

Tomás let go of him, muttered some swear words under his breath, and then pulled out his phone. "Read this."

He tossed the phone to Jaime. Ángela rested her chin on his shoulder to read it too.

Querido Tomás,

Jaime and Ángela's lives are in grave danger.
If they stay here, they will die. If they go to
you, they might survive. We must risk the lives
of our treasured children to keep them safe.
It sounds idiotic and perhaps it is, but please
understand we think it is the only way. I know
we're asking more of you than any parent
should have to ask of their son and nephew.

We are desperate. Parents without another
choice. Parents who love our children so much
we have to let them go.

Jaime scrolled the screen up and then reached for Ángela's hand. She didn't pull away.

I feel like I'm losing all my children, but at least
I know you're safe and I want the same for
Jaime and Ángela. We love you all so much, we'd
rather not be together than lose anyone else.
    Please take care of them, Tomás. Please be
the parents we can no longer be.

With great love,
Mamá and Tía Rosario

"So they do care," Ángela said in a small voice as Jaime scrolled the screen up to read the e-mail again. "I worried they didn't. That they wanted to get rid of us."

"I thought the same thing," Jaime agreed in the same low and ashamed voice. How dare Diego put that idea in his head in the first place? But mostly, how could Jaime have been so gullible to believe anything Diego said?

"Forward this to my e-mail." Jaime handed Ángela the phone after reading it a second time.

"So you see?" Tomás said when he got his phone back. "They're trusting me to take care of you. I can't do that if you're trying to get yourself in trouble."

"I don't want to get into trouble. I want to help Don

Vicente," Jaime insisted. He knew what was at stake, the danger he would be in. But he hadn't been there for Miguel and Abuela. No matter what everyone said, he did play a part in their deaths. With Don Vicente, he still had a chance. He could make things right.

"Still not happening. Abuela would roll over in her grave and the fact would kill our parents if, despite all their efforts to keep you safe, you throw it all away."

Tomás swore and waved him off in disgust before bolting out the door.

Jaime stood there unable to move as he replayed the scene.

Ángela put an arm around him, making him realize he was shaking. "He's scared. Scared for all of us. Too much uncertainty."

Jaime understood that. He knew the fear, the helplessness. He remembered all too well what he and Ángela went through to get here—things they hadn't even shared with anyone else because it was too painful. But he also knew he'd never forgive himself if he did nothing.

"Can I sleep in your bed tonight?" he asked.

"Brush your teeth and get your pillow." She kissed him on the top of his head just like their mothers used to do.

Her bed was meant for one person, not two adolescents and a dog. But Jaime had spent half his life sleeping at Ángela's house, and the other half with her and Miguel at his house when Tía worked late. There was nothing weird about it. Instead, it was the most comfortable he'd felt in a long time. Except for that one miserable night he was sure he'd lost her for good, he'd slept next to her all through their journey. Now he realized how much he missed her gentle breathing and presence. When she brushed a strand of hair away from his face, a move their *mamás* had learned from Abuela, he wondered if she'd missed him too.

He didn't hear Tomás enter the trailer that night, but they heard him leave at dawn.

"They're heading to the hearing," Ángela said as if she knew he wasn't asleep either.

He digested the statement for half a second then rolled off the bed, changed into his jeans, and pulled the hoodie over the T-shirt he'd slept in.

"Take your phone."

He nodded, placing the phone in his pocket and tucking the sketchbook Diego had given him into his waistband.

"My play is tomorrow night. Please don't miss it," Ángela said.

"I won't."

"Be careful."

He held her gaze for a second, looking into her eyes that were like their *mamás'* but at the same time uniquely her own. She couldn't be more family if she tried.

"*Te quiero*," he said.

"I love you too."

And he left the trailer without another look.

A couple of silhouettes moved inside the barn light. Jaime bet anything Tomás was giving Mel and Lucas last-minute details about the cattle and horses. Tomás's truck stood in front of the trailer, just a few meters away from Jaime. No one would see him. Except Jaime had a feeling they weren't taking Tomás's truck. That truck was old and rickety. No, they'd go in Meester George's sleek, six-tire vehicle. The one parked in front of the big house, a hundred meters away.

There wasn't time to think or plan. Any second, Tomás would turn around and see Jaime from the barn. Any moment, Meester George would come out of the big house to start the engine.

Jaime pulled the hood over his head to hide his face, a superstition from when he was little and thought if he couldn't see then he couldn't be seen, and crouched low as he dashed to the expensive truck. He braced his hands on the top of the sidewalls and vaulted into the bed. He landed on the hard ridges of the black bed-liner and tucked into a tight ball in the corner shadow created by the cab.

Not a few seconds later, Meester George opened the kitchen door. Jaime kept his face hidden but could tell by the footsteps who it was.

"Tom, let's go!" he called out to the barn.

"Please, Mr. George," Doña Cici said from farther away,

probably from the door. "Bring my husband home."

"You better start cooking because we're celebrating tonight." The booming voice came from right above Jaime. Just like with the rattlesnake, he didn't dare move the tiniest bit.

The rancher got in the truck and started driving to the barn. The truck barely stopped when Tomás got in. The roar of the diesel engine drowned out any further noise as they drove down the track to the highway. Still hugging the shadow under the cab, Jaime stretched against the width of the truck to brace himself and keep from rolling all over the place and banging his head. Meester George's truck had much better suspension than Tomás's but still it was a bumpy ride.

They turned onto the highway and the terrain became smooth as ice. He rolled onto his back, tucked his arms under his head, and watched the sky lighten.

They couldn't have driven for more than half an hour when Meester George pulled off the side of the road. The truck leaned heavily on Tomás's side and Jaime contracted back into armadillo status, trying to be invisible.

It didn't work.

"Why don't you ride in front with us?"

Jaime remained still. Maybe Meester George was talking to a hitchhiker they came across on the side of the road. Except a sharp poke in his shoulder said otherwise.

"C'mon, get in."

With nothing else to do, Jaime uncurled himself and accepted the hand Meester George offered to climb out of the truck bed.

In the passenger seat, Tomás had his arms crossed over his best shirt and only tie. His face angrier than it'd been last night.

"*¿Qué diablo piensas?*" he hissed before Meester George followed Jaime into the truck.

"I help Don Vicente," Jaime said with his chin up, and in English. Tomás turned away, but not before muttering a few choice words that if Abuela had heard, would have earned him a mouth washing.

"Welcome aboard, son." Meester George clapped a hand on Jaime's shoulder before putting the truck back in gear.

"No, not welcome, not happy," Tomás said in English, slowly so Jaime would understand. "You're staying in the car. Stay in car."

"Now, Tom, you can't do that," Meester George reasoned. "You leave a kid in a car for a few hours, that's called child abuse."

Tomás swore again and turned to face out the window. Jaime hadn't understood everything the rancher said, but he got the gist. He was going to the trial and there was nothing Tomás could do to stop him.

He turned to Meester George; anything to keep wondering if Tomás was right and he'd just doomed himself to imprisonment, deportation, and assassination.

"How you see me?" Jaime pointed to the bed.

"I noticed your scrawny lump as soon as I went to open the door back at the ranch."

"You knew he was there from the start and you let him come with us? How could you?" Tomás said through tight lips. He ran his hands through his gelled hair.

"I know he's your brother and you're worried, but I'm still your boss. You don't talk to me like that," Meester George scolded as he shifted his large cowboy hat. "I let him come 'cause I know you would have done the exact same thing if you were in his shoes. You Rivera brothers stop at nothing to help the people you care about. I would like to think that's a good thing."

Jaime only got part of what Meester George said, but knew it was important and complimentary. At any rate, it kept Tomás from talking, or swearing, for the rest of the ride.

Nothing stood nearby the detention center except brown bushes, more scraggly than the ones on the ranch. A tall barbed wire fence surrounded the building.

Jaime gulped. Maybe he *should* wait in the truck. Tomás was right. Jaime didn't want to be detained and have to stay here. He wished Ángela had joined them. She would have put her arm around him and made him feel like nothing was impossible with her by his side.

You can do this. You've come too far to stay in the truck. A voice that sounded like a mixture between Ángela and Abuela thumped in his head. He slid out of the truck and took a deep breath.

"Best leave phones behind. Now that everyone has recording devices, I don't think they'll let them in," Meester George said. Jaime hesitated. If he got in trouble, he wouldn't be able to call for help. If he tried to smuggle in the phone and got caught, he'd definitely be in trouble. With a sigh, he dropped the phone in the glove compartment, next to Tomás's.

Meester George stashed his hip pistol under the seat, placed his hat on the dashboard, and together they walked into the detention center. As they passed through the barbed wire fence, Tomás reached for Jaime's hand.

Inside the building, Meester George and Tomás showed their IDs, but the guard didn't ask Jaime for anything and waved him through the metal detector. The device beeped and flashed an angry red light when Jaime went through. The look of panic and horror on Tomás's face must have mirrored his own.

The guard however didn't even raise an eyebrow. "Do you have anything in your pockets?"

Heart thumping, Jaime pulled out the sketchbook from his waistband. The guard flipped through the book, half bored, before handing it back to Jaime once he passed through the detector a second time, beep-free. He and Tomás let out simultaneous sighs of relief and then, still in sync, together muttered, "*Gracias a Dios.*"

In the waiting area, they met with Meester George's lawyer, Hope Mariño, who greeted Meester George with a shake of his hand, but Tomás and Jaime each with the traditional kiss on the cheek. She stood taller than Tomás and could easily be mistaken for a *gringa* with light brown hair and skin so pale she'd burn if the sun so much as winked at her.

"You must be Jaime, *mucho gusto,*" she said in flawless Spanish, but with a distinctly Caribbean accent.

"May I ask you something?" he asked the lawyer in a low voice.

"*Claro que sí, mi'jo.* What's up?" she whispered back.

Jaime's shoulders relaxed just a bit. No, this was no *gringa*. She was one of them, a Latina, with all the self-assurance and determination he knew from his own family.

"Is it safe for me to be here?"

She laughed. Not a mean laugh but one that was sweet and relieving. "This isn't the movies. No one's going to organize a prison break and take you hostage."

"But—"

"This hearing is about Vicente. No one's going to care about you." She gave his hand a squeeze and switched to English to discuss the court procedures with Meester George.

A different guard led them into an empty white room. Behind them, the doors slammed shut with an ominous click of locks being secured.

They were trapped.

Tomás put his arm around Jaime. The height difference between them wasn't so obvious anymore but he still felt like a little kid needing his big brother to protect him.

A few seconds later, though it felt like hours, the door on the other side of the empty room opened with a buzz. The guard showed them down a hall and into the courtroom.

Maybe because it was a detention center instead of a courthouse, but this room looked nothing like the fancy courts on TV: just a desk at the front, two tables, and two columns of folding chairs. No jury. No fancy furniture. Good. Less intimidating.

Señora Mariño waved them to some chairs in the back while the hearing ahead of them took place. Across the aisle and a few rows up, a dozen men in orange jumpsuits sat in a cluster supervised by two guards. Jaime searched for Don Vicente and had to look a few times before he found him.

Three weeks in prison and without his cowboy hat, Jaime's friend was barely recognizable. Bits of white hair stood up in random patches as if some balding disease didn't know how to spread evenly. The brown, leathery skin hung on his face, giving him thick jowls he hadn't had before. And he slouched. Something that after centuries of horseback riding, Jaime never thought he'd be capable of doing.

He wanted to rush over to the man and comfort him as he had comforted Jaime after the news of Abuela. If only Jaime could tell him everything that had happened. About the new ranch hands and learning how to ride. About finding his friend Joaquín and the trouble she'd been through in a different detention center. He wanted to tell him that nothing on the ranch had been the same without him.

As if he could feel Jaime staring at him, Don Vicente looked over his shoulder. Jaime and Tomás waved and Meester George nodded. Don Vicente blinked a few times, as if he were outside and the sun's glare blinded him. Jaime kept waving and smiling. A few of the other inmates snickered and one even waved back. And then Don Vicente finally seemed to trust his eyes and he smiled in return. He braced himself against the empty seat in front of him and hoisted himself to a more upright sitting position with his shoulders square and back straight.

Even with the fancy lawyer jargon and words he'd

never be able to pronounce, Jaime could tell the hearing before them wasn't going well. When the other lawyer's client, Juan García, was summoned, two men in orange jumpsuits stood up. Both were named Juan García, both were from México, and the lawyer didn't know which one was her client.

"*Qué desastre,*" Señora Mariño whispered in his ear as she shook her head.

The other lawyer agreed to represent both of the Juan Garcías, but Jaime thought they would have been better off representing themselves. This lady's paperwork was all disorganized, the judge had to keep repeating herself, to which the lawyer kept saying "I don't know," which even Jaime knew couldn't be good.

When the judge made her decision, Señora Mariño shook her head again. They all rose from their seats as the judge stepped out of the room.

"*¿Qué pasó?*" Jaime asked as they settled back in their seats.

"Judge has to pee," Tomás answered.

"No, I mean with those other guys, Juan García squared?" Jaime asked.

"It's not good," Señora Mariño answered him. "Immigrants are not like criminals. They're not entitled to a public defender and it's hard to get anywhere without a lawyer. *Pero esta tipa,*" she used her lips to motion at the other lawyer, "is a disgrace. One Juan got caught shoplifting some food, she couldn't get him out. The other Juan, his bond got approved for twenty thousand dollars. His family will never come up with that money. They're both stuck here, or wherever they get transferred to. This judge is tough and that lawyer didn't help."

They rose from their seats again when the judge returned. Señora Mariño seemed to look at all the men in orange jumpsuits, and resisted the temptation to sigh. Jaime sighed for her as he squeezed his sweaty palms. Señora Mariño's words, "This judge is tough," repeated in his head.

But as soon as Don Vicente's case was called and Señora Mariño began talking, the difference between the lawyers was astonishing, even if Jaime didn't understand most of what she said.

"Your honor, my client Señor Delgado is honest and hardworking. He is the kind of man everyone wants to have as a neighbor and is a real asset to the community."

The judge nodded and looked through some of her papers. "How long has Mr. Delgado lived in the United States?"

"Over sixty years, your honor," Señora Mariño responded without having to consult any files. "There's a record of him having worked in a mustang roundup that took place sixty-two years ago."

From where Jaime sat it looked like the lawyer handed

the judge a photocopy of an old newspaper article. The photograph from the big house. The one that showed a handful of men leaning against a fence as they stared at the wild-eyed mustangs. How had she known it took place sixty-two years ago?

"Has he been employed all this time?"

"At Dundee Ranch. Mr. George Dundee Senior hired him the day that photo was taken."

"But he never filed any taxes?"

For the first time Señora Mariño's confidence faltered. "No, your honor. He never earned enough."

A silence fell over the room as the judge reviewed her papers. A breath caught in Tomás's throat.

"What happened?" Jaime whispered. He thought it had been going well.

"The government doesn't like people who don't pay taxes," Tomás explained in a low voice. "Even if you're undocumented, you're expected to pay a percentage of what you earn."

Jaime grabbed his brother's hand and gave it a squeeze. It couldn't be over.

"Your honor, if I may?" Meester George stood and motioned to the front of the room. The judge nodded her head, inviting him to come forward.

"George Dundee Junior," the rancher introduced himself. "Vicente Delgado has lived with my family longer than I can remember. It's true he never earned enough to file taxes, but that's only because he's never accepted much pay. So I pay him in other ways. When he admires a mare, I buy him her foal. If his wife says her back hurts, I get them a new bed. The kitchen is always stocked, the local feed store bills me for any clothes he needs, and I have him and his wife on my family's health care plan. There isn't anything in the world I wouldn't give him, but he's not into material things."

The judge leaned forward and addressed Don Vicente. "Is this true?"

Don Vicente stood to address the judge. His voice came out raspier than usual. "*¿Para qué necesito dinero cuando tengo todo lo que quiero?*"

Instantly a small man with a thin mustache who was seated near the judge translated the Spanish: "For what do I need money when I have everything I desire?"

The judge nodded for Meester George and Don Vicente to sit back down and then turned to Señora Mariño to continue with the case.

Señora Mariño presented further facts and papers, and every time the judge asked a question, she had an immediate answer. The judge listened intently, glanced at her forms, and nodded in agreement several times.

And then Jaime's heart stopped at the sound of his name.

"Jaime Rivera," Señora Mariño looked at him and continued to speak in slow, understandable English. "Mr. Dundee told me you'd like to help. Please come tell the judge about Vicente Delgado."

Tomás grabbed Jaime's arm and shook his head no. Jaime hugged his sketchbook to his chest and stood. He walked to the front of the room, feeling all the eyes on him. Tomás and Meester George. Señora Mariño and the disaster lawyer. Don Vicente and all the inmates. The security guards and the judge.

When he passed by Señora Mariño, she whispered, "You can use the interpreter if you want." She nodded to the mustached man who had translated for Don Vicente.

Jaime shook his head no. If he was going to do this, it had to be this way.

There was no bible to swear an oath, like they did on TV. Instead, Jaime stood in front of the judge with his back to the rest of the room. His legs began to shake.

"What is your name?" the judge asked

"Jaime Rivera."

"And who are you?"

He took a deep breath and made an effort to speak in his best English. "I Don—sorree, I am Don Vicente's friend and family."

"And what do you have to say about him?"

Jaime turned to the sketchbook in his hands. His legs

stopped shaking and he knew this was one thing he could express correctly. He opened his sketchbook and showed the judge the illustrations of Don Vicente's life, based on the stories he'd gathered from everyone in their community.

"I no speak English good," he explained. "But I leesen. People talk about life of Don Vicente. I draw what dey talk, um say."

He pointed to the first sketch, the one Diego's dad had told him while in the principal's office.

"Deez picture, car get stuck in snow. Don Vicente and horse save man from snow. Take man home. Save life."

He skipped one and flipped to the next page. This story had come from the local sheriff. Jaime had been hesitant to approach law enforcement, but Doña Cici had insisted the story was crucial and that the sheriff was nice. He was. He gave them all jelly doughnuts and orange Fanta. "Police look for gone boy. Don Vicente see foot . . . " He paused, not sure how to say the word he was looking for.

"Yes," the judge looked through her papers and pulled out a letter. "Your local sheriff wrote a letter telling us how Mr. Delgado found footprints in a dry arroyo, which led Search and Rescue to find the lost hiker."

"Yes, help find boy." He wanted to explain that Don Vicente understood the land and the animals, knowing things no one else did. But that was too complicated to explain.

He settled for turning to the next image. That person hadn't been home but Doña Cici had told him the story anyway. "Deez horse have baby trouble. Horse and baby no die."

"Tell me about this one." The judge pointed to Jaime's favorite drawing, the one he had skipped because he was saving it for last: the one he'd made after visiting Sani, Carla's great-grandfather.

"Don Vicente always help people, says all people his family. Here, Don Vicente make *arnés*—"

The interpreter immediately responded with the similar word in English. "Harness."

"Yes. He make harness and put *televisión* on horse. Take *tele* to sick friend. Sixty years, friend still have *tele*."

A chuckle came from the back of the room. Meester George shook his head in disbelief as he suddenly realized what happened to the wedding present his parents had given the old man.

The judge herself smiled as she continued to thumb through the other drawings and testimonies. When she came to the end, she handed the book back to Jaime. "You drew all of these?"

"Yes, judge," he nodded.

"You're very good at depicting events through your art."

"Tank you. I want show Don Vicente good man. Important man."

The judge leaned forward slightly and pushed her

reading glasses up her nose as she looked at him. "And why do you call him 'Don Vicente'?"

Jaime didn't blink. "In Spanish, 'don' eez for 'respect,' 'doña' is respect for woman. Everyone respect and love Don Vicente."

The judge nodded. "You may return to your seat."

Jaime stood and extended his hand like he did with Meesus at school. "Tank you, Doña Judge."

She tilted her head in surprise before accepting his handshake. Walking back to his chair, Meester George mimed clapping while Tomás tried to hide his embarrassment with his hand.

"You're lucky you're a cute kid," Tomás mumbled.

"I was just being polite—" he whispered back.

The judge glanced through the papers in front of her one last time before looking up to address the whole room. "After reviewing this case, reading the character references, and experiencing such captivating drawings, it is my decision to release Vicente Delgado on the proposed four thousand dollars bond."

A cheer exploded in the courtroom. The inmates who understood English clapped Don Vicente on the back. The old man stood, shook Señora Mariño's hand, and left the courtroom with a guard.

"Wait, where is he going?" Jaime asked.

"He's changing back into his regular clothes." Tomás

put his arm around Jaime in his rough, teasing way. "You didn't think they'd let him keep the orange jumpsuit, did you?"

Señora Mariño gathered her files and with a proud smile started heading toward them. Every inmate in the room extended a hand to her. She passed out her business card to each one while the other lawyer hid her sulking by hiding in her disorganized avalanche of files.

They exited the same way they came—through the white lockdown room, and bypassed the metal detectors to the waiting area by the front doors. There stood an office with a window where Meester George handed over the bank-issued check he had gotten the day before and signed the papers presented to him.

"You were great, Jaime," Señora Mariño said, placing a hand on his shoulder. "We'll see each other soon as we start preparing your application for the Special Immigrant Juvenile Visa."

Jaime opened his mouth to say something and then shut it. Señora Mariño must have read his mind, because she whispered, "Tomás told me you don't know if you want to stay here." Jaime shifted from one foot to the other. He didn't want to seem ungrateful for everything his family and Meester George had done, but . . .

Señora Mariño looked Jaime in the eye and said, "Just because we get you papers doesn't mean you have to stay here forever. Maybe things in Guatemala will change and it'll be safe for you to return or even just visit your parents."

"*¿De verdad puedo visitar a mis padres?*" he repeated her words in awe.

"*Claro,*" she reassured. "Once your papers are in order you can leave and return to the United States whenever you like. You can even choose not to return if you don't want to, but at least then that will be your choice, instead of the choice being made for you."

The possibility of visiting his parents changed everything. To be able to see them again, and still return to live safely with Tomás if he wanted. He thought that could only happen in his imagination.

"Do I need to worry about qualifying for this Juvenile Visa thing?" Jaime asked.

"Do you trust me?" she asked back.

"Yes, definitely."

She winked. "Then you don't have to worry, *mi'jo.* We're going to make sure you get to stay as long as you like."

She said good-bye to Meester George and Tomás and left.

Prison had not done Don Vicente any favors. Even with his cowboy hat back on, he seemed too old, too weak. Nothing like the man who spent all day on a horse, and all night with birthing cows. His chest sunk in like a hollow crevice and yet he seemed to have finally gained weight and developed a belly; his beaded belt that Sani had made for him was two notches looser. Again Jaime noticed how he didn't hold himself as straight as he used to, making him smaller and frailer than he had been.

Meester George greeted him first with a handshake and a pat on the shoulder. "We've missed you, Cente."

"*Gracias, hijo. Por todo.*"

They stood like that for a few seconds until Meester George nodded and released his hand.

Then Tomás grabbed the old man in a tight hug and didn't hide his tears. "You know how crazy it's been without you? Don't ever leave me again, *me oyes?*"

"Next time, listen to me when I say Manuel Vega's herd ain't worth their salt."

Tomás buried his face in the old man's shoulder. "I'm so sorry. I shouldn't have taken that road. I didn't mean . . . "

"I don't blame you." Don Vicente patted his back like he did to his horse Pimiento. "Who knew they would be there? I was so grumpy, I know you were just trying to get me home sooner."

"I'm sorry. I'll make it up to you."

"There's nothing to make up. We're going home now. That's all that matters."

Tomás let him go and blinked like he was agreeing, but Jaime knew his brother better than that. Knew that Tomás would do things, even if they were little things, to make sure the old man knew how much he cared.

Jaime walked slowly to Don Vicente and wrapped his arms around the old man. His shoulder blades and spine poked Jaime's hands. Don Vicente rubbed Jaime's back as if it were Jaime who needed the comforting.

"It was very brave of you to come here. The judge liked you," the old cowboy said.

Jaime smiled. "I wanted to make a difference. I had to try."

"And you succeeded. Your art is very moving." Don Vicente reached into his pocket and pulled out not only the two drawings Jaime had sent him, but the sketch Jaime had done quickly before they went to look at the bull calf. The sketch of Don Vicente on Pimiento.

"You kept it!"

"It's what made me wake up every day and not aim for the sunset."

CHAPTER TWENTY-NINE

They stopped for some food on the way back (hamburgers for Don Vicente and Meester George and pizza for Tomás and Jaime. Pizza!) and then continued on to the ranch. They let Don Vicente ride shotgun with Meester George while Jaime and Tomás shared the cramped back seat. Meester George talked endlessly in English about his new grandchild while Don Vicente replied in Spanish. Both understanding each other perfectly, but refusing to break into the other's language. Stubborn old men.

Jaime snapped awake as the truck slowed down and Meester George called out in his loud, booming voice.

"Well, what have we got here?"

Jaime leaned forward. They turned onto the ranch road and Meester George pulled the truck to a complete stop.

There stood Ángela with Vida, looking a bit hesitant as she held the bridles of Pimiento and Picasso.

"Oh mercy, there is a God." Don Vicente used the handlebar above the door to ease himself out of the tall truck. The spotted gray gelding let out a neigh from deep in his belly. The reins slipped from Ángela's hands and the Appaloosa trotted over to his human friend. Don Vicente collapsed against Pimiento's neck and hugged him tight.

Jaime followed behind and gave his cousin, who still held Picasso's reins, a big hug. "You're amazing. I wish I'd thought of this."

Ángela shrugged, though she seemed pretty pleased with herself. "I ditched school and texted Tomás to see when you were on your way. Mel tacked them up."

"*You* ditched school?"

"Today, family seemed more important." She smiled.

Don Vicente detached himself from Pimiento's neck and gave Ángela a hug too. Then, without even using a stirrup, he grabbed the saddle horn and swung his leg around with the grace of a dancer, landing perfectly centered in the saddle. "Now I'm home."

He took two deep breaths and then turned to Jaime in his old, gruff way. "Well, are you just going to stand there looking at Picasso?"

Jaime smiled and mounted the horse—with a stirrup. Baby steps. "*Ven, Ángela*, you can sit behind me."

"You know I've never ridden a horse," she said, half scared, half surprised.

"Better get started then." Jaime removed his foot from the stirrup and held the reins tight in his right hand. Ángela looked back toward the truck just as Meester George and Tomás drove away down the track.

"It's just like riding a train, right?" she said as she grabbed the back of the saddle and Jaime's left hand. She accidentally kicked Picasso as she swung her leg around, which caused him to side step. Still, she scampered on until she was upright behind Jaime's saddle and holding onto his waist.

"Sorry, Picasso," she apologized to the piebald for kicking him.

Don Vicente nodded and then led Pimiento away. Vida trotted ahead of the horses with her nose to the ground, round belly filling out her ribs, and her tail posed high in the air.

"Looks like we're going to need to prepare for some new lives coming soon," Don Vicente said.

"Tomás said calving season was over," Jaime said. It surprised him that Don Vicente wasn't aware of that already.

"Ángela knows what I'm talking about."

"*¡Qué!*" Jaime tried to turn and glare at his cousin.

Ángela laughed and slapped him on the leg. "He's talking about Vida, *bobo*. I wasn't sure, but her belly is getting bigger."

"She's going to have puppies? How did that happen?" Jaime tried to turn around again.

Ángela sighed. He could even hear her rolling her eyes. "You really need me to explain it to you?"

"No, I mean, we found her almost dead, with her insides sticking out. I didn't think she'd be able to have puppies."

"Obviously she had a good vet sewing her up."

Yes, she did.

"I'm glad you saved her. I'm glad you're here with me," Jaime said in a soft voice.

"It was a joint effort." Ángela wrapped her arms tight around his waist and placed her chin on his shoulder. "It's not too bad here, is it?"

The horses climbed up a hill. With the scattered bushes and open landscape, they could almost see all the way back home. To both of them.

"It's okay, for now," Jaime said.

They watched Vida dart this way and that, chasing lizards and following the scents of larger animals. Her one ear cocked and alert, she looked truly happy and full of life.

EPILOGUE

"Oh my goodness, I'm so nervous. What if I forget my lines?" Ángela squirmed as she adjusted her habit before her opening scene.

"You'll be fine," Jaime reassured her. After all, she only had two lines and if she forgot them, someone else would probably chime in. Still, he let her grasp his hand, proud that when she started to feel stage fright, she'd sent one of her friends to get him from the audience.

"You'll stay in the wings, even if you're not supposed to be here?" she asked.

"I'll watch the whole play from wherever you want me to," he said.

She nodded and squeezed his hand tighter. The house lights went down, the orchestra played a few bars, and then the stage lights went on. Unlike the movie, which Ángela made him watch four times that week, the play started with the nuns at the abbey. Jaime thought for sure he'd have to shove his cousin onstage, but as soon as the music changed, she strolled out there with the other nuns, full of more pride and arrogance than any humble nun was supposed to have. And the audience loved it.

Her facial expressions, her holier-than-thou attitude, her stance, all of it worked perfectly, as if she were playing the lead role instead of Abbey Nun Number Three. When Ángela said her two lines, the audience roared in laughter.

The scene ended with loud cheers from the audience, and the nuns exited before breaking into silent squeals once off stage.

"You can go back to Tomás, thank you," Ángela whispered.

"That's it? You're done?" After all that fuss in the weeks leading up, that had been her two seconds of fame?

"Shh. Of course not, I'm in loads more scenes. But that's the only one where I talk. Now go."

He didn't argue. He slipped out the door that led back into the auditorium and found his place again next to Tomás.

"How is she?" his brother asked.

Jaime didn't know what to say. She was Ángela, and apparently that meant something different every minute. But at least she proved that no matter how much she changed, when it came down to it, she knew where to find him. He was happy about that.

At the front of the stage and off to the side, a spotlight illuminated Meester Mike as he signed the play with elaborate arm gestures and facial expressions. His dance-like interpretation captivated Jaime just as much as the play. Jaime searched the auditorium for Sean and instead spotted Carla singing along with members of her family. Freddie seemed very intent on watching the play, unlike Diego behind him who made rude comments that kept the woman next to him shushing him every minute. When an usher finally asked them to leave, Jaime gave a silent cheer.

Seven children marched on stage and Jaime immediately recognized Tristan from the bus as the oldest boy. With his chest held high, he introduced his character with snobbish defiance. A blond boy sitting a few rows in front of Jaime turned around and rolled his eyes once he caught Jaime's attention. Jaime rolled his eyes back in agreement and waved at Sean. Now that Jaime knew Tristan wasn't after Ángela, he wasn't that bad.

The next time Ángela came out, Sean turned and pointed to Ángela on stage before waving both hands near his face, the sign for cheering. Jaime grinned and applauded back. He was proud of her too.

Ángela appeared a few times in the play, each time wearing a different costume and a different persona as she played a servant, a high society lady, a Nazi, and then again her original nun.

As the Von Trapp family pretended to climb over cardboard Alpine mountains, the rest of the cast came on stage to sing the final song, and the lyrics encouraged everyone to keep going until they find their dreams.

The audience leaped to their feet and cheered. Tomás let out a rancher whistle that could be heard in Guatemala. Jaime had to admit that even though he'd seen the movie too many times that week, they did a great job with the play.

Flowers in hand, they strolled to the front of the stage to wait for Ángela. On the way, Tomás leaned over the orchestra pit with a small bouquet of pink, yellow, and white carnations, and handed them to the lady playing the alpenhorn. "It's a good thing I got your autograph before you hit the big time."

Meez Macálista laughed. (Maybe by next fall, Jaime would be able to say her name right. On the other hand, he liked the way he said it just fine.)

"In music, it's all about timing. Today I'm famous, tomorrow it's back to grading."

"So you better eat while you can," Tomás said wisely.

Meez cringed. "Are you cooking again?"

Tomás looked offended. "And make that same mistake

twice? No way! Actually, Doña Cici is making a celebratory dinner for Ángela, and she knows how to use a stove."

"Will there be enough?"

Jaime and Tomás laughed. Since Don Vicente's return, Doña Cici hadn't made a single meal that hadn't been large enough to feed all of Nuevo México.

"You won't starve," Jaime reassured her. He noticed Ángela come out from backstage and grabbed the bouquet of pink roses from Tomás's hand. He swept her up in a big hug, almost lifting her up off her feet. "You were great. Definitely the best Abbey Nun Number Three."

"You don't think I was too obnoxious?"

Pues . . . "It worked well with the character."

Ángela narrowed her eyes at Jaime. She took a big whiff of her roses and sighed at their scent. She motioned toward Tomás, still teasing and laughing with Meez. "So, has he asked her out yet?"

"Just to join us at the ranch for dinner. Doña Cici cooks so much, he's just being nice."

Ángela shook her head and rolled her eyes. "You're so clueless. Just keep in mind we might need a bigger house."

Jaime shrugged. The trailer was just a container. It wasn't what made it a home. "That's not a bad thing, is it?"

She draped an arm over Jaime, giving him a half squeeze, half pinch. "Not as long as our family's there."

AUTHOR'S NOTE

When I started preschool I didn't speak English, and the only other non-English speakers were twins from India. As the daughter of Cuban refugees, I speak Spanish as my first language Although I learned English quickly, there were moments of frustration and misunderstanding. Like Jaime, I struggled to make the "th" sound in words like "three" and "thank you"; to this day I sometimes say "sanguich" instead of "sandwich."

My family moved several times when I was a child. When I started one new school, I used every way I knew to ask to use the bathroom and didn't understand what the teacher meant when she kept insisting that I "sign out" first. At another school, I received a hate letter for no other reason than being different.

Jaime adapted much better to his new environment than I did. By having a teacher who checked up on him and a friend on the bus, Jaime had the support I never had. I can only wish every child entering a new school system could have those friendships.

All children in the United States, regardless of their immigration status, are legally entitled to education. New Mexico is an English/Spanish bilingual state, with the highest percentage (twenty-nine percent) of Spanish speakers per capita in the United States, yet unfortunately, it ranks one of the lowest in quality of public education.

Immigration policies in the United States seem to be changing daily, but these changes are often not for the better. A person in Guatemala filing for legal status in the United States might have to wait more than ten years for the papers to be processed; that is too long for a person whose life is in danger or whose children are starving. Opportunities under the Obama administration that were available for undocumented immigrants are continuously changing, and it's becoming harder for them to stay in the United States legally. But it's not impossible.

At the moment I am writing this, children like Jaime and Ángela can apply for the Special Immigrant Juvenile Visa (https://www.uscis.gov/green-card/special-immigrant-juveniles/special-immigrant-juveniles-sij-status). Alternatively, if a lawyer can prove that the child's life is in danger if they return to their birth country, or there isn't a family member capable of caring for the child in that country, then the chances of that child staying in the United States are considerably better. However, good immigration lawyers are expensive and sometimes even they are not enough.

One of the best ways for people to show their support for immigration is to read and be aware of what's happening. If there are immigrants in your community, make them feel welcome and get to know them as people, not just immigrants. There are programs for adults to become foster parents while the legal system determines whether a child can stay in the United States or not—an alternative to remaining in a detention center. Together as a community, immigration awareness can be raised.

We are a nation of immigrants. If it weren't for immigrants, most of us wouldn't be here. No matter how things change for the worse, we must keep our hope. Hope that there is a way, hope that things will get better. When we give up on hope, we give up on life.

References

American Immigration Council. "Immigrants in New Mexico." October 13, 2017. https://www.americanimmigrationcouncil.org/research/immigrants-in-new-mexico.

Butterworth, Rod R. *Signing Made Easy (A Complete Program for Learning Sign Language. Includes Sentence Drills and Exercises for Increased Comprehension and Signing Skill)* New York: Perigee Books, 1989.

Florence Immigrant & Refugee Rights Project. "Getting a Bond: Your Keys to Release from Detention." May 2013. http://firrp.org/media/Bond-Guide-2013.pdf.

Gómez, Grace. Immigration lawyer at Gómez Immigration (http://www.gomezimmigration.com/). Personal communication.

Love, Allegra. Immigration lawyer at Santa Fe Dreamers Project (http://www.santafedreamersproject.org/). Personal communication, June 20, 2017.

New Mexico Voices for Children. "Immigration Matters in New Mexico: How Kids Count." June 2012. http://www.nmvoices.org/wp-content/uploads/2012/07/KC-immigrant-full-report-web.pdf.

Rice, Cathy. *Sign Language for Everyone: A Basic Course in Communication with the Deaf.* Nashville, TN: Thomas Nelson Inc., 1977.

Santa Fe Dreamer's Project. "New Americans: New Mexico Immigrants Make Us Stronger." 2017.

Shaw, Jerry. "Illegal Immigration Figures in New Mexico." *Newsmax,* September 24, 2015. http://www.newsmax.com/FastFeatures/illegal-immigration-New-Mexico/2015/09/24/id/693112/.

The Young Center for Immigrant Children's Rights, https://www.theyoungcenter.org/.

U.S. Citizenship and Immigration Services. "Green Card Through Registry." https://www.uscis.gov/greencard/through-registry. (This program is for people like Don Vicente who have been in the United States for a long time.)

U.S. Citizenship and Immigration Services. "Special Immigrant Juveniles (SIJ) Status." https://www.uscis.gov/green-card/special-immigrant-juveniles/special-immigrant-juveniles-sij-status. (This program is for children like Jaime and Ángela.)

U.S. Customs and Border Protection. "Border Patrol Sectors." https://www.cbp.gov/border-security/along-us-borders/border-patrol-sectors.

U.S. Customs and Border Protection. "Detention Facility Locator." https://www.ice.gov/detention-facilities.

Further Reading for All Ages

Picture Books

Colato Laínez, René. *Mamá the Alien / Mamá la extraterrestre.* New York: Children's Book Press, 2016.

McCarney, Rosemary. *Where Will I Live?* Toronto, Canada: Second Story Press, 2017.

Phi, Bao. *A Different Pond.* North Mankato, MN: Capstone Young Readers, 2017.

Sanna, Francesca. *The Journey.* London: Flying Eye Books, 2016.

Poetry

Argueta, Jorge. *Somos como las nubes / We Are Like the Clouds.* Toronto, Canada: Groundwood Books, 2016.

Engle, Margarita. *Lion's Island: Cuba's Warrior of Words.* New York: Atheneum Books for Young Readers, 2016.

Middle Grade

Agosín, Marjorie. *I Lived on Butterfly Hill.* New York: Atheneum Books for Young Readers, 2014.

Freeman, Ruth. *One Good Thing About America.* New York: Holiday House, 2017.

Gratz, Alan. *Refugee.* New York: Scholastic Press, 2017.

McGee, Alison. *Pablo and Birdie*. New York: Atheneum Books for Young Readers, 2017.

Medina, Juana. *Juana & Lucas*. Somerville, MA: Candlewick Press, 2016.

Osborne, Linda Barrett. *This Land is Our Land: A History of American Immigration*. New York: Abrams Books for Young Readers, 2016.

Young Adult

Abdel-Fattah, Randa. *The Lines We Cross*. New York: Scholastic, 2017.

Andreu, Maria E. *The Secret Side of Empty*. Philadelphia: Running Press Teens, 2014.

Fraillon, Zana. *The Bone Sparrow*. New York: Disney Hyperion, 2016.

Grande, Reyna. *The Distance Between Us: Young Reader's Edition*. New York: Aladdin, 2016.

Film

The Walt Disney Company. *The Girl Who Spelled Freedom*. 1986.

Glossary

Spanish is mostly a phonetic language and the words are pronounced how they're spelled. However, some letters are pronounced differently in Spanish than in English. For example, Jaime's name is pronounced "Hi-Meh" and Ángela is "Ahn-hey-la". That said, Spanish speakers love it when you make an effort to speak to them so don't be afraid to try some Spanish!

Abuelo/Abuela: Grandfather/grandmother.

Abuelitas: a plural form for "grannies."

Acabo de hablar con: "I just finished talking to . . ."

Amigos: a word every Spanish wannabe speaker should know, "friends."

Arnés: a "harness," especially one used for horses.

Arte: "art," Jaime's favorite subject.

Así se hace: an exclamation similar to "That's how it's done."

Ay no: "oh no" and a common expression that can be said in various tones to change the meaning.

Bello durmiente: the male version of "sleeping beauty."

Bien: "good" or "fine" and the answer you would give if someone asks how are you.

Bobo: a dummy or stupid person, but more endearing than insulting.

Bruja: a witch or spiritual person who often uses spells to accomplish what she wants.

Bueno: means "good" but can also mean "so" or "well then" at the beginning of a sentence.

Café y frijoles: coffee and beans.

Cajeta: a caramel traditionally made from goat milk. It can be liquid and held in jars or in chewy candy form.

Cállate: a command to "be quiet."

Capulín: the New Mexican/Mexican word for the berry "chokecherry" but may go by other names in other places.

Centro de inmigrantes: Immigration center.

Chico: The word for "kid" or "boy" so Jaime calling his bathroom friend "Choco-chico" is like calling him "chocolate boy."

Chinchines: traditional musical instruments in Guatemala similar to maracas. They are made from gourds and often painted in bright colors.

Chisme: gossip.

Ciencia: science.

Cómo se dice: "How do you say . . . ?"

Ciudadanía: the thing Jaime isn't sure he wants, "citizenship."

Claro: "sure" or "of course."

Claro que sí: a version of the above but with more emphasis and assertion, "Of course!"

Comal: a griddle used to make corn or flour tortillas but can be used for cooking other things as well.

Cómo están las cosas: a question to ask, "How are things?"

Contacto: "contact" or as in "to make contact with someone."

Curandera: a healer or witchdoctor, similar to a *bruja*, often uses herbs for cures.

De: most often indicates "from" or "of."

De todo, piano, guitarra, flauta: the first part, *de todo,* means "of everything" and in the context used means "a bit of everything." The following words are, "piano, guitar, flute."

De verdad: a question or confirmation meaning "truthfully" or "really."

De verdad puedo visitar a mis padres: literally translates to, "Really, can I visit my parents?"

Desgraciado: this word doesn't have a good English translation, but means "disgraceful," "disrespectful," and "bad-mannered."

Diario de Greg: Días de perros: Spanish title for *Diary of a Wimpy Kid: Dog Days.*

Don/Doña: a term of respect for a man (don) or a woman (doña).

Dulce de leche: a sweet dessert similar to caramel.

El señor: "the man" or "the mister" and can also mean "the boss."

Es por tu culpa: a question asking "Are you at fault?"

Está vivo: "He/she is alive," or in question form, "Is he/she alive?"

Estadounidense: a citizen of the United States and a preferred term over *americano* when really all of the citizens of North and South America are "Americans," not just those from the United States.

Estás aquí: a question, "Are you here?"

Fantástico: if you guessed this means "fantastic," you're right!

Flauta: the word for "flute" but can also mean "recorder." To tell the difference, some people will say *flauta transversal* or *transversa* for the flute that is played to the side of the mouth and *flauta dulce* for a recorder or other flutes that are held vertical.

Fútbol: The sport most of the world calls football but in the United States is called soccer.

Futuro: the future.

Gracias: a must-know word, "thanks."

Gracias a Dios: an exclamation, "thank God."

Gracias, hijo. Por todo: the first part is "thanks, son," followed by, "for everything."

Grapadora: a stapler.

Gringo/Gringa: a person (*gringo* for a man, *gringa* for a woman) who is white, from the United States or not Latino. *Gringo* is not a bad word or insult.

Guayabas: guavas, tropical fruit the size of tennis balls.

Hermano/Hermanito: means "brother" and "little brother." In Spanish, you can make most nouns diminutive (little) by adding "ito" for a boy or masculine noun and "ita" for a girl or feminine noun.

Historia: history.

Hola: another good word to know which is pronounced, "oh-la" and means "hello."

Inmigración: immigration.

Jodón: a slightly bad word to call someone who's being a pain.

La Bestia: the nickname for a train in Mexico that brings many immigrants riding on top of it to the United States. Its name means, "the beast."

La frontera: literally "the frontier" but refers to the Mexico-United States border.

La migra: a nickname for the immigration officers that try to prevent people from crossing the borders without permission.

Latino: a person from a Spanish or Portuguese speaking country or a descendent from such country. Because of the colonization of the Americas, Latinos can be descendents of European, African, Asian, and Native ancestors and can be of all colors and ethnic backgrounds.

Los Estados Unidos: The United States.

Mamá: mom or the mother.

Masa: any kind of dough, but in this case made out of corn or flour to make tortillas.

Matemática: can also be called *matemáticas* and means "mathematics."

Media loca: this does NOT mean "made crazy by the media" but rather a girl who is acting "half crazy" or "kind of crazy" (for a boy, you would say *medio loco*).

Me oyes: a question that literally means, "you hear me?" but implies "you understand?"

Mercado: a market where you do your shopping.

Mi familia: one of the most important things to Jaime, "my family."

Mi hermano: my brother.

Mi hijo: "my child" or "my son," but can also be a term of endearment said by anyone.

Mi'jo: A term of endearment often said by an older person to someone younger. It's a conjunction of "mi hijo" (my child), but you don't have to be related to say it or have it said to you.

Mira: literally means "look" but can also mean "hey."

Mucho gusto: a nice thing to say after you've been introduced to someone, "nice to meet you."

Muerte: death.

Música: music.

No lo quiero: "I don't want it."

No me digas: can be used as an agreement "Don't tell me about that," or statement, "Don't tell me."

No que va: an expression that means "no way!"

No puedo escribir en español: "I can't write in Spanish." Unfortunately, a lot of youth in the United States who have Spanish-speaking parents or grandparents never learn Spanish.

Nosotros: us.

Nuestra amiga: "our female friend." (If you say *nuestro amigo*, that means "our male friend.")

Nuevomexicanos: New Mexicans, many of who are Mexican/Spanish descendents or Native Americans.

Oye: An exclamation like "hey" but literally means "listen."

Oye hombre: another exclamation, "hey man."

Pandilleros: gang members.

Papá: dad or father.

Para qué necesito dinero cuando tengo todo lo que quiero: "What do I need money for when I have everything I want?"

Para ti: for you.

Pepián: a traditional Guatemalan meaty stew.

Perfecto: a good and easy word to know, "perfect."

Pero: "but" or "however."

Pero esta tipa: this uses a bit of slang, "but this woman/chick." For a man, you can say, *pero este tipo.*

Pero solamente hasta que regrese Don Vicente, verdad: "But only until Don Vicente returns, right?"

Picante: hot as in spicy. Mexican food is often much spicier than Guatemalan.

Pimiento: a pepper, also the name of Don Vicente's horse.

Por fa: this is a slang word for *por favor* ("please") and is the same as saying "pretty please."

Por qué estás de mal humor: "Why are you in a bad mood?"

Por supuesto: "of course" or "naturally."

Pues: this can mean "well" or "because," especially at the start of a sentence when you're not sure what to say.

Pues, sí: an agreement such as, "well, yes."

Qué: in question or exclamation, it means "what" or "how."

Qué desastre: "What a disaster."

Qué diablo piensas: almost a swear word, "What the devil are you thinking?"

Qué haces aquí: a question, "What are you doing here?"

Qué hora es: a common thing to teach in Spanish classes, "What time is it?"

Qué maravilla: "how marvelous," but in the context used it is sarcastic.

Qué pasó: "What happened?"

Qué piensas: literally means "what are you thinking," but in the context used, it carries the implication of "What were you thinking?"

Qué te pasa: means "what's going on with you" or "What's up with you?"

Querido/Querida/Queridos: the words mean "dear" and it changes if you're addressing a male, female, or several people. It's the word you use to start a letter but can also be used in other contexts you'd use "dear."

Rancheros: ranchers.

Sabes jugar un instrumento de música: this is an incorrect way to ask "Do you know how to play a musical instrument?" The correct form would be, *Sabes tocar un instrumento de música.*

The verb *jugar* does mean "to play" but it's used for playing with dolls or a sport, not musical instruments.

Se busca ranchero: means "rancher wanted" when hiring.

Señor/Señora: "mister/missus" but can also mean "man/woman."

Serpiente: a serpent or snake.

Sí: another good word to know, "yes."

Sopapillas: a traditional puffed and fried bread in New Mexico, eaten as either part of the meal or with honey for dessert.

Soy: one of the ways to say "I am" or "I'm."

Te quiero: Most often means "I love you" and can be a family, friendship, or romantic love. But it can also mean "I want you."

Tele (la tele): the abbreviation of *televisión*, similar to "TV."

Tienes la forma: "Do you have the form?"

Tío/Tía: Uncle/Aunt.

Tocar: literally means "to touch" and is the correct verb to use when referring to playing musical instruments.

Trabajador sin remuneración: "indentured servant" or someone who works without getting paid.

Una familia mexicana: a Mexican family.

Unir: "unite" or "join."

Universidad: university.

Ustedes están muy flacos: Doña Cici's favorite complaint and something often heard said to children, "You guys are too skinny."

Vamos ya: "Let's go now" or "Let's go already."

Vamos rápido: "Let's go, quickly."

Ven: an order to "come."

Viejita: a "little old lady."

Vida: the name of Jaime and Ángela's dog, that also means "life."

Y: "and." If used by itself as a question, it can also mean "so?"

Ya sé que eres la que manda: a way to say "I know you're in charge" when someone is being demanding.

Yo gusto gatos: A literal but incorrect way of saying "I like cats." The correct way to say it would be, *A mí me gustan los gatos.*

Yo soy la que manda: "I'm the one in charge."